Women of Darkness

Also by Kathryn Ptacek
published by Tor Books

Blood Autumn
In Silence Sealed
Shadoweyes

Edited by

KATHRYN PTACEK

Women of Darkness

A TOM DOHERTY ASSOCIATES BOOK
NEW YORK

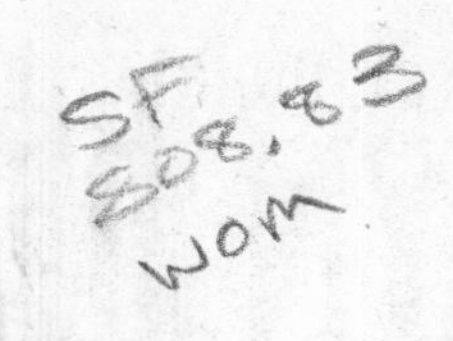

WOMEN OF DARKNESS

A TOR BOOK
Published by Tom Doherty Associates, Inc.
49 West 24 Street
New York, NY 10010

Library of Congress Cataloging-in-Publication Data
Women of darkness / edited by Kathryn Ptacek.—1st ed.
p. cm.—(Tor horror)
"A Tor book"—T.p. verso.
ISBN 0-312-93096-8 : $17.95
1. Horror tales, American—Women authors. 2. Fantastic fiction, American—Women authors. 3. Women and literature—United States.
I. Ptacek, Kathryn.
PS648.H6W6 1988
813'.0872'089287—dc19 88-19728
CIP

First edition: December 1988

0 9 8 7 6 5 4 3 2 1

Acknowledgments

Introduction, copyright © 1988 by Kathryn Ptacek.

"Baby," copyright © 1988 by Kit Reed. By permission of the author.

"Ransom Cowl Walks the Road," copyright © 1988 by Nancy Varian Berberick. By permission of the author.

"True Love," copyright © 1988 by Patricia Russo. By permission of the author.

"In the Shadows of My Fear," copyright © 1988 by Joan Vander Putten. By permission of the author.

"The Spirit Cabinet," © 1988 by Lisa Tuttle. By permission of the author.

"Hooked on Buzzer," copyright © 1988 by Elizabeth Massie. By permission of the author.

"Little Maid Lost," copyright © 1988 by Rivka Jacobs. By permission of the author.

"Mother Calls But I Do Not Answer," copyright © 1988 by Rachel Cosgrove Payes. By permission of the author.

"Nobody Lives There Now. Nothing Happens." copyright © 1988 by Carol Orlock. By permission of the author.

"The Baku," copyright © 1988 by Lucy Taylor. By permission of the author.

"The Devil's Rose," copyright © 1988 by Tanith Lee. By permission of the author.

"Midnight Madness," copyright © 1988 by Wendy Webb. By permission of the author.

"Monster McGill," copyright © 1988 by Cary G. Osborne. By permission of the author.

"Aspen Graffiti," copyright © 1988 by Melanie Tem. By permission of the author.

"Sister," copyright © 1988 by Wennicke Eide Cox. By permission of the author.

"Samba Sentado," copyright © 1988 by Karen Haber. By permission of the author.

"When Thunder Walks," copyright © 1988 by Conda V. Douglas. By permission of the author.

"Slide Number Seven," copyright © 1988 by Sharon Epperson. By permission of the author.

"The Unloved," copyright © 1988 by Melissa Mia Hall. By permission of the author.

"Cannibal Cats Come Out Tonight," copyright © 1988 by Nancy Holder. By permission of the author.

Contents

Kathryn Ptacek	Introduction	ix
Kit Reed	Baby	1
Nancy Varian Berberick	Ransom Cowl Walks the Road	14
Patricia Russo	True Love	36
Joan Vander Putten	In the Shadows of My Fear	43
Lisa Tuttle	The Spirit Cabinet	53
Elizabeth Massie	Hooked on Buzzer	68
Rivka Jacobs	Little Maid Lost	77
Rachel Cosgrove Payes	Mother Calls But I Do Not Answer	116
Carol Orlock	Nobody Lives There Now. Nothing Happens.	124
Lucy Taylor	The Baku	139
Tanith Lee	The Devil's Rose	148
Wendy Webb	Midnight Madness	179
Cary G. Osborne	Monster McGill	190
Melanie Tem	Aspen Graffiti	197
Wennicke Eide Cox	Sister	213
Karen Haber	Samba Sentado	227
Conda V. Douglas	When Thunder Walks	251
Sharon Epperson	Slide Number Seven	263
Melissa Mia Hall	The Unloved	271
Nancy Holder	Cannibal Cats Come Out Tonight	290

Introduction

A few years ago, I was glancing through a number of the most current dark fantasy/horror anthologies residing on my bookshelves. And since I am in the habit of counting various and sundry things (a habit which can drive the others around me batty), I started tallying the number of women writers included in them.

In one anthology I found to my surprise that there were no women writers at all, in a second and a third just one or two. There were too many like that. Only in the latest volume of a well-known anthology was there more than a couple—half of those contributors were female.

And I thought that low number of women in the first three volumes, and most others as well, was curious; somehow, considering the number of women writing in the field, there should have been more. I didn't really think the editors had deliberately not chosen women writers, but neither did I think that women had not sent their stories in.

From a glance at the book racks we all know that male horror *novelists* outnumber women, at least as of this writing, but when it comes to the short story, women write and publish just as regularly as men.

So why weren't there more women in the anthologies I saw?

I don't know.

I do know, though, that from that moment I wanted to do something about it.

I wondered what it would be like to do an anthology of dark fantasy and horror—with all the stories written by contemporary women writers.

And that's something which has never been done before.

Sure, there've been anthologies with all women contributors, but those included Edwardian and Victorian writers as well. Few living writers, or even those of the mid twentieth century, were represented.

I knew then that I wanted this to be as modern, as up-to-date as it could be.

I wanted the anthology to be a *showcase* for the women horror and dark fantasy writers of today.

And so here it is at last, *Women of Darkness,* with all original stories.

The range is fairly wide, from very quiet dark fantasy to some that are definitely not that. Many are about families or family members, or about the relationship between man and woman; some are from a woman's point of view, others aren't. Most take place in today's society, with its own current of unleashed horrors, while still others reach into our distant past.

But no matter the subject, the stories all bear one common characteristic.

They are chilling.

And because of that, I suggest that you read these stories on a cloudy grey autumn afternoon when the wind is blowing the leaves in red and yellow billows outside and moaning under the eaves, and making that long straggly rosebush tap-tap on your windowpane, or perhaps on a cold dark evening as snow falls silently outside, muffling sounds, when you're curled up before the crackling fire and are the only one left in the house. You think.

But whenever you read the stories by some of the best women writers around today, I hope you enjoy them as much as I did.

Kathryn Ptacek
Newton, New Jersey
April 1988

BABY

by Kit Reed

Kit Reed is a former Guggenheim fellow and the first American recipient of a five-year literary grant from the Abraham Woursell Foundation. Her eleven novels include *Captain Grownup, The Ballad of T. Rantula,* and *Fort Privilege*. Her most recent story collection is *The Revenge of the Senior Citizens * Plus*. Her latest novel, *Catholic Girls,* is being published by Donald I. Fine, and her story "Winter" is included in the new edition of *The Norton Anthology of Contemporary Literature.* She lives in Connecticut.

A new short story by esteemed writer Kit Reed is always a welcome event, and this one proves no exception.

✦ ✦ ✦

When her sister came home from the hospital with her new baby, Elva could not make herself visit. She shied away from disaster like a contemplative avoiding crowds, not because she couldn't handle it but because it got between her and that which she was trying to be.

What made her think this was a disaster? Babies were revolting; love must make mothers blind. Rilla loved this thing even though it had ruined her waistline and was wrecking her life. Elva caught intimations—feeding problems, trouble with Rilla's husband, Stanley, who had not taken to the thing; Rilla's joyful accounts took on a desperate note. Therefore when Rilla called she always found excuses: new boyfriend, extra hours at the health club, new responsibilities at work. Let Rilla be the martyr mother, giving up everything for her young. Elva had worked too hard and come too far to let anybody's baby slow her down.

She was trying to be a perfect person, serene and glossy, even glamorous, a collector of men. Nothing interfered with her eight hours' beauty sleep, which she followed with an hour in the bathroom; neither fire nor flood could prevent her from the long bath, during which she washed her hair, shaved everything that didn't belong, including certain details along the hairline, and steamed her face. While her hair dried she worked on her nails and did makeup, and at the end of the hour she emerged, perfect, prepared to dress for the day's conquest, the night's victory.

How could she go into Rilla's house, with its chaotic atmosphere, the large and noisy dog, and the crying baby; how could she rest in a place where nobody slept in peace? How could she make her toilette in a bathroom that stank of baby powder and worse, or maintain the inner peace that kept her pretty face unlined?

What if their big dog jumped up on her, and ruined her skirt?

What if Rilla asked her to hold the baby?

What if she had to touch its diapers?

What if it cried?

Details like this could turn a beauty into an old woman overnight. It was responsibility that made pretty women ugly, motherhood that robbed them of their youth. When babies moved into their lives, men moved out.

It was too much to think about.

But this was her only sister's very first baby.

Yes, she was putting it off.

Rilla called again. "Do come and see us," she said, and when Elva murmured apologies she tendered the bait.

"Stanley and I are going to give you a party. A big one," she said.

If you were beautiful, you had to let the people see you, or else there was no point. She could wear her red linen, or if it was dressy, her black silk . . . "Oh Rilla, I don't know if I . . ."

Rilla sweetened the bait. "We have found a wonderful man."

Elva said, cautiously, "How wonderful?"

"Looks like Matt Dillon."

For him, the chiffon shot with gold. Beautiful. "Oh Rilla, I don't know."

"Clears two hundred thousand a year."

It was this she dressed for: to be admired, complete. But in the background, the baby was crying, which Elva tried to ignore."But you're both so busy, with the baby."

Rilla said hollowly, "The baby is no problem, really."

"Rilla, you sound tired."

"I need you. I mean, you're so good at fashion, I need your help. I want to look wonderful for Rick. I mean Stanley." She tried to sound festive but there was something in her voice that frightened Elva—some breathy flutter that implied troubles past and troubles to come. "I mean, I need you to perk up this party. Oh Elva, I promised Dack you'd come."

"Dack?"

"This wonderful man I have for you."

"Oh, Dack." In almost involuntary assent, Elva put a hand to her throat, in which a soft pulse beat, hinting at new conquests, the excitement of the chase, romantic thrills.

So it was that Elva Richmond, self-proclaimed beauty and the best-dressed woman in her large town or small city, took two weeks off to go and help her younger sister take care of her new baby in Skokie, Illinois. She didn't bother to tell her employers that she was going for a party, or that the new baby in question was already six months old. She took two suitcases and a zipper bag in which she had hung her four best party dresses—contingency changes of costume, with matching accessories.

Perhaps because Rilla was tied up and couldn't meet her at the airport, perhaps because Stanley wasn't available and she had to take a cab, the low redwood house with its big front lawn looked strange and a little sinister, everything in the yard sere and brown, and the whole place somehow neglected, as if everybody had been too preoccupied to deal with it, too pressed to take a look around outside. She approached cautiously, but no dog came, although its spoor dotted the yard. Here and there were other ugly details: what looked like dead birds under the rosebushes, the delicate skeleton of some small animal upturned right next to the door.

On the front stoop Elva fought down feelings of foreboding. "I knew I shouldn't have come."

Gosh, she thought when her younger sister met her at the front door. *This thing has made her old*. "Elva, thank God you've come."

In the old days Rilla had been the prettier, but that was all gone now, chased away by the creases lack of sleep and worry had made in her face. She was, of course, holding the baby, had it plumped over her shoulder so that Elva had to wait until they were inside to get a good look into its face.

"Here he is," Rilla said, her face suffused with adoration. As if presenting the crown jewels, she turned so Elva could see. "My darling boy."

It was a perfectly acceptable-looking baby, ordinary except, perhaps, for the glint in the eyes; it didn't look like much to Elva, but Rilla took on as if she had here the Kohinoor diamond, or the crown prince.

Love, thought Elva, is definitely blind.

"Isn't he beautiful?"

It yearned, straining as if to spring from its mother's arms into the unwilling Elva's. "Oh no you don't."

"Oh Elva, he likes you."

Under her sister's stern eyes, she made as if to pat its head and was startled by how quick it was. "Don't!" Shuddering, Elva withdrew her hand as the baby tried to close its wet mouth on it.

"What's the matter?"

"He snapped at me."

"Don't be ridiculous, he's just a baby," Rilla said, adding, on a note that seemed determinedly offhand, "Babies are all mouth."

Something made Elva ask, "Where's the dog?"

Wildly, Rilla shrugged. "Oh, you know."

So there was that, she thought that night, collecting herself in the guest bed with wet tea bags on her closed eyelids and her hair-waving clips firmly in place. There was the way Rilla seemed to dote on it, and the fact that she loved it so much that she cooked and served dinner one-handed because she couldn't bear to put it down. When Elva remarked on this she said, "I just like to have him where I can keep track of him," but would not say precisely why. There was also the fact that Stanley had not come home for dinner, nor did he come home to bed. As far as Elva knew, he had never come home. There was as well the sound of the baby's nocturnal wailing, grimly persistent and suddenly stilled.

Even so, there were a hundred people coming to the party, and what's more, Rilla had several Polaroids of Dack. Definitely worth coming for, Elva thought, deciding at the same time that she had better go into Chicago and buy a more impressive dress. In the morning they were going to start making hors d'oeuvres to put in the freezer against the day of the event.

On the way back from the bathroom at dawn she stepped on something that crunched, drew back and shook her bedroom slipper free. In the dimness it looked as though she'd hooked her toe on the rib cage of some small animal. At the far end of the hall she saw, or thought she saw, something moving—a flash of white flickering around the corner, something small and pink disappearing last, like a hairless mouse, but it was dark and she was half-asleep so she did not investigate, but instead went back to bed. On second thought the thing gave her the creeps, but in the morning when she checked, all she found was a little heap of toys.

"By the way," she said that afternoon. "Is Stanley away?"

Rilla stood at the kitchen table, stuffing mushroom caps. She moved adroitly, even though she had the baby slung at her hip. Mother love had made her gaga; cherishing her firstborn, she seemed indifferent to everybody else. "Not exactly." Putting down the mushrooms, she held the thing to her face, nuzzling it. "Isn't he *beautiful?*"

But Elva persisted. "Is he coming to the party?"

"I don't think so," Rilla said.

"Have you and Stanley broken up?"

"He just can't come to the party, okay?"

This was the moment Elva had been afraid of; in a minute Rilla would hurl herself into Elva's arms and sob out her story; she would have to hold Rilla and the baby and say, "There, there"; she could already feel the muscles in her jaws contracting, the beginning lines that worry drew, the weight of her sister's problems making her old. Very well. With no Stanley, there would be no party. She would hear her sister out, say whatever seemed appropriate, and escape this very night. But nothing happened. Jogging the baby, which was mouthing her forearm, Rilla just went on stuffing mushroom caps. Elva was going to have to broach the subject herself. "Are you getting a divorce?"

"Not exactly," Rilla said and lifted the baby so she could nuzzle it, glowing with love which was not necessarily returned.

"Since there's—ah, trouble," Elva began delicately, "naturally you'll want to cancel the party, right?"

"Lord no! I mean, oh no indeed." Rilla reached for another bowl of mushrooms with a frantic laugh.

"I mean, don't do this on my account." Elva was already wondering if there were any other ways she could meet Dack. Maybe if she called him to cancel the party, they could meet. "You've got too much to handle now."

"Babies take a lot out of you," Rilla admitted with a haunted look.

Escape was near; Elva could hardly wait to get away. "Give me your list and I'll make the calls."

But the infant gurgled and Rilla lunged, cutting her off from the phone. "Oh no you don't."

"But without Stanley—"

"Why do you think I'm having a party anyway? The baby needs—"

Alarmed, Elva said, sharply, "What?"

Rilla covered hastily. "I mean, I need a new man."

"What about the baby?"

Rilla's laughter was light and artificial, but her face gleamed with pride. "He's the most wonderful, beautiful, fabulous baby in the whole wide world."

"But he's wearing you out. You need to get a sitter, Rilla. You need to get away. He has to learn to be self-sufficient. You can't let him ruin your life. To begin with," she said, increasingly exasperated, "to begin with, you could put him down."

"Oh no," Rilla said, hugging the thing closer. Its bare legs dangled and its little pink feet stirred against her belly like baby mice. "I can't put him down."

"You're bigger than he is and it's your house."

Rilla's face was suffused with a strange pride. "Drop it, Elva. Let it be. When you're a mother you'll understand."

Something about this chilled Elva's blood. When she looked at the baby she thought its eyes were glittering, but the power of its infantile concentration was so forbidding that she had to look away. Clearly there was something going on here. If only she could get her sister alone, she thought, but she and this child of hers seemed to be joined at the hip, like Siamese twins, in a symbiotic relationship that a nonmother like herself did not even want to understand.

What's more, there was no time that day that they were not taken up with preparations or the baby's feeding or the baby's outing, or the baby's evening bath. If he would only take a *nap*, Elva thought, but at naptime Rilla curled up on the sofa with him, exhausted, leaving Elva alone in her uneasiness. They were so close—mother, child—that Elva left the house simply to escape their intense communion, which was how she found herself in the little gorge at the back of the lot, a tiny declivity which she jumped so she could go walking in the woods. It was also how she happened upon another upturned rib cage and shuddered because it was of a size and shape that recalled Rilla's shaggy Newfoundland, which on all her other arrivals had jumped up on her with enthusiastic paws, muddying her dress. Could this be—was this? Fighting revulsion, she stirred the leaves until she heard something rattle and her fingers closed on what she already knew to be a set of metal tags.

She ran back to the house with her heart pounding, threw open the door, prepared to confront her sister and then be on her way to home and safety, her dressing table, her own bath, but she was brought up short by the fact that there were two voices coming from the living room —her sister's and a man's.

This then, accounted for the shattering of her concentration and her failure of will: the burning need to make herself right before a mirror so she could go in and meet him. She was already certain it would be Dack.

Imagine her surprise when she emerged in her silk blouse and her silver earrings, with her hair just so, to discover her sister jogging the baby and talking over its head to a police officer: something about a missing child which she dismissed in part because the implications were disturbing and in part because the lieutenant was tall and clearly impressed by the way the shape of her earrings echoed the pattern in her blouse. He was also adorable.

"Well," she said, "how do you do?"

The lieutenant was clearly drawn, but he was on business. He finished writing in his notebook. "So that's all you know."

"Yes," Rilla said, but her mind wasn't on it. She kept jiggling the baby. "That's all I know."

Elva whispered, "Maybe he'd like to come to the party."

Rilla brightened. "We're having a party tomorrow night."

He was looking at Elva. "I'd love to come."

In her sister's arms, the baby bubbled and hummed.

So she might have gotten away then, come off clean and gone home to her life, but did not because of her own cupidity. Here was a man who admired her, who would be coming tomorrow night for Rilla's party, and whether or not they hit it off in the long run, there was also Dack. In one of Rilla's Polaroids he had his shirt off; with any luck she could get him to take her away right after the party; she'd think of some story to explain why before they'd even met her bags were all packed. Meanwhile all she had to do was stick it out through tonight and tomorrow. She looked sternly at the baby, which looked at her. *We're only going to have to put up with each other one more night.*

She thought she caught a difference in its expression, something specific to her—a yellow, malevolent, directed glimmer of—what?

By the time the officer left it was time to have dinner, which Elva in a fit of guilt ordered from Domino's Pizza, although for reasons which were never quite clear Rilla insisted on her meeting the delivery person at the end of the drive. Warmed by the light from the TV, the sisters ate in silence, switching off the newscast because it was all about the missing toddler. News like that was bad for the baby, Rilla said, and when Elva said, reasonably, that she could put him to bed so he wouldn't have to hear, Rilla gave her a weary look that described all the hardships of its six months of life and hers of motherhood. All she said was, "Bad news makes me feel bad."

"Look." Baby or no baby, Elva had to find out. "What happened to the dog?"

"The dog. Oh, the dog." Rilla was pretending to be vague, but it was clear she was severely shaken. She covered the baby's ears.

"I found a skeleton and some dogtags."

"Oh," she said mournfully, "so that's what happened to the dog."

All Elva's suspicions hit bottom, assuming a clear shape.

She knew. "My God," Elva said, afraid to speak its name. "You're going to have to do something about him!"

Rilla's arms tightened around the thing. She shook her head in a passion of denial. "He's only a little baby."

"I don't care what he is."

Besotted with love, Rilla hugged and rocked, rocked and hugged. "He's my baby," Rilla said.

"Then he's your problem. I'm getting out of here."

"Dack."

"Right after the party," Elva said.

Without knowing why, Elva found it necessary to wear her best boots to the bathroom shortly after midnight, and while she was sitting on the toilet with the lights off, she was disturbed by unfamiliar sounds. When she came out there was indeed something in the corridor—an armature of some kind; it was small and light and toddler-sized; it rattled when she bumped into it. In the near darkness it could almost have been a skeleton, but fear kept her from bending down to see. Instead she looked up quickly and saw something small and pale flittering around the corner, heading for her sister's bedroom: the flick of a nightshirt, the slither of a tiny foot.

The baby, she thought. *She put it down after all.*

In her head there was a warning bell ringing, faint but fearsome, but by this time Elva was too upset to do anything but lock herself in her own room and take a sleeping pill because the big party was the next night, and she had to get—all right, she thought, I have to get my beauty sleep.

This was how it happened that she overslept, and woke in mid-afternoon to a house so silent that she thought everybody must have fled it in the night. When she came into the hall long shadows fell at bizarre angles, striping the perfectly ordinary little house and turning it into something more, or different—a place in which, since she had been foolish enough to ignore danger signs, she could logically expect what happened next.

She had been wrong about the silence. It was not complete. Faint sounds she could not identify came from the master suite where her sister had slept with her husband, Stanley, until Stanley went away.

"Rilla?" she called, and received a strangled answer—not words, exactly, but definitely her sister's voice.

"In here," Rilla managed finally.

"Rilla?"

"I need you."

Just what I was afraid of, Elva thought.

"Rilla?" she called, following the sound down the crazily tilted hallway to the bedroom, through the half-opened door, and into the master bath, which was where she found them, mother and child, what was left of Rilla locked in the dreadful act of nurturing, apparently paralyzed but still alert and gaga with mother love, dying Rilla slumped against the tub.

"Rilla, how horrible!"

"He's my baby," Rilla said.

Behind Elva, the door swung shut; the lock engaged in an inexorable click. Slowed by sleeping pills, mesmerized by the baby's glare, she could not escape.

Instead she waited while it finished, regarding it. There was power in the fiery eyes when it nudged the remains of its mother and looked up. She saw determination written on the mouth and signed in the bloody saliva dripping from the jaws. It wasn't going to let her leave.

It was her baby now.

She knew she ought to do something: scream, run, stamp it to death, but she knew as surely as she tried that it would destroy her, or at the least it would destroy her looks. She knew she ought to break the door down with her bare hands if she had to, get out while she could, and knew it was already too late. She also knew there were a hundred people coming to the party tonight.

Now that it was finished, it began hitching toward her in that strange, three-pointed crawl that ordinary babies had—arms, bottom, arms, helped along by adorable curling feet. It put up its rosy little hands, begging to be picked up. It blinked, with its eyes overflowing with baby love, its mouth promising a baby kiss.

A hundred people coming, and she hadn't finished the hors d'oeuvres. That nice lieutenant. Dack.

It was waiting.

A hundred.

It was kind of cute.

"There, there." She put out her arms and it sprang. She was startled by its pleasing warmth as it locked its legs and arms around her midsection like a homing creature, surprising her with its soft weight. "There, there," she said. "There, there. We've got a hundred people coming, mmm? A hundred, mmm . . ."

"Mmm."

"Mmmmm?" She joggled the thing and it began to hum. "Plenty for both of us."

RANSOM COWL WALKS THE ROAD

by Nancy Varian Berberick

Nancy Varian Berberick lives in a small rural town in the hills of northwestern New Jersey with her husband and teenaged son, two dogs, and two computers. She quit the business world at the end of 1984 to go freelance. Her fiction has appeared in *Amazing,* TSR's three *Dragonlance* anthologies, and has been excerpted in *How to Write Tales of Horror, Fantasy, and Science Fiction*. Another short story appeared in TSR's *The Art of DRAGON Magazine*. Her novel, *Stormblade,* will be published in September 1988. A second novel, *The Jewels of Elvish,* will appear early in 1989.

Nancy provides us with a dark glimpse of a small town in New Jersey, out by the Delaware River. Perhaps not very different from her own town or even mine.

✦ ✦ ✦

Dre: my husband's name has always held the magic to make me smile. Bowdre Carson. I can still hear his mother calling him. She would stand at the back door of the enormous old house. "Bowdre!" she would call, pause, and then louder: "Bowdree!" The *dreee!* would rise, skirling into the summer blue sky, losing none of its demand for distance. Dre would stop what he was doing at once. He'd grin sheepishly, and shrug, then scramble off to answer the summons. And always, before he left, he would stop to pull one of my long black braids and then dance away laughing. I didn't know it then, of course, but I probably loved Dre even in those golden days when being eight made the summer last forever.

I never longed, as many of my friends did, to leave our little town in the hills of western New Jersey. For me there were no bigger and better things to find than Dre and little Petersons Run. The years spent away at college were obligatory and I quickly put them behind me. Returning to Petersons Run to teach seemed right. I like completed circles. And after my first year at the grammar school "Karen Keller" became "Karen Carson" and I was happy.

My days moved to the songs of children, skip-rope rhymes, and learning tunes. *"A" my name is Alice and my husband's name is Al* . . . and *Lincoln, Lincoln, I've been thinkin', what's that stuff that you been drinkin'* . . . or *I before E except after C*. And, still, as it had been during the time that Dre and I watched the years move along outside the wide classroom windows: *Ransom Cowl walks the road, Ransom Cowl can see! Ransom Cowl walks the road, and he comes for thee!* And the *thee!* would rise, high, almost hysterically high, and end in giggles and gasps.

Ransom Cowl was Petersons Run's own mass murderer.

He haunted the nights of the town's children with a delicious fear, mitigated by the nearness of parents murmuring in soft conversation, and the completed ending of the terrible story. Ransom Cowl had met justice. Strapped into a huge, ungainly wooden chair he went, assisted by killing voltage, to a quicker death than any of his victims had met. And each child knew that when a story is ended, it is ended. No one seemed to remember that the little rhyme chanted in schoolyards to the cadence of a skip rope was the curse of Beckon Cowl, spat out into the hot July dust the day her grandson was executed.

✦ ✦ ✦

Jason's Meadow was named for Dre's maternal great-grandfather. The house, one hundred fifty years old and still in good condition, had been in his family since it was built to hold his great-grandfather's brood of seven children. It was a large, neatly laid-out clapboard at the edge of the four acres of Jason's Meadow that remained to Dre's family. The house came to Dre in the normal course of things, and both of us were happy to continue our lives together in this place where we'd played during our childhood. Another circle complete, I would think, as I went about cleaning the many rooms. Our children would grow up here, and theirs. My roots, when they are set, are set deeply.

I listened to the sighing of the snow in December, the insistent piping of cardinals in May, and the winding *chirrrr* of cicadas in July. These were the songs of my life until dirges came to replace them.

✦ ✦ ✦

That year, though I was grateful for the summer school classes that provided extra money, I was also grateful that they would soon be over. Two more weeks, I thought as I took the steps of the front porch. Two more weeks!

I could sense Dre's mood before I saw him. I knew he was in the kitchen at the back of the house, brooding over a beer, before I called out. "Too many years together," he used to say when I did what he called reading his mind. He'd laugh and shake his head and swear that there was no use keeping secrets from me. I didn't read his mind, of course, and we both knew it. It was just cumulative knowledge. He could do the trick, too, but didn't very often.

"Dre?"

"Back here, honey." His voice was flat, dull, empty of anything that would tell me his mood. Still, I knew.

"You're home early." I dropped my book bag onto the sofa in the living room, scooped up the mail from the coffee table, and went through into the kitchen. July sunlight splashed soft squares of gold across the wide planked floor. The earthy scents of basil, thyme, and oregano interlaced under the sun's heat with the marigolds' musk and drifted in from the kitchen garden.

Dre pushed his beer aside and sat back. His dark thick hair was rumpled, his wide mouth, usually so generous with his smile, was a grim, hard line.

"Bad day," he sighed.

It was a standing joke between us: how bad could a day be on a police force of four men when two of them took turns napping from boredom? But there was no laughter in Dre's green eyes today.

"What happened, hon?"

"The cemetery's been vandalized."

"Oh, no."

"Yeah." His eyes were filled now with disgust.

"Badly?" I filled a tall glass with ice and poured myself a soda.

"One grave's been dug up."

"Ugh! Any ideas?"

"Not a one. That's why I'm home early. Just stopped in to get a bite to eat. I'll be out late tonight, Karen."

"Why?"

Dre shook his head. "It's not going to be fun, but Pete

and I have drawn what you might call a graveyard shift tonight." For the first time a smile, wry at his own bad pun, lighted his face.

"I'll fix you a sandwich. Want something to take for tonight?"

"I don't think I could eat a thing tonight. Coffee would be nice, though."

I didn't know where the thermos was, but I got to my feet, determined to root through attic and cellar until I found it.

"Thanks, Karen."

"Sure." I paused in the doorway. "Which one? Which grave?"

Dre pulled in a chest full of air and let it out in a gusting sigh. "Ransom Cowl's."

I didn't say "ugh" this time. Chills crawled up my arms, my stomach was suddenly too tight and full of an old childhood fear. I heard, in my mind, the rhythmic slap-slap-slap of a school yard skip rope and the voices of young girls singing an old song that was peculiar to Petersons Run alone.

My determination to search through the dark attic and the musty cellar flagged a little, but I would not send him out into the night without his coffee. Dre must have seen the squaring of my shoulders because his "atta girl" followed me down the hall.

✦ ✦ ✦

A lovely New Jersey night can turn threatening and ugly in only an hour. The dusk's promise of a clear evening went unfulfilled. Grey clouds hung, leaden and sulking, over Jason's Meadow. The approaching storm's power breathed in the air. The potent humidity of a steamy night crept into the house. In the hall the old Regulator clock groaned once and struck three times.

Startled by the weighty, echoing bongs, I realized that the volume of Shakespeare had fallen, unnoticed, from my hand. Though the night was warm, I shivered. I was listening. I had been listening, though not consciously, through the last scenes of the fourth act of Hamlet. The words, lovely, amusing, intricately woven, had passed through my mind, leaving little mark. My breathing had become soft, cautious. Polonius went to his death unremarked by me, and Hamlet made his discourse with his uncle about the fate of men and worms unheeded by me.

I was listening, and now I knew what it was that I listened for. Dre was not due back yet from his cemetery stakeout. But like the night waiting for the storm, I waited and listened for his return.

Even as I realized this, I heard his car, the soft hum of the Volvo's engine on the long driveway that wound from the road to the house. Relief gusted through me and my breath came in a choppy sigh. I closed the book and went to the front door to watch the swinging arc of the Volvo's headlights sweep the elms that huddled near the garage.

The car's door chunked closed. A moment later I heard Dre's feet crunching on the driveway's gravel, the only sound in the thick, hot night.

"Honey?" I called.

He was a dark patch of night, moving closer to the house, his head down, his shoulders hunched.

"Dre?"

A cicada started up its whirring somewhere nearby. I gasped; my hand flew to my throat. A cricket piped its monotonous song, high, higher, high, under the front porch. My pulse jerked and thumped under my fingertips. The insects sounded too loud in the waiting stillness.

"How'd you make out, Dre?" Thunder growled in the western sky, lightning flashed, throwing the garage and the elms into startling silhouette. Close on that flash came another, and I saw Dre's face, pale and drawn. His eyes were dark pits of shadow. This time I could not read his mood. I shivered again in the hot night air and stepped out onto the porch.

"Come on in, honey, I'll fix you some coffee."

"I'm tired, Karen. I just want to go to bed."

He did look tired. His feet were dragging, his shoulders slumped. When he passed me I heard the soft slither of dirt dropping from his shoes. He smelled of dark earth and sunless places; the pungent scent of crushed weeds clung to him.

I followed him up to bed and didn't think to ask why he had abandoned his graveyard shift early.

✦ ✦ ✦

The voice was high and thin, an echo of voices I had heard drifting in from the playground through the open windows of my classroom.

"Ransom Cowl walks the road! Ransom Cowl can see!"

In my dream I shuddered. Cold sweat traced clammy paths down my neck, between my breasts.

"Ransom Cowl walks the road!" Now the tinny echoing quality of the voice was gone. The words were spoken in a quavering old voice filled with groaning and hatred. I could not breathe. It was as though a hand pressed down upon my chest.

"And he comes for *theeeee!*"

I screamed. And behind my scream I heard the crackling old voice tell me that I could scream until my throat bled, I could scream until my eyes, clenched against the dread and terror, threatened to burst. It makes no difference: Ransom Cowl still comes.

He was filthy with evil, he wore it like a shroud, bore it like a shield. He laughed, and that laughter was the knell of church bells, tolling in mourning. He howled, and the howling was the sound of Death triumphant.

Putrid and stinking of hopeless, midnight places, rotting grave clothes still clinging to his wasted body, he shambled to the bed. His lifelessness chilled me to the bone, sucking from me all that was warm and alive. My heart slammed hard against my ribs, a terrified rabbit in a cage of bones. My ears were filled with the sound of my own racing blood. His scabrous hand, scraps of decayed flesh shivering on the white bones of his fingers, touched my lips.

"Lovely," he said. I heard the word as a doom pronounced, a sentence handed down. Nausea twisted my stomach and bile burned a searing path to my throat.

Thunder growled in the distance. A storm prowled close to the valley.

His face came close to mine and I could smell the rotten stench that gusted from his decaying, gap-toothed mouth. It was the stink of something long dead in the bushes, moldering and putrefying. Then I saw, the shock of the sight racing through me like an electrical current, that he had only empty, gaping sockets where his eyes should have been.

"Oh, God, no!" I screamed, and I was, at last, awake.

As though my scream had been the power that called

it, lightning danced at the window, tossing huge, unrecognized shadows across the walls of my familiar bedroom.

There was a hand on my face.

"Karen." Dre's voice was soft, inquiring. His fingers stroked my cheek, moved up to brush my hair back from my face.

"Dre—I—it was—"

"It's all right," he whispered, leaning closer to me, curling his leg over mine beneath the sheet. "It's all right, it's all right."

"A—a nightmare—" I shivered, trembling hard as if from a bone-freezing cold.

"I know. It's all right." He tucked his chin over my shoulder and buried his face in my hair, offering the comfort of his nearness, of his body. But when his hand moved up to my breast, when his lips brushed gently against my ear as he murmured, "Lovely," my blood turned to ice.

"Dre."

"Lovely Karen." He sighed.

"No. No, Dre." I turned away from him and felt his leg move away, his hand draw back to my shoulder.

"It was just a dream, Karen."

"I know," I said, my voice a quivering whisper. I did know. And he had always called me "lovely" just before his lips moved from my ear to my neck, to my shoulder. But "lovely" had new echoes that I hated and feared.

I told myself that the dream would be gone in the morning, leaving not even a shadow of fear to be remembered by. I apologized silently to Dre, knowing that he would understand.

And he must have understood, for I heard his even,

gentle breathing before long. I did not sleep that night, but listened to the rolling progress of the storm as it marched into our little valley.

✦ ✦ ✦

When the phone rang my mouth was full of toothpaste. "Dre?" I called through clenched teeth. He didn't answer me, but must have answered the phone because it went silent after three rings. I finished brushing my teeth, washed up quickly, and pulled my robe closer around me. As I racketed down the stairs, I cursed the alarm clock I hadn't heard and decided that Dre and I were getting no better a breakfast than juice and cold cereal this morning. He was already in the kitchen, slouched in a chair. His elbows were on the table, his hands covered his eyes. It was not an unfamiliar pose: Dre tried to protect himself from the morning for as long as possible.

"OJ, honey?" I asked.

"No."

"Cereal?"

"No."

"Who was on the phone?"

"Pete's wife."

"Clare? What's up?" Yet even as I asked the question, I recalled, from some odd tangent of memory, that I hadn't asked Dre why he'd come home so early last night. I nudged the refrigerator door closed behind me and put the orange juice on the table. "Sure you won't have any juice, honey?"

"No!" The word was a bullet fired through the morning silence. Startled, I dropped the glass I'd been holding.

The little bright shards scattered across the wooden floor, glittering in the sunlight. I held my breath and watched them spin and tumble.

"I'm sorry, Karen. I'm sorry."

He might have been, but I saw nothing of it in his eyes. They were dark holes in a face that was too pale. There wasn't enough room for apology in those eyes, crowded as they were with confusion and a haunted fear. Quietly, I swept the broken glass from the floor.

"Dre? What is it?"

"Pete didn't get home last night."

"Well, but—didn't you drop him off?"

His answer came fast. "Yes, of course I did."

"At the house?"

"At the road. He wanted to walk in."

"But—" I shook my head and took another tack. "You guys didn't stay very late last night."

"I think the wrong one of us is the cop in this house," Dre said coldly. He didn't look at me when he spoke. His eyes, those pits of confusion, were riveted to the table. The forefinger of his right hand traced the ancient pattern of some child's homework, engraved long ago into the soft pine planking.

"Dre."

"Leave me alone, will you, Karen? I'm tired, and I don't know where Pete is. Clare is upset. Will you stop by to see her on your way to school?"

I was late already, and for a moment my conscience warred between declaring a convenient illness so that I could spend the day with Clare, and the fact that my students would be dismissed early today because I couldn't find a substitute teacher at this hour. Clare—or perhaps it was the students—won.

"I'll call in sick, Dre. They can spare me for a day, I'm sure."

His "atta girl" was perfunctory, barely grunted. I put it down to his concern for Pete and kissed him briefly on the top of his head. He moved his hand as though to touch mine, but the gesture died with his sigh.

✦ ✦ ✦

Clare hadn't immediately fallen into the "My God, He's Dead" syndrome. She worked her way toward it through the "My God, He's Cheating on Me" syndrome first.

By the time she'd reached the point of aggressively asserting that Pete was "a good man, a wonderful husband, he'd never cheat on me—*never!*—he loves me, loves the kids . . ." we'd gone through too many pots of coffee and eaten too many cookies. The evening sun slanted in through her kitchen windows, seven o'clock mellow. There was nothing left to face now but the fear that Pete was dead. When she finally acknowledged that fear, Clare's voice was a cracked whisper from which hope leaked fast.

"He's *not* dead, Clare."

"But where is he then? Where?"

I didn't know. I didn't know where Dre was either. He hadn't called at all that day. I snatched at this and patted Clare's trembling hand with an assurance I hardly felt.

"We haven't heard from Dre yet. Surely we'd have heard if something were wrong. Come on, come on, now."

She'd sent the two children to stay with her mother. I didn't know whether or not she'd told them that their father hadn't come home the night before. I thought now that the children would be just the comfort she needed.

But when I offered to pick them up and drop them off she only shook her head.

"No, Karen, not now. Not yet."

Her thick blonde hair was a tumbled mess. She'd piled it carelessly atop her head this morning and it fell now, in fits and straggles about her face and neck. She'd been plowing her fingers through it all day. Her face, one I'd always thought of as pretty and plump, looked haggard and bloated now. Without her makeup, in fear's harsh light, she appeared far older than forty-two.

"Karen, call the station for me? Call them to see what's going on? I can't stand this waiting anymore."

I didn't want to do it. I didn't want to hear the dispatcher's patient kindness. But I couldn't watch Clare gnawing at herself, either, poised to leap for a phone that hadn't rung all day.

The dispatcher's voice sounded like that of a mother who assures her frightened child that it was only a dream, only a nightmare, that there's really nothing to worry about. She hadn't heard from Dre all day, but, yes, he'd been out with the others looking for Pete.

"There are lots of people looking for him, Clare," I assured her as I hung up the phone. "The police, the whole auxiliary staff." It didn't make her feel better. Though Clare hadn't wept all day, tears threatened now in eyes bruised from exhaustion. Her lips trembled, her hands moved in unconscious jerks through her hair. I made a quick decision.

"Come with me,"

She looked puzzled. "Where?"

"Home. We'll wait there."

"No."

"Clare."

"No! I want to be *here*."

"Then I'm going to run home and leave a note for Dre. I'll get a few things and spend the night."

She didn't refuse that. Her gratitude poured from her eyes in the first tears I had seen all day.

✦ ✦ ✦

The storm was a terrible one. Between the house-shaking blasts of thunder I heard rain lashing against the window of Clare's guest room. Lightning splashed the room with a baleful glare, threw the furniture into huge silhouette. Shadows staggered across the walls. I'd asked Clare if she wanted me to sleep with her, thinking she would want the comfort of another person nearby. I regretted her refusal more for my own sake than hers. It was a long time before I slept.

"Ransom Cowl walks the road."

The dream was upon me, smothering me like a thick woolen blanket. The tremorous old voice whispered in my ears, drifted around in my sleeping mind.

"Ransom Cowl can see."

In my dream I moaned.

It had been on all the local news stations, even the national news had carried the story for one day. *In the small New Jersey town of Petersons Run a local man is accused of murdering six women.* A serious, grim voice, newscaster-perfect in its enunciation, rolled through the dream.

And yet, how did I know this? How could the words of a broadcast that was older than I am whisper now in my dream?

My dream world began to rumble, to shake, like the quavering old voice that spoke the rhyme. "Ransom Cowl walks the road."

The six women had been butchered. It was a term too

frequently used these days to mean brutally murdered. These women *had* been butchered. Like heifers for market, they had been neatly, cleanly taken apart. There had been no evidence of a killing wound. They'd been butchered alive.

"And he comes for *theee!*"

Death-awkward, he staggered across the guest room and stopped at the bedside. His fingers were ice upon my face. His nails, longer in death than they should have been in life, rested lightly on my cheek. A relentless, dread-filled ache seeped through me as his lifeless chill passed through skin and blood and bone. It touched deep inside me, reaching for the core of who I was.

Ransom Cowl scratched against the surface of my soul, chipped away shards of reality. I could not have screamed had I wanted to. And I did not want to this time. It seemed then that everything within me, my heart, my lungs, my mind, everything that *was* me, halted, paused, listened. Horror was crouched, ready, waiting to burst the boundaries of the thing I call my soul. It never did. My pent breath, ready to erupt in a ranting scream, sighed tremblingly away.

"Lovely," he said, his voice a grating rasp. "Lovely." He leaned nearer, filling my whole dream with the stench of his breath, and the rotting stink of his body. The white bone of his skull gaped in places through the putrefying flesh that had once been his face. Then, as on the night before, I did scream.

And, as on the night before, I was suddenly awake. My husband stood at my bedside.

"Dre!"

"Right here, Karen."

"How—how did you get here?"

His smile was slow and familiar. "I found your note, of course. I didn't want to spend the night alone."

I couldn't blame him. I sat up and reached for his arms. The storm had passed, leaving behind a sweet, clean breeze. It plucked now at the curtains, made their yellow rosebud pattern dance like a field of flowers in the wind.

"How did you get in?"

"Pete had his key."

"Pete! You found him!"

"Sure did."

"Where—?"

"Tomorrow, Karen. It's late and I'm tired."

"What time is it?"

He sat on the edge of the bed, pulled off his shoes, and rose to unzip his pants. "Four. Now hush and let me in."

I moved over in the little double bed, made room for him, and cuddled next to him. I had turned away from his comfort the night before. I wouldn't tonight.

But he made no advance, simply settled down beneath the sheets and turned his back to me. "Good night," he mumbled.

Fair is fair, I thought wryly, and turnabout, they say, is fair play. I kissed the back of his head. "Good night."

I dreamed again, and heard only whispering, murmuring, and laughing. Snatches of the old rhyme drifted in and around these sounds, but I didn't wake until morning.

✦ ✦ ✦

Bacon sizzled and spat in the pan. Coffee sent its familiar comfortable smell throughout the house. Despite the hour he'd arrived, Dre was up and humming around the kitchen, lurking near the stove for the first cup of coffee.

"You must be exhausted," I said, giving the bacon a final shake.

"Too wired to sleep."

I could understand that. It was why I was awake, rambling around in an unfamiliar kitchen, making breakfast. "I've made enough for Clare and Pete. Should I wake them?"

Dre shrugged.

"Where did you finally find Pete?"

Dre poured his coffee and took a seat at the table. "It's a long story, Karen. Wait until he's had a chance to explain to Clare. I'll tell you when we get home."

Had Pete been with some woman? Had he been cheating on Clare? I felt a sudden flare of anger, remembering her torment of fear. The anger must have shown on my face because Dre chuckled a little.

"Don't go jumping to conclusions, Karen."

"No, you're right." I smiled at him, feeling suddenly sheepish, and noticed that there was a smear of mud near the counter where he stood. "Dre, you're tracking up Clare's kitchen."

He glanced down at his feet and shrugged again. "Sorry."

His shoes were filthy, and dark stains smeared the legs of his pants. Where had he found Pete, anyway? "Oh, Dre, what a mess! See if you can find a broom. I'm going to see if Clare and Pete are awake."

✦ ✦ ✦

My light tap at the bedroom door went unanswered. I knocked a little harder and waited. There was no sound from within. Maybe we should just have breakfast, I thought, leave a note, and call them later. I was anxious to get home anyway. But I tried one more time.

"Clare?"

I tapped again at the door. "Pete?" Nothing, not even snoring. The door was ajar, and as I turned to go back down the stairs my shoulder brushed against it. It opened with a creak and a sigh. A yellow line of sunlight from the bedroom window widened on the floor at my feet.

"Anybody awake?"

No one stirred. Shrugging, I reached for the doorknob, thinking to pull the door shut. I caught a glimpse of the room and saw only Clare lying still in the middle of the large bed, her hand flung over the side.

Was Pete up already? I listened, but heard no sound from the bathroom. "Clare?"

She didn't move. The morning breeze stirred at her window, fluttering the curtains. I wondered, suddenly, if she was all right. I'd made enough noise out here to wake the—

"Clare?"

I stepped into the room, not caring now that I was invading private territory. The white shag carpet was splashed with mud and something red.

"My God." My throat was tight and dry, my blood hummed and pounded in my head. Clare's blood was splattered all over the carpet. She was not all right.

The room spun around me, nausea churned in my stomach. The once-good smells of bacon and coffee drifted up from the kitchen, sickening me. I clamped my hands across my mouth as vomit rushed up against my teeth with its acid sting.

No one part of Clare was connected to another. The pieces of her lay on the bed, like parts of a toy ready for assembly. Everything was laid out neatly, arms near the torso, legs where they should be, her head upon the pillow. Her lovely blonde hair splayed across sheets that were crimsoned with her blood.

I wailed. "Dre! Dre! Dreeeee!"

I bolted from the room, gasping, moaning a "no-no-no" chant of denial. I dashed my knee against the door. Pain burst like a fireball and raced along my leg but I did not stop. I scrambled for the stairs and took them running, stumbling twice. My leg screamed pain from my ankle to my knee but I righted myself, still gasping "No-no-no!" I could not think about what I had just seen, I could not allow those pictures back into my mind. My only thought was to get to the kitchen and Dre.

"Dreee!" I gasped, falling to my knees at the bottom of the stairs. *No-no-no!* My mind coughed the words over and over, stuck in a groove of repetition. *No-no-no!*

His back was to me when I staggered into the kitchen. I fell against the table, grasping its edge as though it were the edge of a cliff. I heard the fat spattering in the frying pan, smelled the acrid stink of bacon burning.

"Dre! My God, my God, Dre! She's dead!"

When he turned he was Dre. And yet he was not Dre.

"I know." His voice was hollow, deep and cold. His eyes, Dre's eyes, were pits, holes, empty of any emotion. Even as fear's icy finger skipped up my spine my stomach clenched against a sudden flood of adrenaline. His face was changing before my eyes, shifting, wavering.

"Dre—"

The flesh of his face thinned. His jaw became more square now, his face longer. Dre's dark hair turned, before my horrified eyes, to slatey grey. His straight white teeth became ravaged by decay. I could smell the stink of his breath from across the kitchen.

I'd seen the pictures, grainy black and white newspaper

photos. Every child in Petersons Run had sought them out at one time or another. When I was young it was almost a rite of passage: find a picture of Ransom Cowl, look at it, and try to suppress the giggling squeal of fear that you hoped your friends thought was only pretended. But I'd seen more than pictures. I'd seen him two nights running in my dreams.

No-no-no! The chant started up in my mind again. Breathless and terrified, it was a child's denial.

"Yes," he said, his voice as cold as winter's ice. His fingers gently caressed the shining edge of a carving knife. "Yes, yes."

He did not shamble now. He had the strength of Dre's body, Dre's strong legs, powerful and muscled. He leaped for me, throwing himself across the table, the knife gleaming silver in the sunlight.

I scrambled around the table, keeping it between him and me. "No! Dre! Dre!"

But he was no longer my Dre, and there was no emotion to respond to my pleading. There was only Ransom Cowl, muttering "Lovely, lovely, lovely," and a voice, ghostly and cracked with age, whispering that Ransom Cowl could see.

My knee throbbed where I had smashed it against Clare's bedroom door. My hands shook, palsied with fear. Breathing in short, panting gasps, I wrapped my fingers around the back of a chair and took two retreating steps until the small of my back touched the counter. Fat from the burning bacon spattered against my arm, bit my skin with needle-sharp, fiery teeth.

"Lovely, lovely."

Dre's prelude to love, growled from the rotting throat of the thing before me, made me furious. It was violation, a rape of moments that had been beautiful. My fury gave me the strength I needed to act. Clutching the chair with one hand, I reached for the frying pan with the other.

The thing laughed, a guttural sound, and lunged around the table.

No-no-no! my mind gibbered. *No-no-no!* I hurled the spitting frying pan at the thing's face, laughed and screamed to hear its howl of pain. It could be hurt! My heart cringed at the knowledge. Of course it could be hurt; it was, in some awful way, Dre.

It still had the knife, grasped in fingers that were rotting before my eyes. It leaped from where it was crouched on the floor, hitting me low. I crashed to the floor, my elbow smashed against the stove, my head thumped against the floor.

No-no-no! I clawed at its face and pieces of skin came off in my hands. Bile rushed up my throat. I spat it out and forced my heaving stomach to calm. The Dre-thing lay across me full length, its face touching mine, its knees thrusting in attenuated kicks against my ribs. The knife in its right hand caught the light. The gleaming blade was all that I could see.

"Lovely, lovely, lovely."

It was going to kill me and my death would be a horrible one.

I thrust upward with all my strength but I could not move the thing. I twisted, screamed, kicked, but I could not free myself. My hand, in its flailing, found the frying pan. I clutched at its handle, raised it, and brought it crashing down on the thing's skull. The stinking face snapped away from mine, the body sagged and rolled off me. It was stunned, and I scrambled to my feet.

The knife! It lay a few inches from the creature's hand. *No-no-no!* It seemed that the screaming child in my mind already knew what I was about to do. *No-no-no!*

But I couldn't listen to it now. I couldn't take the time to consider what I was about to do. I simply did it.

The knife made horrible thudding sounds when I plunged it into the Dre-thing's chest, and wet, sucking sounds when I pulled it out. I did not butcher it—though the word would later be used to describe what I did. I killed it. I sent it back to the unholy grave it had come from, howling and screaming like a sidhe wailing across Irish moors.

And when I was done, it was not Ransom Cowl who lay beneath my hands. It was Dre. My Dre whom I'd loved from childhood, who had been all I'd ever asked from life. His head was smashed, his eyes seemed to stare, still frozen with terror, at my hands. His blood spattered in sticky drops from my fingers, tapping the first faint beat of a dirge that would haunt me all my days.

I wept for him, and wept for myself. Then I climbed to my feet. I staggered across the blood-smeared kitchen, moving numbly to the phone. *Police,* I thought, *I must call the police . . .* Victim, bereaved, and killer, I did not know what else to do.

I lifted the receiver. The dial tone sounded like the first whimpering echo in a long, black tunnel of loneliness.

TRUE LOVE

by Patricia Russo

Patricia Russo lives in North Bergen, New Jersey, and is employed at and attends New York University in New York City. At the moment she's going for a master's degree in linguistics, with a goal of getting a degree in anthropology. This is her first professional sale, although she's had a number of stories published in small-press magazines, including *Haunts, Z Miscellaneous, Space and Time,* and the *Minetta Review.*

Patricia's tale is one of the shortest included in the anthology, but packs quite a punch, nonetheless.

✦ ✦ ✦

The fellow swept in like a grenadier, whipping his cloak and stamping his feet and calling for ale in a loud voice, so naturally I gave him an eyeing while filling the tankard. He was a tall, lean, black-bearded chap, with a crooked scar down one cheek and an easy smile aimed to set any girl's heart to beating fast. Without so much as a nod to the men gathered round the fire, he sat himself on the hearth bench and stretched out his legs, so that the firelight flashed from silver buckles on his boots. If the fellow isn't a highwayman, I thought, then I'm a princess. And he didn't half drink like one, emptying three tankards before thinking to ask after some beef and sausage.

I wasn't surprised when old Bill took his pint and ambled over to the fire, for I'd marked him watching the fellow, too. He stood there, quiet, just watching the flames, for a couple of minutes. Finally the stranger gave him a sidelong glance, then another.

Shifting about on the bench a bit, he cleared his throat. "It's heading down Lincroft way, I am," he offered.

"Oh, aye?" Bill said and took a pull at his pint. "'Tis a long road, and a dusty one."

"That's no lie," the fellow said. "But I've got me a little miss lives on Flaxhill Road, and I reckon she'll make my journey's end sweet enough."

Some of the men sitting round the table by the fire burst out laughing, and the fellow flashed them a broad smile. Bill nodded, sort of slow and sad, and said, "Aye, love's sweet. And all the sweeter if the maid loves ye back."

"If she don't, then I don't know what love is," he said. "Hark ye, the wench's no common maid. 'Tis the daughter of the house herself, and her love'll make my fortune for me." He shook his empty tankard in the air. I took my time walking over with the pitcher.

"True love," Bill said dryly.

"True as any I ever had," the fellow snorted. "Let me tell ye, one girl's like another, no matter her quality. Sweet words in her ear, a skillful hand under her skirt, and it's true love to her, sure enough." As I was filling his mug, he jerked his chin at me and asked, "Hoy, missus, how much is it for a night's lodging?"

I straightened up before I looked at him. "This is no inn."

"No? Yet I spy a pallet in yon corner. I'll wager 'tisn't taken."

"I give ye my say already," I said, and was turning away when old Ned piped up from the end of the table.

"Now here's a woman ye won't get round with sweet words, lad. Nor sharp ones either, if the truth be told."

"No?" Rising, the stranger took the pitcher from my hand and dropped me a little bow. "A lass'll give ye the strings from her bodice if ye only ask her right, and I reckon a woman's the same, just a mite more choosy, perhaps. Now, ye seem a good-hearted woman, missus. Ye'll not throw a weary man out into the dark night, specially one as has got good silver to pay for his bed."

"It's how ye got that silver that's worrying me," I told him plain. The smile dropped from his mouth like a lead weight down a well.

"Ye'll be whistling another tune when I'm a gentleman," he said, real quiet. "Ye'll take my money and thank me for the privilege of doing it, ye and everybody else in this county."

"I'll be safe in my grave long before ye're ever a gentleman," I said.

The fellow threw his head back, his black eyes aflame. "I tell ye, woman, the girl loves me dear."

"Aye, and too dear for her, ye'll turn out to be," I said. "I know how easy a young girl's pulled astray by a handsome man's sweet words." Bill looked away a moment, for he was first cousins with my husband, Rob, who took up with a woman from Langleyford not a year after we were married, and soon after that disappeared altogether.

I didn't usually give much thought to Rob, but this fellow put me in mind of him in an odd way. He had the same sort of set to his shoulders and the same sort of tilt to his head—and the same sort of swagger to his talk.

"Never saw nor heard of an alewife yet who'd refuse my coin," he said. He dug a couple of shillings out of his waistcoat pocket and tossed them on the bench.

Sticking my fists on my hips, I gave him back as hard a look as he gave me. "I can read ye like a riddle, boy," I said. "Ye're one of those as thinks any woman they can't get round by love they'll win with money."

A couple of the old men hooted, and Ned banged his mug on the table appreciatively. Curling his lip, the fellow said, "Ye'll be telling me that ain't the way of the world next."

"It ain't always."

He gave a cocky laugh that sounded just like the one my Rob gave when I told him I knew all about his woman up in Langleyford, and settled down before the fire again. "Much an old woman like you'd know about love or money."

A powerful wish rose up in me to see this fellow cut down to size. Though my best cutting days were long gone, I said, "Tell me what ye know about love, then."

Cocking his head, he clasped his hands together behind his neck, and said softly, "My love is like a cherry without no stone."

Bill gave him a keen look, for riddling's a proper passion with him. This were a simple one, and Bill answered it real slow and easy. "Well, yer love's like a cherry blossom, then, I see."

"Aye," he said. "Pretty and pink and ready to be plucked." Grinning at me, he said, "And my love is like a yellow apple washed in a white wave."

Now he thought he were smart, but that weren't no hard one neither. "She's like butter in a churn, is she?" I said.

"Aye." He laughed. "Soft and sweet and just waiting to be patted all over." He crossed his ankles, and the firelight gleamed red on his silver buckles. "And my love is like a little room, black as night outside, and bright as day within."

There weren't much of a trick to that, considering how his thoughts were running. So I said, "Ye think she's a treasure chest, I take it."

"Ah, she's the chest, and the treasure, too." Sitting up a bit, he threw a glance around the room. "Look here, I've given ye three. Who'll give me one?" But he was really talking to me, and everybody knew it. When his gaze came round to me, he said, "What about it, missus? Will ye riddle me for a bed?"

Now I know I shouldn't've done it, specially with Bill right there and him so good at riddling. But I thought if I set the fellow one he couldn't no way know the answer of, I'd be rid of him fast and fair and no complaining.

So I thought it out, then told him this: "I sat on my love, and I drank of my love, and my love, he gave me light. I'll give any man his lodging tonight, if he can read my riddle aright."

The fellow took his chin in his hand and looked real solemn. After a bit he got up and started to pace. "Hold on, missus," he said when I got to tapping my foot. "I got to think on it a minute. And since the riddle's in three parts, ye've got to give me three guesses at it, ye know."

So's not to have no arguing when he lost, I agreed. The fellow carried on pacing and mumbling to himself for a minute or two.

"Well," he said, when he finally stopped and looked at me. "First I was thinking yer man could be a sailor, and it were his sea chest ye was sitting on. But I couldn't get no further. Then I thought, it could be Love were the name of a horse, and it were him ye was sitting on, and his trough ye took a drink of. But then the light part stopped me, ye see." A little smile curved his lips, and he paused a moment before he went on.

"But then I thought of this, missus. Ye'll agree that a man's land's as much a part of him as his hands and eyes, and likewise whatever's on it." He looked around, and no one said him nay. "So I'll read it like this: ye sat on a chair weaved of withies that grew on yer love's land, and ye drank of ale brewed from the malt in his barn, and ye picked rushes from his fields for yer light. Well, missus? Tell me true, did I unriddle yer riddle or no?"

Now I was in a rather tight place. I could see Bill turning the answers over in his mind and nodding, and everybody seemed to think the fellow'd hit it fair, so all I could do was sigh and said he'd done it. I picked his shillings up from the bench and made up the pallet.

I saw him off next morning early, and glad I was to be shut of him. He made me remember a load of things best forgot. But wouldn't ye know it, even with him gone the thoughts kept nagging at me, sneaking into my head whenever my back was turned, ye might say. So, toward the end of the day, but before the evening custom started wandering in, I took the key from round my neck and unlocked the back-cellar door.

Shutting it quick, I locked it again behind me and went down the steps in darkness. I found the chair by touch and sat with a bit of trepidation, but it was firm and solid under me. 'Tis near forty years old, that chair, and nary a wobble to it. A fine piece of work, though I say it myself.

Striking a match on my shoe, I held it up and hunted for the box of candles. I recollected I'd left it by the chair. Feeling around underneath, I found the cup and a dusty bottle of wine, and lifted them. The match burned out, and I had to strike two more before I found the box. When I opened it I saw there was but one candle left, the skinniest and sorriest of the lot. I lit it, and the flame flared and flickered, making the shadows shake like aspen leaves. I was never a great hand at wick making, even as a girl.

Aye, the candles gave me the most trouble, for he were a lank fellow, with little enough fat to his flesh. I got grease enough for but five tapers, boil away however long I might. Skin and bones, my man was, all the days of his life.

Ah, but his bones was fine. I patted the white arm of the chair and leaned against the smooth curved ribs of its back with a sigh. Then I dug the cork out of the bottle and poured myself a cup of wine, careful not to spill any out the holes.

"Here's to ye, Rob," I toasted him, before I raised his skull to my lips. "The light and joy and support of my old age—all ye never was to me in my youth." And I drank deep of the sour wine, so as not to think of certain sweet words that curdled long ago.

IN THE SHADOWS OF MY FEAR

by Joan Vander Putten

Joan Vander Putten has held a number of sales jobs over the years, selling everything from door-to-door cosmetics to encyclopedias, the latter while she was pregnant. She has also worked at a crisis center. She's made short-story sales to *Devils and Demons,* a number of small-press magazines, and a chapbook entitled *Perdition Press*. Her first novel is completed, and a second one is in progress. She lives in Shoreham, New York, with her husband and five children.

Joan certainly proved to be the most persistent of all those who sent me stories; her patience finally succeeded.

✦ ✦ ✦

I open my eyes, and I am afraid. Again. Each day the fear licks me awake, follows me around the house, like an unwelcome pet. It is nearly ready, I think, to metamorphose into something tangible. But not yet, I sense, not until it wrings the last ounce of courage and sanity from my soul. It hounds me, a living thing at my side, ever present, as I move from room to room in Felicia's house; the house she so loved and invited me to live in with her. *My* house now, my lonely house, since her death.

Listening, I hear only the gentle kiss of the Gulf's waves as they meet the sandy beach below my window. I could swear to a movement at the edge of my vision, but when I turn quickly to catch the phantom I see only a lamp, a chair. The beast hides in the shadows of my fear, cautious as a stalking lion. Its origins are unknown to me, yet of one thing I am certain. It intends to win. I sense this with every nerve in my body, every pore that sweats icy anxiety.

I rise from Felicia's bed, noting that sometime during the night the mattress has become metal spikes. My skin is pricked and bleeding slightly. There is no pain, and I head for the bathroom. All the doorknobs in the house have become miniature skulls; their tiny teeth nip the heel of my hand as I grasp them, and the small bites never heal. The water in the basin becomes blood that stains my face red when I wash, making me use the drinking water in the refrigerator to scrub myself clean. I can never really get clean. My toothbrush is a small, steel rake that combs blood from my gums in tiny streams. I rinse and spit out repeatedly, until my spittle is no longer red-flecked. Still, I imagine I see blood.

Why do you do these things, Felicia? I refused to spill one drop of your blood. But if it is my blood you want, take it, with my assent. Take whatever it is you want of me. I am yours, and always will be. Oh, my darling, if only you knew your tortures go unheeded, perhaps you would stop these silly games of spite.

I have grown inured to Felicia's spite. Nothing the house, Felicia's house, can do hurts me, regardless of what orders she gives it. I am sure it is her spirit, seeking a vengeful justice, which plagues me.

But I no longer care about her tricks, for the fear is all-consuming, blinding me to slow changes of objects around me. The fear is not part of her tricks. It is part of *me,* joined to me, like a sinister Siamese twin. It tolerates no scrutiny, allows me no peace. Helpless to defend myself against it, I am slowly sinking into its hopeless depths.

And day by day, I find myself caring less.

I remember the days before the fear, the days when I laughed, and played, and loved my beautiful Felicia. Oh, *how* I loved! Too much, some would say; others, not enough. And because of my love I suffer now—and will for all eternity, I am convinced. But to have had the love of Felicia for even so short a time, to know that while she loved me I was complete—ah, that must suffice. But it does not, and the fear nibbles at my mind. The memories of her beautiful features and shining hair fade, lost in the whispers and mists of the past, escaping my outstretched fingers.

To have her here now, to feel her silken hands soothe and banish the constant trembling of my limbs, for that I would gladly deliver my soul into the hands of the hulking menace which is my constant companion. But it can never be, for my Felicia floats, slave to the whim of the tides, ever straining at her anchor.

I weep, sometimes, guilty with the knowledge it was wrong to put her there. But I could not bear to think of her young body ravaged by worms and ants, deep under the firm soil where I could never visit. Due to my forethought, we can spend happy hours in each other's company. Only occasionally, when I visit, do some bold fish swim over to bid us good day. For the most part they avoid us, choosing instead to explore other mysteries of their watery home.

Soon it will be time to leave for our tryst. I anticipate the daily appointed time I have set, and know that Felicia expects me there at the stroke of ten, much as a wife awaits her husband's nightly homecoming.

The fear will trail me into the warm Gulf, a hated sleuth that dogs my steps. But once I am with Felicia, it is strangely impotent. When I am with her, it skulks into the shadows of the deep—hiding, perhaps, among the brightly colored coral—impatient for my ascent, when it can leech itself to me once more.

I hurry to the bedroom to dress. I choose the shirt Felicia loved, the bathing suit she picked out. But when I don my clothes they flame up, scorching my body before they disintegrate, leaving a film of black smoke covering my skin. I must wash again to cleanse myself. Perhaps if I felt pain I would not be so annoyed by the delay they cause.

As it is, I feel nothing. Nothing except fear.

I sigh, and dress in other clothes. These behave normally, and it seems that for the time being the house, or Felicia, is done with tricks. I leave quickly, unwilling to keep my dearest waiting.

✦ ✦ ✦

My boat breaks free of its tethers and runs across the waves, like an eager pup seeking its mistress. It, too, was Felicia's, and seems to know the place she rests; it stops, almost unaided, at her exact position on the charts. I prepare to dive, anxious fingers fumbling with the oxygen tank on my back. The fear dives with me. I try to outdistance it with fast strokes of my flippers, and as I swim to the ocean's floor, I see the outline of my love's pliable, eternal home grow nearer. The fear slips further and further behind until I escape it completely. Although I know it merely lies in wait for my return, I am free, for a while, and I swim toward my darling.

Felicia's arm waves gracefully and I fancy she greets me, rather than admit she moves from the capricious tide. I embrace her gently, careful not to squeeze too hard. Bloated, her smooth skin rubs against the clear plastic bag encasing her, her body filling it almost completely. It was an oversight to neglect calculating how badly the water would swell her; the bag should have been larger. But she doesn't mind—not now, nor will she ever. Her silent swaying calls forth images of an embryo cozy in its placenta.

And here she will stay, that I may adore.

But her current situation is hazardous, I suddenly realize, when I see holes nipped in the plastic surface by curious fish. I frown, curse my stupidity and lack of forethought. Soon, I fear, the fish will shred the plastic enough to reach my beloved; another thing I failed to take into account when I conceived what seemed, in the heat of the moment, the perfect solution. Before they can harm her, I must take action; find a place where we can be together always, undisturbed and undiscovered. That is my goal, my only goal, my reason for living only to be with Felicia. At the present, my mind is empty of alternatives to her current predicament. Later, when not distracted by her nearness, I will puzzle it through, find the ultimate and only answer for us both—a place where we can finally be together for all eternity, never separated. But for now, my attention is focused on Felicia.

The green fungus on the plastic distorts her face, making it look pleated and sickly. Wiping it away, I gaze at her beauty. I am able to see beyond the water's destruction; her exquisite features are branded in my memory by love's blind vision. Blonde hair, once bleached by the sun, floats lackluster and lackadaisically around her head. Her wide eyes still accuse, although each day they become more like raisins lost in the puffy dough of her face. And her mouth, her perfect, rosebud mouth, still forms its round scream of horror, though silent these many days.

You have not yet forgiven me, my beautiful Felicia. Will you ever? You must. For now I am all you have, and you are mine alone. Why, my dearest, why did you drive me to this? We could be making love now on the beaches' warm sand, swimming in the Gulf's azure bath, instead of meeting secretly in its sepulchral depths.

What made you grow tired of our love, torment me with the threat of ending it? From the first time we kissed I knew that our destinies were inextricably woven together, meshed finer than the silk of your favorite mauve scarf, the one with which I ended your life.

"Marry me," I had asked.

But you only laughed, and called me silly.

"Come live with me," you said. "We'll have all of the fun, and none of the commitment."

So I did, even though it was your commitment I needed.

We lived in your house by the sea, with no one but the gulls for company. Our love nest, you called it. As the days went by, my life with you became my only memory. It blotted out my past, with its unhappy history of cruel women who left me—or *tried* to. None ever succeeded. I couldn't let them, of course. The pain would have been too great. But none, Felicia, *none,* I swear, did I love as much as you. Of them all, you are the only one I have wanted to keep.

As I explain all this to my love the water around us darkens, as if something blocks the sun from above me. I look up, just in time to catch a monstrous shape dart behind a coral reef. My fear, lying in wait to pounce upon me when I leave. But while there is oxygen in my tanks, I will remain. I check my gauges, surprised to find the oxygen supply so quickly diminishing. Did I bother to check it before I dived, or have I a death wish? No, no death wish. For my own death would end forever this last, tenuous tie between us, and that I could not bear. I must live; for it is only through my own life that Felicia will continue to exist. Without me, her memory, her very *being,* would deteriorate into nothingness. The escaping air hisses warning bubbles into the water above me and I resume my adoration. Time grows short.

Ah, Felicia, while you lived, we had such happy times! You bewitched me, spinning your magical web of enchantment ever tighter around my heart, until I thought it would burst from loving. Then, one day, you voiced your boredom with our love. I was slashed by your words, as the throats of those other women were, by my knife.

"I'm going out for a while to have some fun," you said.

"Fun? Without me?" I couldn't understand.

You laughed, but it was not your silvery, moonlight laugh. It was cold and derisive, filled with a loathing that made me shudder.

"You naive, romantic fool," you said, your beautiful eyes slitting into blue gashes, your perfect lips stretched in a sneer. And those were your last words.

I could hardly see your scarf for the tears in my eyes, but my pain helped me pick it up and wind it around your neck. No knife for you, my dearest. No ugly, gaping wounds that wept blood, not for the woman I had hoped to marry. Your body would be unscarred, preserved in its perfection.

Those same tears blurred my vision of your face as we kissed good-bye, a moment before you lost consciousness. Was that kiss as bittersweet for you as it was for me? I couldn't see.

The darkness has returned, hovering above and now closing in, it seems, on every side. My fear is finally solidifying. I will ignore it as long as I can. The water ripples strongly, as if trying to tug Felicia from my grasp. I continue our conversation, aware of a giddy light-headedness.

Do you remember, my love, our last, moonlit ride, to this place? I carried you to the boat over my shoulder. It was so late, and there was no one on the beach to see us. I held you in my arms with your head cradled close to my chest as your boat reluctantly took us to where we must part.

I don't remember where I found the bag—I think it was in the basement, near all the cartons from your recent move. Were you, too, running from someone? We were both solitary souls. Me, running from the authorities, who would never understand why I *had* to do what I did. They'll never catch me. I know well how to cover my tracks. But you—who were you running from? Or was it something you were running to? I don't think even you knew. You had no friends, you said, no relatives. I felt sorry for you at first, before I realized that it would make you fill your life with only me. In the end, it turned out to be a fortuitous circumstance.

On the boat that night, I thought to bring an extra anchor as well as the bag, and I was pleased with my preparations. I had not expected to be able to think so rationally. Seeing you now, I question if I did.

What I did *not* expect was your untimely revival. You certainly surprised me, my dear, when your eyes fluttered open. It unsettled me to discover I had removed the scarf before it had completed its work. You tried to scream, but your poor voice was so hoarse, remember? And you were weak—you could hardly struggle at all when I slipped you in the bag and tied it closed, before attaching the anchor. I waved at you as I dropped you overboard—did you see me? It was such a dark night, it's understandable if you didn't; and you sank so fast you could've easily missed it anyway.

I pause in my visit, catching, from the corner of my eye, a massive form approaching. My fear has never been so bold before, and I am amazed, stunned in disbelief at its brash behavior. A small voice in my head screams at me to escape, that danger is near. But I am dizzy, and too late realize that it is from lack of air. My muscles fail to respond and I float weightlessly, next to Felicia.

Suddenly my fear is upon me, as quick as an intake of breath. It slices between my love and me, sending me tumbling away with its force. I spin in slow motion, whirling about like a black rubber top. My body trembles, feels boneless and all too mortal. It refuses to obey commands, and I cannot move.

It is not my fear that has so rudely separated me from Felicia, or perhaps it is. Death seizes my beloved, unaware she is already beyond its grip. For a selfish moment I am glad that she, and not I, has been chosen for its cold kiss.

A thought insinuates itself into my brain's fuzziness, nibbling at the edge of my fading awareness. Can it be? Is death the specter that has haunted me all this time, only death, nothing more? Confusion blurs my physical and mental boundaries until they mesh with the scene before me. I do not know where I end and it begins. It is then, as I watch the specter stealing my darling, that I realize there is something worse, much worse by far, than the fear of death. How stupid I have been not to recognize it until now! It is something I have known since my first meeting with Felicia.

No, I scoff at my stupidity, death is not my albatross, my nemesis, the fear that now engulfs me. Death holds no terror. The *greatest* terror, my biggest, and *only* fear, is life! The thought of life without my Felicia plummets me into a heart-sinking despair. Loneliness has been the demon shadowing me as I move through the emptiness of my days, tormenting my every waking hour.

As I watch, Felicia is shaken about. She looks for all the world like an excited bride dancing with her energetic groom. Flecks of her skin swirl about, tiny snowflakes in a maelstrom. One leg floats lazily downward, tired from the dance, and its skin splits like the casing of an overstuffed sausage when it lands gently on the abrasive sand. It settles, a meal for the small fish who begin nibbling at the exposed muscles.

The intimate union continues in water so filtered with blood I can hardly see. My fear devours my dearest, engulfing, possessing her totally, as I never could. As the two slowly fuse into one entity, they are locked in a perpetual embrace which excludes me. Seeing their unity, my emotions roil like the churning, bloody water around my darling. I, who have loved so deeply and so faithfully, am soon to be left alone!

Jealousy catapults me toward the vicious lover that schemes to part Felicia and me. As I sensed from the first, we must always be one. I will not allow her to be taken from me, leaving me to live with only my fear for company. I will join Felicia and we three will bond in an unholy trinity of eternal love, if need be. Thereby will I thwart the marriage that should have been ours alone.

My fist punches through the water, and I cannot tell if it has hit anything solid. I hear a gurgling scream, and a great black hole punctuated with gleaming points of white fills my vision.

I welcome it rapturously, knowing that within its silent depths lies the demise of my fear. I have triumphed.

Oh, Felicia, I am coming.

THE SPIRIT CABINET

by Lisa Tuttle

Lisa Tuttle is an expatriate Texan now living in London. She's been writing scary stories for most of her life, with the first one appearing in print when she was only nineteen. A collection of her short stories, *A Nest of Nightmares,* was published by Sphere Books in Britain in 1986 and will be published in the U.S. by Tor. Her other books include two novels, *Familiar Spirit* and *Gabriel,* a collection of science fiction stories, *A Spaceship Built of Stone,* and an *Encyclopedia of Feminism*. Her stories have appeared in *Shadows* 4 and 10, and *Night Visions* 3.

She claims she's never seen a ghost, but says she spends a lot of time lurking around ancient sites and historic houses, in hope. Her story came in when I had just made my first antique purchase—a Victorian cabinet that bears more than a passing resemblance to the one in the title.

✦ ✦ ✦

Frank and Katy Matson had no sooner moved to London than they found a haunted house. At least, Katy called it haunted. Frank did not, then, believe in ghosts, and his wife's superstitions amused him. He thought it was a cute idea, but he didn't take it seriously, when Katy dragged him away from a discussion of terms with the landlord to exclaim, "I just saw a man—not a man, but a ghost! In the front room! This house is haunted!"

"Oh, dear, do you really think so? Well, if that's how you feel, I can just say it's not quite what we had in mind—"

She grabbed his arm and gave him one of her blazing, slightly nearsighted looks. "You will not! We'll take it!"

"But you said—"

"Yes, yes, of course! That's why! I've always wanted to live in a real haunted house—haven't you?"

Frank could not honestly say he had, but Katy's enthusiasm then, as so often, made up for his lack.

"It's perfect, just too, too perfect," she burbled happily. "To live in London, in an old, old Victorian house, with our very own, genuine English ghost! Oh, wait till I write to Melissa—she'll just curl up and die with envy!"

So they rented the house which, leaving aside the question of ghosts, was in fact exactly what they wanted in terms of size, price, and location. It was a short-term rental: only three months away from their own house back in Atlanta while Frank attended a company training program, and Katy explored London.

At least, she had intended to explore London. But that first week, although the weather was mild and sunny, she scarcely budged from the house. London had many charms, but they could not compete with the lure of a real ghost. As soon as Frank had left in the morning Katy began her vigil. She wandered through the house, returning again and again to the front room where she had seen, so briefly before he vanished, the bearded man in an old-fashioned suit. But he did not reappear. As she drifted restlessly through the sparsely furnished rooms, Katy, in her long skirt and gauzy white blouse, looked rather like a ghost herself.

Then, one evening as Katy sat in the front room, an unread book in her lap, listening to the muffled, hollow sound of Frank singing in the bath, something alerted her. Something—a flickering on the edge of her vision—caught her attention. Not stopping to question, she rose and walked to the door, then turned to look back into the room.

Everything had changed. Instead of a well-lit, underfurnished space, she saw before her a shadowy room filled with heavy, dark furniture. The glow of a coal fire in the grate showed her a small, stocky, bearded man standing very still and staring at her. She had the impression that there were other people in the room, but she found it hard to shift her attention from the man in front of her to look. She had seen him before. He was her ghost.

Katy took a step forward and put out her hand as if to touch him, but she never had the chance. As soon as she moved, everything was gone. The room was once more in her own time: normal, well-lit, familiar, and empty.

Katy closed her eyes, clenched her fists at her side, and smiled, blissfully. It was true. He was real. And he would be back.

That experience gave her the patience she needed. Now she truly believed, and instead of trying to catch her ghost, she was willing to wait for him to catch her, instead.

As she explained to Frank: "It's no good trying to see him when he doesn't want to be seen. It's not even like he comes to me, but more like I go to him—that he calls me to his time. Well, I told you how the whole room changed! He wasn't coming into our house—he was letting me visit *his*. Oh, I can't wait—I mean, I know I've *got* to wait, but I'm so excited—until it happens again!"

She knew by the way her husband smiled at her explanation that he didn't believe in her ghost. But he didn't disbelieve, either. They had been married very happily for three years, but for all that they shared they still had separate lives. His was made up of computers and sales, vintage cars and airplanes and money. Hers was less material, more fantastic and old-fashioned, built up out of books and movies, dreams and fears and history. Frank could not have lived in Katy's world, but he enjoyed glimpses of it, just as he enjoyed the scent of her perfume and the flash of rings on her slender fingers.

Two days later, on a Saturday morning, Frank was in the kitchen frying bacon and pancakes, and Katy was wandering around in an early-morning haze, trying to remember where she had put her sunglasses, and just what it was she wanted them for. As she stepped into the front room, it changed.

Katy froze. She was afraid, not of what had happened, but of what she might do. She was determined, this time, to stay longer and see more of the past, and she couldn't risk ending the miracle by doing something wrong. She moved nothing but her eyes.

Dark: heavy draperies covered the window, and a coal fire gleamed redly in the grate. There was only one other source of illumination: an oil lamp turned very low, hardly more than glowing through milk-white glass, set on a round table at the far side of the room. There was a lot of furniture in the room, dark, heavy stuff, and people—

The man she had seen twice before was standing in the same place, near the center of the room, in front of the fire. He was looking in her direction, and there could be no doubt that he saw her. He seemed neither surprised nor frightened by her presence. He looked at her steadily, as if keeping her there by an act of will. Katy held her breath, waiting to see what would happen.

She felt, like a command along her nerves, the impulse to go to him. But she resisted it, afraid that any physical motion would return her abruptly to her own time.

Then he beckoned, extending one dark-suited arm, fingers curved in toward himself, and she understood that the urge she felt to walk forward was coming from him.

So, hesitantly, Katy took one step. Nothing changed. Still she could feel him willing her forward. Another step, and another. In a moment she would be close enough to touch, but now he nodded at her to stop. His eyes looked straight into hers, telling her something, but she could not read the message. Slowly and deliberately he turned his head, looking toward the window. Katy imitated him, turning her own head, and she saw four or five other people sitting around a table. She couldn't make out any details, not even if they saw her, so she took a step closer.

And found herself blinking in the sudden morning light of a cool, empty room, feeling as if she had just fallen a very great distance in a very short time.

She shuddered. For the first time she felt afraid.

Frank listened to her story, keeping an eye on the breakfast preparations. When she had finished he said, "We could move."

"Oh, no! Why should we?"

"If you're afraid," he said gently.

"But I'm not afraid. Well, only for a minute. I guess I just wonder if it's a good idea to live in a haunted house."

"I thought it was what you wanted," said Frank. "If it isn't—"

"It is. It still is, in a way. It's an amazing opportunity. I'd never forgive myself if I ran away. But it worries me a little because I don't know what's happening. I'm not just seeing a ghost—*he's* seeing *me*. I think I'm traveling back in time somehow, back to the Victorian era, or whenever it is. Which is something I've always dreamed of—you know that! But for it to happen in this way . . . I don't have any control over it. I have to trust him, a stranger. I can only do what he wants me to do."

"No," said Frank, as unemphatic and practical as ever. "That's not exactly it. You can't choose when you go back, but you can choose how to respond. You do have control. You told me that you knew when he wanted you to do something, but you didn't *have* to respond. He lets you know what he wants, and you decide whether or not to do it. He's not controlling you any more than I am when I say, 'Let's go down to Windsor today.' He's giving you suggestions, not overpowering your will. And you've already figured out that you can come back to our time by making the slightest physical movement of your own. So if you're worried, you know what to do: turn your back. Leave the room. You can always escape. He can't stop you from moving; he can't keep you there."

Katy gazed at her husband, wondering how much he believed. Was he simply humoring her? Was this a game they were playing together?

"I wish I could share it with you," she said. "I wish you could go there with me."

"So you don't want to move?"

"I don't want to move. I'm not afraid anymore." She smiled. "I can't wait to see what happens next!"

But she did have to wait. That was the point. She was waiting on the will of a ghost. This could become a ridiculous obsession, Katy told herself, but she wouldn't let it. She decided to leave the house every day when Frank did, and explore London as she had always intended.

There was so much to see, and so many ways of looking at London, but she had her own particular interest now. She was in search of Victorian London. Everywhere she went she wondered if her ghost might have walked down this street, seen that building. Such thoughts seemed to bring him closer. Her reading was chosen with him in mind, too: fat paperback volumes by Trollope, Dickens, and Eliot were always tucked into her bag. She wondered if she would be able to learn, from furnishings and clothing, what year she had been enabled to visit, and went to the library to browse through illustrated books and old fashion magazines. One such rainy day Katy found an engraving from 1869 which made her catch her breath. There was something very familiar about it—what did it remind her of? She looked at the title: "At the Séance."

Then she understood. *That* was what had happened in the front room of her house back in Victorian times. They were having a séance. That explained the darkness, the people sitting in silence around a table. They must be spiritualists, and the bearded man, the man who saw her, was the medium. As for herself, she was the ghost.

She had to stop herself from laughing out loud in the library. But of course she was a ghost. Why not? Spirits had to come from *somewhere*—why not the future as well as the past? As a woman of the 1980s she was as insubstantial to a man of the 1860s as he was to her. Both were real, but not at the same time. Had any ghost ever felt itself to be a ghost? Ghosts were not the remains of dead people—the whole theological issue could be avoided—ghosts were people living elsewhen. Ghostliness was not a permanent state, not a matter of unquiet souls, but was a matter of perception, the result of passing momentarily through some time and place not your own.

Pleased with herself for figuring it out, Katy began to delve into books about spiritualism, but she found no reflection of her ideas. Certainly the spiritualists of Victorian times never imagined they might be in touch with the living, or the yet-to-be. Their faith was in a contact with the spirits of the departed: the dead could live again, speak again, through them. And as most spirit messages concerned the happy time they were having in the afterlife, it seemed that the spirits themselves agreed with the prevailing view that they were dead.

If, in fact, there were any spirits at all. For as she read on, even allowing for the bias of modern, rational writers, the history of spiritualism appeared a mass of self-contradictory absurdities, and the most outrageous, and obvious, deceptions. Most mediums were shabby con artists, deceiving a public eager to believe. She read about mediums who practiced simple conjuring tricks, or used their feet like hands; about spirit voices produced by hidden phonographs or a confederate using a speaking tube from another room; about ghosts made of paper or bits of clothing moved by invisible wires . . .

"But *I'm* no trick," said Katy to Frank that evening. "I'm real, and so is he. My medium must have had genuine psychic powers, to be able to make contact with me. Even if he didn't know what he was doing . . . do you see what that means?"

"Tell me in the cab," said Frank. "If we don't leave now, we're going to be late for the theater."

She couldn't even remember what play they had decided on. "I'm sorry," she said, feeling guilty. "This is all I ever talk about these days . . . I know it must be boring for you."

"I like hearing about it," he said. "I like knowing what interests you—how else can I share it? If you ever stop talking about him, I'll think the worst: that you're having an affair with that bearded geek."

"He's *not* a geek!"

"Uh-oh," said Frank. "It *is* an affair."

She laughed and denied it, but she was blushing. Because sometimes it did feel like the buildup to an affair, the way she was always thinking about him, wondering when she would see him again, trying to find out more about him, fantasizing conversations with him.

"He's not my type," she said. "I like tall skinny blonds—you know that. Besides, he's dead. It's more like reading a really good novel, but only finding a few pages at a time. Or like being a detective."

"Okay, Sherlock," he said. "Just don't forget your faithful Dr. Watson."

"Maybe next time it happens I could shout, 'Watson, I need you!' "

"I'll come running."

Although part of her cherished the specialness of her experience, Katy would have liked to share it with Frank. It might make the experience less special, but it would make it more real, she thought. And because she felt safer with him nearby, she continued to avoid spending much time in the house alone.

She made her next discovery in one of the junkier antique shops of Camden Town, where she had gone to browse among the postcards, china, jewelry, and other small bits and pieces which would make nice souvenirs and gifts for friends back home. She couldn't look at anything large or expensive, but as she eased her way around the dusty chairs and ancient tables which made the tiny shop an obstacle course, she found herself noticing a particular piece of furniture. It wasn't particularly attractive, and she couldn't think at first why it had drawn her attention. It was some sort of cabinet or small wardrobe, a squarish box with two doors, standing less than four feet high. Katy moved closer, putting out her hand, and, as she touched the wood, she knew.

She had already seen it—or its ghost-double—in her own front room. Aware of it then only as a dark, unfamiliar shape between herself and the people at the table, now, as she felt it solid beneath her hand, she recognized it beyond any doubt. It had been *his*.

Without even a token protest at the price, she paid for it and took it home with her in a cab.

Frank was not pleased. "Shipping stuff home is expensive, you know that. We *agreed*. And it's not even like this is some great antique—it's crummy now, and it was crummy when it was new. No matter how cheap it was, it's not worth it. The wood is bad, and just look at the workmanship—look inside at these shelves, just look at the way they—"

"It wouldn't have had shelves in it originally," she said. "That's why they don't fit right. Someone put them in later—it's obvious. I thought we could take the shelves out."

"Take them out? Why? What did you think we could use it for? Why did you buy it?"

Katy shrugged, suddenly uneasy. She had let her enthusiasm run away with her again. "I don't know . . . I wasn't really thinking about using it, or taking it back to Atlanta. In fact, I don't particularly want to take it home with us—we might as well leave it here. But I had to buy it, I just had to, as soon as I saw it. It belongs in this house—it was here before. I recognized it as soon as I touched it. And when I knew it belonged here—well, I just couldn't leave it sitting in that junk shop, I really couldn't. I had to bring it back here to this house."

"A present for your ghost? Oh, all right, Katy. How can I be jealous of a ghost? As long as we don't have to worry about shipping it to America, I won't ask what you paid for it. I hope it wasn't much." He gave her a hug of forgiveness, and brightened. "It might be useful, anyway, while we're here. You must be tired of keeping half your clothes in a suitcase under the bed. We could put sweaters and jeans and things in here, on the shelves. Wonder what it was used for before the shelves were put in?"

"I think I know," said Katy. The idea had come to her as she held the box steady in the cab; she remembered something from her readings on spiritualism. "I think it was a spirit cabinet, and that my—medium used it for the séances he held right here in this room."

Frank arched an eyebrow. "He kept his liquor in it?"

"Not that kind of spirit, silly." She hugged him back, and took advantage of his restored humor to launch into an explanation. "Mediums had things called spirit cabinets. I'm not sure exactly how they were meant to work, or the theory behind them, because the book I read implied that they were just another opportunity for faking ghosts. Somehow or other the ghost was supposed to materialize inside the cabinet, and the sitters could talk to them—but not touch them—and look at them there. Maybe some of the cabinets were like magicians' boxes, with false backs or bottoms, but I had a good look at this one before you got home, and there's nothing like that. If anyone ever got in this box, it must have been in the ordinary way."

"You think you might be able to get your ghost to materialize inside it in *our* time? Do you want to hold a séance?"

"Oh, no, nothing like that." There was something almost shocking in the idea of that well-dressed Victorian gentleman crouching in the cabinet, pretending to be a ghost—even if he *was* a ghost. "I hadn't even thought about using it. It just seemed like the right thing to do when I saw it, to buy the box and bring it back here. It's a link, you know, another connection to the past." She moved away to examine the cabinet again. She took hold of one of the shelves and tried to move it, but it gave not at all under the pressure of her fingers, no matter how she tugged. There were four shelves, each one a thick, solid plank tightly fixed in place.

"These shouldn't be here," she muttered, almost to herself. Then she looked at Frank. "Will you help me take the shelves out?"

"Take the shelves out? What for? I thought we were going to use it for our clothes. If we take the shelves out, it'll be totally useless, just an ugly box taking up space."

To Katy it seemed obvious that the next step, after returning the cabinet to its home, was to restore it to its original condition, but she saw that Frank was fast losing sympathy with her ghost story. He had been so good about it all along, and he was so seldom annoyed with her, that she did not persist. She wasn't giving in—in a few days, she thought, she would approach Frank about it again, or even take the shelves out herself. Once it was done he would have to accept it. But for a while she would go easy, try not to be obsessive.

"Let's leave it here for now, all right?" she said. "I should clean it out really well before we start putting our clothes or anything in it."

"You're right," he said. "Wouldn't want any ghost-moths getting in our clothes . . ." He grinned, and she smiled back, and saw him relent still more. "Maybe it *should* be in this room," he said. "If that's where you think it belongs. The bedroom is awfully small and . . . I guess it looks kind of nice in here."

"It belongs here," she said. "And I know where I belong."

"Yeah?"

"In bed with you."

In the middle of the night—two o'clock by the glowing radio-alarm clock—Katy woke suddenly, as if someone had spoken her name. But Frank was sleeping peacefully beside her, and although she listened, straining her ears against the silence of the house and the distant, outside noise of traffic, she could hear nothing else. Yet she knew her awakening had not been by chance—she knew she *had* been called. And she knew that if she went into the front room, she would find her bearded medium presiding over another (or perhaps it was always the same) séance, with all those long-dead Victorian ladies and gentlemen waiting silently, hoping for Katy's appearance.

She lay in the darkness, smiling. She wondered if, this time, she would speak to them. She turned her head on the pillow to look at Frank, and wondered if she should wake him. The compulsion to go into the front room became stronger.

It's my own compulsion, she told herself. No one else was controlling her. She could stay in bed and go back to sleep. Nothing but her own curiosity, her own desire, made her move.

She looked again at Frank, thinking of taking him with her. But he didn't believe, and Frank had not been called as she had been. What if his presence spoiled it?

Katy got up and reached for her robe, moving carefully so as not to disturb her husband. She was in no danger, she told herself. She knew what to do. She could return to her own place and time whenever she wanted, merely by making some motion not directed by the medium. The difficulty, really, was in letting herself be directed in order to stay in the past a little longer.

Next time, Frank, she thought. When I've figured it out more. She blew him a kiss, and walked out of the room, down the short corridor, and into another time.

As before, there was a coal fire glowing and the lamp turned low in the stuffy, overfurnished room. Again, the stocky, bearded man stood before her and beckoned, silently drawing her into the room. When she turned her head this time, again by his direction, she immediately picked out, among all the extra furnishings her room lacked, the spirit cabinet, standing in exactly the same spot where she had put it.

The recognition gave her a small thrill of accomplishment. Yes, she had done that, she had done her part in making this connection between past and present possible. She felt even more pleased, even more necessary, when the bearded man indicated that she should climb into the cabinet. She understood what was happening—after all, she had read about séances and spirit cabinets—and so she did not pause or object, but climbed inside quite willingly. She did not mind when he shut the doors and she was in total darkness. In a moment, she knew, he would open the doors again and display her to his audience. But although pleased and excited, she was also just a little bit uncomfortable. The cabinet was an awkward size, and she hadn't been able to get entirely settled before the doors were closed. She didn't want to spoil the séance by moving, but she was afraid one of her legs was getting a cramp.

✦ ✦ ✦

The police thought it must have been a bomb, although none of the neighbors reported an explosion, and the rest of the room was undamaged. Only an explosion of the most tremendous force could have driven solid wooden planks, two inches thick, right through the woman's body like that.

The husband had found her, early in the morning, and the police put it down to shock when he claimed responsibility for her death, because nothing he said made any sense.

"It's my fault," he kept repeating. "She told me—she told me how it worked. If only I'd taken out the shelves right away, when she told me, she could have come back alive."

HOOKED ON BUZZER

by Elizabeth Massie

Elizabeth Massie was born in 1953 and, except for college, has always lived in Waynesboro, Virginia. Married for fifteen years, she has a daughter and a son. She's a part-time artist, a full-time teacher, and has directed, written, and choreographed children's theater. She is also an active member of Amnesty International's Urgent Action Network. She wrote her first horror story in the tenth grade, but received a C− because the teacher didn't like the sentence fragments she used to describe the protagonist's demented mental state. She's had stories published in *The Horror Show, Grue,* the anthology *Bringing Down the Moon,* as well as a number of other markets, and has done nonfiction for *Starmont* and *Horrorstruck.*

In this Southern tale Elizabeth demonstrates that she possesses a fine sense of the bizarre. I don't think you'll forget Angel soon.

✦ ✦ ✦

"Glory.

"Glory."

Nubbed fingers stroked the scratched window; lips made tiny, moist patterns in the dust of the glass. Wide eyes panned the street below, waiting, watching.

Feo was late.

Angel took a slow breath. Her throat rumbled. "Glory," she said, and shifted her weight against the radiator. "Praise Him, Amen."

There was movement down on the street, and Angel started. But it was only a cat, a knotted patch of fur winding about the tires of the newspaper delivery truck.

"Glory," said Angel, sighing.

Behind Angel, a child's battered record player throbbed with the wailings of the Savior's Salvation Seven. Angel's thick finger stubs pawed the window in rhythm with the music. She knew the lyrics, they were as much a part of her as Mother or Buzzer, but Mother had never sung and so neither did Angel. Mother had felt her own voice to be poor, and so singing along with the Salvation Seven would have been a blasphemy. Angel was sure that her voice was even more unworthy than Mother's.

Feo was very late.

Angel tapped her stubs and closed her eyes. The music began to pull at her, pushing her legs gently into the vertical ribs of the radiator and then sucking her away. She rode the current, thinking of Mother and of Glory. Hearing Mother and Brother Randolph.

"Angel," said Mother.

Angel said, "Mother." She closed her eyes more tightly, and saw Mother on the sofa in the tiny living room of Mother's trailer. Mother wore a wool shift. There were large sweat rings under her upper arms. Brother Randolph sat beside her.

"Angel," said Mother.

Angel was beside the wall, the tiny toes of her dirty sneakers pointed toward a toy top in the middle of the floor.

"Don't you dare, Angel," said Mother.

Angel took a step and moved slightly from the wall. Mother frowned, the fat around her eyes squeezing them to slits.

"Train the child, Amen," said Brother Randolph.

Angel's hands moved outward for balance as she took another sliding step. She looked from the top to Mother and back again. The Salvation Seven sang on the shelf.

"Angel!" said Mother.

"Self-denial," said Brother Randolph. "Glory to the child that withstands earthly rigors and temptations and to the mother what leads that child in the way."

"Glory," said Mother. "No, Angel!"

Angel hesitated, then reached out to the top. She picked it up and looked at Mother.

Mother roared from the sofa and grabbed her, shaking the top free. Angel gasped. Mother grappled the prong end of an extension cord from the floor and plugged it into the socket beneath the record-player shelf. The other end of the cord was a frayed mass of wire.

Brother Randolph nodded sadly and said, "Buzz her. Amen."

Mother drew Angel close.

After a moment, Brother Randolph said, "Glory."

Mother dropped the cord. "Amen," she said. The Salvation Seven's gospel cantation cut a piercing, frantic current in the air.

"Put her by the wall," said Brother Randolph. "We'll try again."

"Glory," said Mother.

"Buzzer, Amen," said Angel. She opened her eyes and looked again at the street below. The cat was gone. And Feo was very, very late. Feo was supposed to be bringing the groceries today. He was the landlady's brother. He was nineteen, two years younger than Angel. Angel felt a holy love for Feo. It burned in her when she saw his face through the door. God was in Feo. Feo's eyes were green, like pastures in the Bible.

Angel turned up the gospel music. The voices shook the newspapered walls. Someone next door hit the wall with a heavy object. Angel went into the bedroom and lay down on the frameless twin bed. The music pinned her to the mattress. She looked at the ceiling and drove herself to climax with a Prelude II. Sweaty and panting, Angel rolled off the bed and knelt to give thanks.

✦ ✦ ✦

Feo sat on the edge of the bus bench and watched as the small assembly of shoppers filed through the door and climbed the bus steps. He turned his face away then, so the bus driver would not wait for him. He held a bag of groceries between his knees. In his jacket pocket was the change from the purchase. He was in no hurry to return with the food.

Goddamn freak.

Lizzie was expecting too much. She was the one who usually got the freak's groceries, but Lizzie had gotten an idea when Feo had gotten the note, and when Lizzie had an idea it was like riding downhill on a snowplow. No getting off until the ride was over.

"Goddamn freak," muttered Feo. He pulled his knees together and something inside the bag gave way. Lizzie had said, "The death of me you don't care to do for your family."

"You see her, Lizzie?" Feo had answered. "You see her face? Her fingers?"

"Blood is thicker than looks."

"She's crazy. They kicked her out of the halfway house, said she's on her own for shocking herself all the time. You heard that."

"I heard that. And I seen her note to you. She wants you. She got money, I know."

"She don't want me." Feo balled the note and shook it

in Lizzie's face. "It says here she wants to pray with me. I get the willies when I see her looking through that door crack. Like she wants to suck me in."

"She got money. Lots, I bet. Holed it up all this time, from disability and from when her mama died a couple years ago. Buy her groceries. Pray with her. She got money, Feo."

"Fuck you."

"No, fuck her. Pray with her, whatever she wants. She got money. And we living in this dumphole with nothing but late payments and cockroaches."

Feo threw the note against the wall. It bounced and rolled back to where he stood. He stepped over it and through the apartment door, swearing softly and fiercely.

✦ ✦ ✦

In the bathroom, Angel switched on the clock radio and worked the knob until she found Reverend Olley of the Truth and Way Mission. Reverend Olley was speaking in tongues and a missioner was interpreting. The radio had been a going-away gift to Angel from one of her many foster mothers. When Angel was six, Social Services had taken her from her mother. Angel had lived in sixteen foster homes over the next ten years. Most of the homes had quietly requested that Angel be sent elsewhere after several months.

The Ryders, however, had not been as concerned with discretion. Mrs. Ryder had been a religious woman, or so she had told Angel, yet when she caught Angel witnessing at Lisa Ryder's slumber party, she had become enraged.

Nine eleven-year-olds had attended the party. They spread their sleeping bags about the basement floor and entertained themselves with gossip and makeup and ghost stories. Angel was forgotten, alone in the corner on a blanket, until she began to talk about Heaven and Glory and earthly rigors. The girls stopped and stared. Lisa Ryder groaned nervously and said, "Not again." Angel unscrewed the bulb from a table lamp and poised her finger above the empty socket. One girl said, "Oh shit, neat." Another said, "I heard she does stuff like this for God or something." Everybody watched, except for Lisa, who dashed up the steps.

Snorts rippled through the gathering. Angel lowered her finger into the socket.

"Praise Him, Amen," she said.

Angel was thrown back from the lamp with an electric pop. She held up her burned finger and the girls cheered. Lisa and Mrs. Ryder thundered down the stairs.

"Demon-child!" screamed Mrs. Ryder. "You aren't welcome here anymore!"

"Go fry yourself somewhere else!" cried Lisa.

"Buzzer, Amen," whispered Angel.

The girls on their sleeping bags rolled their eyes and giggled darkly.

Angel adjusted the volume on Reverend Olley. She plugged the tub drain and turned on the spigot. Feo was late, but Angel was sure nothing had happened to him. Feo was safe in holy arms. Feo would come. Angel stepped into the water and stretched out her legs; her fingers strummed erratically on the water's surface. Sometimes Angel could feel the entire length of the fingers, and she found that to be a wondrous miracle. Angel lifted the stubs to her face and caressed the scars there. At the halfway house they would not give her lamps or cords or batteries. And so Angel was forced to seek Glory without Buzzer. She used a plastic knife that came with her dinner. When she was eighteen, they let her go.

The living room door thumped. Someone was knocking. Angel climbed from the tub and wrapped herself in her terry robe. "Be ready for His call!" said Reverend Olley.

"Glory," Angel said.

✦ ✦ ✦

Feo hit the door again with his boot and looked quickly about over his shoulders. If anyone in the other apartments saw him going in with the freak's groceries, he would kill Lizzie. He couldn't believe he'd wasted as much time as he had already on her. It had been thirty minutes getting the groceries and an hour and a half sitting on the bus bench worrying about taking them back. Then he spent another fifteen minutes telling himself that Lizzie was right. The freak had to have money stashed somewhere in her apartment. And braving her looks long enough to gain her confidence would pay off. If he didn't get the chance to slip anything into his pocket while she was praying, at least he could get a good idea of where things were, and he could schedule a late-night visit later on.

"Come on, freak," he muttered.

There was a soft sound behind the apartment door. A voice said, "Who is it?"

"Feo," said Feo, and in doing so he had a sudden, horrid sensation that he had offered his soul along with his name. He spit angrily on the floor.

The doorknob twisted, and the door bucked on its warped framework. Then it was jerked open, as far as the chain links would reach. The scarred face was in the crack.

"Feo?"

"Got your groceries," said Feo.

"Ah, yes," said the freak. But she did not move from the crack.

"And I got your note," Feo added. "Gonna let me in?" He cleared his throat unintentionally.

The face smiled, then withdrew from the crack. The chain came off. The door swung wide.

Feo stepped in, being careful not to look directly at the freak. He put the bag of groceries on the dinette table in the kitchen corner. The bag fell over and two cans of bean-with-bacon soup rolled out. Feo anxiously snatched them up and stuffed them into the bag. Then he felt the freak behind him. He turned around.

She was fat. Her hair was near white, slicked back into a thin, greasy ponytail. Huge blue eyes dominated the ravaged face. She smelled of sweat and imitation chocolate.

"You come to pray with me," she said.

Feo stepped quickly around her and stopped in the middle of the living room.

"Don't clean up much, do you?"

"God asks self-denial, praise Him."

"Yeah, right," said Feo. "Hey, why don't you show me around?"

"What?"

"Show me around. When people come to visit, you show them around."

He turned back to the freak. Her eyes seemed even larger. Her hands were pressed together in a nubby ball.

He nodded cautiously at her hands. "Why you do that to yourself?"

"Is it worthy?"

He blinked. "I . . . don't know. I guess."

The freak took several steps closer to him. Feo flinched but did not step back. She tipped her head as if studying him.

"Show me around, okay?" Feo managed.

"What do you want to see?"

"I don't know. Anything. Everything."

And then the freak opened her robe and let it fall to the floor. Her huge body was slick and damp.

Feo's mouth fell open soundlessly.

"Bless me. Baptize me. All I have is yours."

"Oh, shit," said Feo.

"I have been worthy. You have come to me. Bless me."

Feo watched as she went into the bathroom. He was horrified and transfixed. She climbed into the tub and looked at him. He walked slowly to the bathroom door. She lay back, her giant breasts falling to opposite sides. "Bless me," she said, and closed her eyes.

Feo went to the side of the tub. He wiped his mouth and clenched his fist. "Shit," he said. Her malformity and willingness was terrifyingly sensual.

"Ah," she said softly.

Feo slipped out of his clothes and kicked them aside. He grasped the sides of the tub and carefully climbed in. He thought of how the money would be a breeze after this; he knew she would give him anything. He thought of the old joke about the woman so ugly that you had to put a paper bag over her head to make love. He laughed out loud, thinking this added a new twist to the joke. Paper bag and a pair of work gloves. Feo's hands moved through water, through flesh.

"Glory," said Angel. "Buzzer, Amen." One set of nubbed fingers reached out of the tub and caught the cord of the clock radio. And with a rapturous wail, Reverend Olley joined the holy lovers.

LITTLE MAID LOST

by Rivka Jacobs

Rivka Jacobs was born in Philadelphia in 1952, but grew up on Key Biscayne, Florida, and also lived in Oregon and in the Southwest Miami area and in Coral Gables, Florida. Shortly thereafter she moved to Huntington, West Virginia, where she completed her college education, a B.A. in history, at Marshall University. She also holds a master's degree in sociology and taught the subject part-time at Marshall. She's been writing since she was twelve years old and has submitted stories to magazines since she was seventeen; she sold her first one in 1979 to the anthology *A Spadeful of Spacetime*. Since then she has sold a number of short stories to various markets.

Another Southern writer, Rivka proves that not everything is necessarily sunny down in the Sunshine State.

✦ ✦ ✦

✦ 1 ✦

Death was not a matter that thousands of homebound motorists thought of on Friday. As the western sky flamed coral and crimson over Miami and her suburbs, as the windshields and chrome of the bumper-to-bumper traffic flashed the sun's final salute, as the expressways emptied car by car into the city's lesser and lesser streets, most of South Florida's citizens rode far away from death.

Above north Biscayne Boulevard's Golden Time Motel,

heaven's great dome began to fade until only a dull pinkish glow remained. The last light, the last automobile surge, the last of the straight world passed the twilight and left this single-story string of twenty rooms to its night.

In the Golden Time's office, behind the gold-speckled Formica counter that divided space in half, Martha, her mother, and her father awaited the Friday evening circus parade.

Martha's father took his standing position center counter, guarding the registry and cash drawer. Martha's mother huddled on her stool in the left corner beside the filing cabinet. She was reading a movie magazine. Martha's father was tall, lean, tanned, hard, and expressionless. He was in his fifties, but the gray had only started to strafe him above his ears. Martha's mother was plump, with continually sunburned upper arms; the result of daily chores on the motel grounds. Her lips were scarlet, her hair was dyed its original yellow and was tightly curled. She was pleasant-tempered but hadn't laughed for a long while.

Martha at fourteen was developing slowly. She wore her browning blonde hair in long bumpy strands and pinned the mass of it with a gold barrette at each temple. Her face was round and her complexion was uneven. Her eyes were hazel, her brows were amorphous, her lips were pink but fleshless. Wire-rimmed glasses straddled her small nose. A female figure was almost nonexistent, with the exception of budding breasts that sometimes ached.

It was just after 8 P.M., now, and in the usual fashion a fringe world began to beat its path to the motel's office door. The bell jangled—it was Rouse, the early-bird pimp. He let the entrance door smooth and narrow to a close. He strutted to the counter and smacked both palms on the Formica.

"Hey now, Mister Mo-bile, Alabama" was how Rouse

always greeted Martha's father, who had brought his family from the Crimson Tide Hotel in Mobile to the Golden Time of Miami in 1970. "Two rooms, please," Rouse spoke-sang with a glint of razor.

The owner refused to look at his customer. He pushed a Bic pen in the pimp's direction. The other laughed and signed.

The bell jingled. Carmella and Rowen sashayed in, snubbing the rival Rouse on his way out. "How ya, honey," Rowen called to Martha.

Martha picked at the gold metallic flakes in the countertop and stared back. Rowen was glitter tonight, arrayed in a pair of deep green satin hot pants and a sequined magenta T-shirt that bulged with breast.

Carmella signed, then passed the advance money to the proprietor. "He don't trust us," she said as she winked at the girl. Rowen made a sound of agreement. They tramped out. The bell gonged.

Martha's stare skated to her father. He was glaring in return. *Don't talk,* said his liquor-red eyes. She knew. And she knew what would happen to her if she did.

The bell chimed. William and two of his followers appeared. The leisure-suited leader introduced them, to Martha and her mother, since her father strictly ignored him.

"This is Todd," he said as he hugged the mascaraed boy wearing silk coveralls. "And Juan." He fanned fingers at the leather-sheathed older man who puffed on a panatela cigar.

She pinned her attention on Juan's expensive jewelry: his single gold earring set her mind spinning in the direction of pirates. Or sixteenth-century swashbuckling heroes who performed in the movies of her dreams.

Her mother smiled at them, murmured, "Nice to meet you," and quickly returned to her *Photoplay*.

"A room for the night." William's voice pranced. He signed in, summoned his companions, and waved a farewell.

Her father twitched his mouth as the trio exited. He knew that the guest list would be much the same until the wee hours of the morning.

Usually she stayed with her parents until dawn, when she didn't have to go to school. She left the bastion of the office only twice; to visit the toilet in her own room. When school opened, she would help until 11:30 P.M., doing homework and sorting the bills. For now, it was three against the world with Martha caught between a rock and a hard place.

She was drifting once more, searching the reaches of an imagined realm while leaning on elbows that barely cleared the counter, when a loud knock sounded. The door gave way ringingly to two Miami police officers. Their uniforms were studded with badge. They radiated spit and polish. One was chubby, red-haired, and ice-eyed. The other was slim and brunet, with dark eyes, close brows, and a high-bridged nose. The first had introduced himself as Hal Tooney, the second as Richard Leon. She straightened, her interest sparked then shyly dampened by the meeting of eyes. Officer Leon stirred her in some way, like the rumble of thunder under clear skies.

"What can we do for you, gentlemen?" her father asked so dryly that it sounded peevish. He hadn't altered his position.

Tooney liked Martha's father and appreciated his manner. "Just checking," he answered with a grin. "What's happening?"

Both men understood that no honest answer could be expected from a motel owner who earned a living off those whom the cops would like to put out of business. "The same," the proprietor replied, as he always did.

"How are you this evening, Mrs. Dalston?" Tooney asked the woman.

"Fine, just fine," she said wanly, and opened her current issue of *The Midnight Globe*. Paper crinkled.

"We came to warn you," Officer Leon broke in, "there's another crackpot killer loose right here in the magic city. The shit will hit the propeller soon—we were ordered to work with the Metro guys, to probe a bit first." Leon was from the Florida panhandle and had some Southern sympathy for Martha's father. "What I mean is, we've been ordered to make the most of the case before the newspapers do."

"What kind of killer?" her father demanded.

Martha's mother peered over the page tops at the cops. Martha listened.

"A ripper. The suspect is male. His weapon appears to be a machete, and it seems he rapes and mutilates victims only between the ages of ten and twenty years. That's all we really know."

"Or all you're prepared to tell us," the man grumbled.

Officer Leon folded his arms and laughed once in a meditative way. "Well"—he looked at the miniature fault line spanning the terrazzo floor beneath his polished shoes—"it's like holding open the jaws of the beast to keep it from biting. I try to help the special people in my territory. What else can any of us do?"

Tooney smirked. "Same old story. It's up to us to make everything even again, so the tourists and wealthy retirees can go on getting their suntans without a care in the world."

"But when does he attack, when is it dangerous?" Martha prodded, thinking of ten days hence and her early morning hike to catch the bus to Dade County Christian Academy.

"Hmmm?" Leon faced her. "You know it's dangerous to loiter at *any* time around here."

Tooney patted his holstered police special. "Every city has a dark side. The prostitutes stopping traffic, the nightriders hassling straight citizens, but especially the cocksu—"He stopped and frowned. There was a moment of putty silence.

Martha glanced at Leon; he was sweating a film but was smiling at her father. "Officer Tooney means," he said, "those gentlemen who fly the light of our city-beautiful streets in the expectation of finding . . . an outlet."

Her father's features were lithic, the veins pulsing in his temples the only sign of stress. His ramrod eyes glistened as they fastened on the cop. "We haven't seen anyone out of the ordinary round here. And Martha hears all kinds of talk so you don't have to insult our intelligence." The belligerence was scarcely veiled but her father always said what was on his mind, nothing more. He suddenly turned from the officers and trudged to the table edging the rear wall. He sat heavily before a manual typewriter. The air conditioner above the typewriter whined. A click . . . click . . . click click commenced.

Martha furrowed her brows apologetically. She juggled a batonlike letter opener she'd retrieved from the desk behind her. "What should we expect?" she asked Leon.

Tooney scowled concernedly though his blue eyes were complacent. "You be careful, young lady. This doesn't have anything to do with prostitution or the drug traffic. This guy is a nut, unpredictable, so do not go *anywhere* alone." This fatherly speech completed, he beckoned his partner with a scoop of his hand.

Leon brusquely nodded at the two women and followed Tooney under the shaking bell. The jalousie windows and steel mesh window guards shivered with the door slam. There had been worse scenes between the cops and Martha's father.

Clacking continued, the air conditioner groaned, then sighed and resumed a steady flow. Martha rubbed the mounds of plastic oranges that were piled and glued in a plastic bowl on the counter. Her mother hid behind her paper.

The bell clanged. And again, and again. Familiar and unfamiliar manikins marched to and fro. It was 1 A.M. when Martha's father arose, his letters completed. More protests: to the mayor, to the governor, to the TV stations, Martha thought.

"You takin' care of things?" He reached the counter, inspected the registry.

She knew he had listened to every exchange between the customers and herself. She shrugged and nodded at once.

"Put these in the mail." He threw the sealed, stampless envelopes on the flyblown Formica.

She gathered them and made a mental note to visit the stamp machine in Señora Blanco's grocery.

He began complaining to his wife in tight, eviscerated whispers. Martha didn't try to overhear; these conferences never concerned her anyway.

The bell barely tinkled.

She raised her chin.

A man entered, and paused by the far wall, beneath a dime-store painting of the Everglades. He swiftly acknowledged a mirror on his left. He approached the counter. She hopped from her stool, opened her mouth to speak, but abruptly lost her voice with a croak. She stared.

Her guest was of medium height, lithe, with an athletic gait. His skin was coffee-colored. Black wispy brows were visible just above a sporty pair of dark glasses, the lenses of which seemed like two huge and black cartoon-character eyes resting on high jutting cheeks and a smallish nose. His cherubic mouth was full; a long cigarette dangled for a moment from his lips while he folded his arms and faced her. On his dark wavy hair sat a black hat that looked like a panama.

He removed his glasses suddenly, and with the same hand took the cigarette in his finger.

She stared. His eyes, in their almond-shaped sockets, were like fleshy living things that seemed to have no shine, no surface. They were like miles and miles of undulating dark velvet.

She choked, closed her mouth, swallowed. A blush rose up her neck, into her cheeks.

"I said, do you rent rooms?" the stranger asked again out of a fog. His slightly nasal voice was spiced by a tangy, rhythmic accent.

"Uh, yes, twenty-five dollars a night but it goes up to thirty-five next week because the tourist season starts then." She spilled the words and stumbled over them, blushing more fiercely.

He smiled with sealed lips, his eyes almost disappearing in their tearlike slits.

She blinked rapidly.

The man seemed to reemerge, to jell in the present for a second time. And now she saw that he wore a navy blue three-piece suit that was soiled and disheveled. That under the coffee stain of his skin he was terribly pale, and there were ominous charcoal crescents under his lower dark lashes.

"I don't want to be disturbed. Is there privacy here?" He pointed in the direction of the rooms.

"Yes, unless the cops get a search warrant."

This made him laugh in a high-pitched, gaspy way. He pressed his lips once more on the cigarette; Martha realized that it wasn't lighted. "I'd prefer the end room," he said calmly.

"That one is—" She had started to say *mine*. "It's occupied. The one next to it also. Number eighteen is empty, though." She turned and reached for the appropriate key impaled on the plaque above the desk, and noticed her parents for the first time since the man's entrance. She dropped the key with a clink. She leaped back, banging into the desk.

They were frozen, as if carved from stone. Her father's back was to Martha; he was bent toward her mother's ear. One of his hands was raised as if to punctuate a sentence. Her mother was staring directly and eerily at her daughter; her topaz eyes were motionless and vacant. In the woman's lap lay the rumpled *Midnight Globe*, crushed by protesting but petrified hands.

Martha gaped until the man at the counter coughed politely. She reanimated slowly, tiptoeing to the registry while watching her parents. "What's wrong, what happened? Am I crazy?" she whispered, returning reluctantly to the stranger.

"I told them to be still," the man explained with a smile. "Now, pick up that key, and I will sign this book." He lifted the Bic pen and watched her until she retrieved the small piece of metal. Then he wrote.

She passed him his key. She hesitantly spun the registry to see what had been entered. "Mr. Sam" was all she read, on line eighteen, by coincidence under junkie Jack Jackson's scrawl along seventeen. "Mr. Sam what?" she asked with intense curiosity as she righted the book.

He didn't answer for several seconds. He seemed to be distracted by something on the wall behind Martha; either her mother's plastic Christ that hung from a wooden cross beside the key rack, or the machete that hung beside the cross. He suddenly drew Martha's clammy face into focus. He sighed lightly. The cigarette was in his fingers again. "Are you here every night?" he asked.

But she was more interested in him. "How did you do that?" She nodded stiffly at the bodies of her frozen parents. "What's wrong with them?"

"It's all in the eyes." He winked at her and held two fingers to the corner of one of his. "I thought it would make you happy. Are you here every night?" he repeated.

"I'm sorry, I didn't mean to ignore you. Yeah, each night." There was no pull of caution when she said this, though she knew she was too naive in these situations. Too trusting, too curious, too ready to grab at the warmth of another human being. "Is it hypnosis?" she urged.

Mr. Sam pretended to brush hair from his forehead as if he didn't know the answer. His inky irises seemed to suck in Martha's attention like twin black holes. "You will see me tomorrow night," he assured her. Then, in counterpoint to this evasion, he filliped like the best commercial hypnotist. Automatically she spun to look at her parents. They were abruptly in motion.

Her father pivoted, anger and confusion tinting his angular features. Her mother gasped; she dropped the paper and slid to her feet. She crossed herself, something Martha had seen her do only in moments of gravest crisis.

Martha again remembered Mr. Sam and ducked under the counter hatch, charging into the empty office lobby as if to catch a ghost. She splayed her fingers and pirouetted, searching air.

"What the hell's wrong with you, girl? Get back over here!" her father ordered.

"Did you see him? Did you see him?" She stooped, and stood upright before her father. "He took room eighteen. He hypnotized you!"

He screwed his face into a do-you-want-the-belt expression.

She blanched, bowed her head. "I'm sorry," she whispered.

"Don't push me tonight, Martha. I won't take any of your crazy crap tonight, you hear?"

"Yes, sir," she muttered, eyes down.

✦ 2 ✦

". . . and I arrived in this city," Mr. Sam was saying with great seriousness, "to find a new spiritual life."

Martha's magnified, tawny irises were miniature pools that mirrored his now hatless head; his oval face and flat, obsidian eyes. She became aware that she was six feet away from her inexplicably indifferent father, that her mother, calmly seated at the desk directly behind her, was totally unaware of her presence.

Mr. Sam casually rested his folded forearms on the counter. "Martha, you're not listening to me," he said with a slight smile.

She started violently at the nasal voice, returned her

gaze to his. "But . . . I . . . but I don't understand what you're saying." She squeaked her palms across the Formica. "It doesn't make any sense," she muttered, tears abruptly blooming, pearllike behind her glasses.

He reached for and patted her small, plump right hand with his left. His eyes were alert as he watched the tears trickle from where wire touched cheek.

"You haven't said anything," she continued, shaking her head. "Nothing real. You're just crazy, that's all," she sobbed.

"Like I said, I'm master of half of everything. And I say, nothing is real unless it is willed. Now come out from behind your fortress." He stepped backward and theatrically bowed with an extended arm, inviting her.

"What time is it?" She tried to break his weaning, dark gaze but could not.

"Leave this place, Martha," Mr. Sam said enthusiastically, "and we can have such a good time."

"But . . . I mustn't . . ." she protested, her weeping dwindling.

Mr. Sam's lids lowered sadly. He appeared hurt. With a deft motion he removed his dark glasses from the right front pocket of his jacket and slipped them on.

Outside, thunder rumbled. The air conditioner moaned as it sponged the increased humidity caused by the exterior tropical shower, and produced cool dryness within.

Martha felt emotionally moved, and she physically moved. The counter end swung up, and down following her passage. Not a sound came from the two adults.

She glanced back; she saw her father ranging behind the barrier. She turned and surveyed the lobby.

Mr. Sam happily squeezed her left elbow and guided her to the door.

✦ ✦ ✦

The gusts rolled great billows of rain against the buildings. Traffic signals danced red, yellow, and green under crisscrossing cables. Sodium crime lights cast waves of fat drops into amber fishbowls. Water streamed gurgling from stone walls, cement walks, asphalt streets and swirled into deepening, rushing gutter rivers. Cars plowed through the storm, their tires half submerged and headlights fuzzy balls of white.

Martha was tucked against his breast, her knees and back supported by strong arms. Her last memory of reality was a clock ticking 11 P.M. over a filing cabinet. The reentry of this strange man with skin less sickly and a manner less subdued had become a dashing over glassy wet pavement, laughter in her ear, liquid flying from behind them.

Mr. Sam halted. He giggled as he set her on her feet, on mushy grass. Sheets of gray became drizzle dots and blowy mist.

A soaked Martha turned and gasped. She distractedly pulled off her streaked glasses; Mr. Sam grabbed them from her and slipped them into his coat pocket.

"This is Morningside Park!" she exclaimed. And suddenly a name occurred to her as she peered at the blurred, spry man at her side. An identity sprouted from the cellars of her memory. "You're Him!" she whispered with a hiss, pointing a finger in his direction. "How else did we come this far so soon."

He giggled again. "Close enough," he said and clasped her in his arms.

She couldn't think of anything else to say. She wasn't afraid. She wasn't sure why she wasn't.

"But," he continued, "I have bagged enough souls for the time being. Now I want to be with you."

"Not me," she said hotly, struggling to free herself. "I'm the stupidest, ugliest girl in my entire class."

"Martha, Martha, don't you know? I was attracted to you from the start."

Another Martha was tugging at her tongue, reminding her that the park was dangerous, asking her what she was doing there in the middle of the night, demanding rationality. She tried not to relax in his grip. "It's not true, is it?" she asked timidly.

In answer, he began stroking her musky wet ringlets.

The breezy air was steamy and scintillant under the park lamps. A banyan tree tossed nearby, flinging droplets. Tropical hedges exuded a heavy, languorous, sweet scent. Frogs croaked and insects buzzed and chirred.

From the corner of her eye she could imagine malignant, milling shapes. Fear overcame pleasure. "Don't you know where we are?" she mumbled into his damp, musty smelling coat. "Let's go back, please."

He worked supple, bony fingers into her hair, winding the soft locks like yarn on spindles. "My dear little virgin, you mustn't be afraid with me. Let me show you . . ." And he again swept her into his arms.

They were galloping once more. Martha sealed her eyes and snuggled her face against his breast. She felt the wind hit them like flapping silk. She was aware of the sounds of brakes and auto horns, the swish of speed on slick streets, the crackling thunder of a low jet.

Flying, yes flying, she thought. They were soon above noise and the air gusted around them.

They halted. She was lowered; her shoes touched cement but she resisted standing and wouldn't open her eyes.

"Martha," Mr. Sam said, "look now."

She straightened and raised her lids. In the dimness of an astigmatic world she recognized the Sea Circus billboard above the publicity-garnering, oversized stuffed shark glowering within its cage. They were at the entrance to a city causeway. She shifted and peered into the gloom, down to the causeway tollbooths. The smell of warm brine coiled around her.

He spread his arms. "Tell me what you would like to do. We can have a lot of fun!"

"I was standing in the office, you came to the counter, you asked me my name, you said you were 'master of half of everything,'" she recited.

"That's me," he confirmed, once more removing his dark glasses.

"Can you turn into animals?" she blurted, stepping close to him so she could see.

"Of course I can. I'm also boss of the little gray pigs. I taught them everything they know," he boasted. He tenderly wiped wet sticky hair from her forehead. "So, what do you want to do?"

"Can we go to the beach, over there?" She pushed at the night sky with an open hand, as if trying to grip the distant shorelines of Virginia Key and Key Biscayne. "They never let me go to the beach."

"That doesn't sound very exciting," Mr. Sam said, shaking his head, but in moments they were descending to the sand beneath the far end of the bridge over Bear Cut Channel. In moments they were strolling along the low-tide exposed strand. Spotty mangrove trees with their algae-furred tangle of legs seemed gnomes ready to leap in front of them. Tiny fiddler crabs scurried en masse from their approach.

He stopped abruptly. He held high two fingers and sliced

air toward the channel that was both the Atlantic Ocean and Biscayne Bay. "Watch," he said.

"But I can't . . ." she began.

"Oh yes." His sinewy arm forcefully held her by the waist and drew her to him.

She relaxed in his embrace and gazed outward amid the soughing of calm waves that lapped silvery at the shore. Whisperings filled the night and sucked away the bridge lights, the crossing cars with their red taillights flowing toward the city; all evidence of the twentieth century.

Clouds scudded and tore, revealing pale stars and a waning crescent moon.

In an instant, gleaming whitish shapes began breaking the moon-mottled surface water. The whole channel was suddenly alive with splashing and diving, tail-dancing yet regulated forms. A squeaking-honking came to Martha's ears.

"Porpoises, hundreds of porpoises!" she squealed, and gripped his shoulder in her delight. "Oh, I want to see them. Where are my glasses?"

He giggled and shook his head. "Would I lie to you? You know they're there."

"No . . ." She tried to shove free. "I want my glasses."

At that moment, as if someone had spoken a magic word, a humid silence fell and smothered the world like saturated cotton. The porpoises were soundless. They thinned, and were gone. High storm clouds blew together and fused once more. Somewhere lightning struck, sending a pale blue echo-flash over the bay.

"The night is almost gone," Mr. Sam said, his tangy voice seemingly melancholy. "I have matters to attend to. We must return." His hand slipped from her waist. He pressed her soft fingers with her spectacles.

Slanting rain spattered the beach and dimpled the choppy, rocking seawater.

Martha flew home to the Golden Time Motel.

✦ ✦ ✦

Martha was preparing for sleep. The time before dawn was her time because it was no time, the limbo of end-beginning. It was five nights since her midnight romp with Mr. Sam. Five nights since the hasty flights that now seemed fancies. She hadn't seen him since.

She struggled into her sleeveless cotton nightgown and thumped into the sultry bathroom, flipping up the light switch. The brightness speared a huge and brown palmetto bug as it balanced on the sink rim. Martha was terrified. The sight of roaches sickened her. Sprays, pellets, traps couldn't get rid of them. Nothing affected the rats, either, that scuffled in the motel's trashy rear lot outside her window.

She eased backward into the shadowy, warm, and sticky motel room. She glanced at the hulk of her long-dead air conditioner; above it, the gridlike guard over her one window seemed like dungeon bars. She found the edge of her bed, sat down heavily, and cried. After several minutes she sobbed haphazardly, and fell silent.

The place seemed oddly cooler. Languid tendrils slithered about her arms and legs and made them feel cooler. She glanced at the window, then at the door opposite it. She studied the black corner behind the door. The murk there seemed to be thickening; it began to revolve like a tornado. She thought she saw two small, blazing white stars in the midst of the whorl. She incredulously wiped her eyes and groped for the night table and her glasses.

The congealing ink cyclone stepped forward. "Martha,

you're not afraid of me, are you?" it asked in a slightly nasal tone.

She recognized Mr. Sam's rhythmic, spicy voice. His pale face emerged; a smear to her. She stood unevenly. "I thought you were gone. I thought I imagined you." She realized that he was indeed there, yet her door was locked and double-bolted. "How . . ." Her mouth remained open on the word.

He was fully corporeal now, and he briskly walked toward her, as if happily approaching a long-unseen old friend. "You know I can change into anything I want," he explained. He was opposite her. "And what I want to do, I do." He cupped a hand on each of her round shoulders. "I've really missed you, Martha. I want to be with you." He was minus hat, glasses, cigarette, and jacket this time. His black satin vest and tie burned into his silky white shirt.

"It's almost dawn," she protested.

He smiled broadly, revealing the tips of many sharp teeth. "There is a time for every purpose. I with the dawn have often made sport. The old sun and I aren't enemies, just opposite ends of the same stick."

"I don't see much sun, either," she mused, not understanding what he said.

"Yes, I know," he said matter-of-factly. "Your life certainly is difficult."

"And I can't sleep sometimes, you know? My father says I sing in my sleep. He starts pounding on the wall to wake me and make me stop."

"Do you sing in your dreams?" He guided her to the small dinette table, pulled out a vinyl-lapped chair, motioned her to sit.

She sank with perfect composure. "I dream I'm a great opera star. That I'm on stage, and I know every language, every part. I hear the applause—but it's only my father's yelling." She puckered her lower lip and looked at her thighs pressed tightly together under the translucent white material. The gown slipped slightly off one shoulder.

Mr. Sam blankly gazed at her as he seated himself, the Formica square between them. "Do you eat here?" He tapped the table.

"Sometimes. My father gives me money and I buy what I want. Señora Blanco feeds me, too. I also get stuff from her grocery." Something buzzed from the bathroom and landed on the white bed sheets. She yelped like a whipped dog and jumped in her chair.

He stood energetically and faced the insect; the thing was suddenly on its back, its legs wriggling helplessly amid the sheet folds. Then it was motionless. "I will tell those little bastards not to bother you anymore," he stated as he reappeared in the chair.

"What?" She found herself chuckling nervously. "You can do that?"

"Of course." His tone was gallant. "I will tell the big boss of roaches to control his gang. From the smallest to the largest, they will trouble you no more."

"Can you make all the rats and bugs march themselves into the sea, like the Pied Piper?"

His eyes were two oil pools. He shook his head. "That's not my specialty. But I have influence."

She smiled until her cheeks ached, then abruptly lowered her eyes. There was a pause, then she asked carefully, staring at the table, "Mr. Sam, do you like me?"

This question spurred him to his feet. He dramatically extended pale, slender hands for her. She was startled and wouldn't move for them. He dropped them to his sides. "Alas," he moaned. "No more. I'll see you tonight, heartthrob. I want to get to know this Señora Blanco."

Martha gazed up, her lids drooping from sleepiness, anxiety, and strain. "You like me?" she asked plaintively.

"My heart, I love you," he replied. *"Buenos días, señorita, bon jour."*

And he was gone before she could move a muscle.

✦ ✦ ✦

"He's so beautiful," Martha managed over her tuna salad sandwich. "He's like a lord or prince." She washed the bread down with a swallow of her milk and Coke.

"Bueno!" Señora Blanco said mockingly. She stumped from her gas stove to the sink, to the cupboard for spices to sprinkle in the pan of paella. She slammed the cupboard door and turned with her fists on her round hips. She was concern incarnate; her bright silver and blue muumuu was tentlike; her huge breasts were heaving, her graying black hair was askew. Sweat spotted her hairline and the skin above her upper lip, stippled her pale neck. "Martha, you be a fool!" she shouted in her thick accent. "I told you and told you not to let this happen. A young child work in that place . . ." Her voice was losing volume, becoming a mumble as she returned to her sizzling skillets and pans.

The dining table was under a window and Martha was feeling the late-afternoon breeze. It had a fresh scent to it, a hot but balmy reminder that another thunderstorm was coming.

"Martha . . ." She slipped into the chair beside the girl's. "Who is he? What else you know about him? Eh? Nothing, right?"

She shrugged, slightly surprised and hurt that Señora Blanco disapproved. She picked at crumbs on her plate.

The woman sighed lugubriously; her large brown eyes and black brows seemed to fuse for an instant. "I do not like this," she stated heavily, and rose to once more attend her brews.

She had known the señora for years. The woman's single-bedroom apartment had been above her Cuban grocery for years. The store was in an older, lower-income neighborhood, and was an easy walk from the Golden Time.

The lady was outwardly typical; a widow who attended Sunday Mass in solemn black, who uttered prayerful exclamations, and cooked traditional holiday meals for her relatives. Martha, however, suspected the señora possessed a deeper, darker side.

Even now Señora Blanco was fingering the necklace chain that disappeared under the muumuu's yoke. Martha knew that an amulet and a crucifix dangled at chain's end, and the amulet little resembled anything Catholic.

The señora's white-walled living room was furnished in a sturdy, wooden Spanish style, simple but elegant. Along the wall opposite the couch were shelves hosting a variety of bottles, pots, jars, and jugs, some wrapped in pale cloth, some resembling used wine bottles sealed again. A few of these jars were made of white porcelain and were tightly lidded. Others were sun-dried clay amphorae, open at the top.

Two corner whatnots, between the bedroom and living room, presented an equally mystifying array of objects: rattles decorated with strings of shells, beads, and bones, primitive apron-shaped bells, shell and bead necklaces, smooth polished stones buoyed in oil-filled marble boxes.

In the señora's bedroom, Martha had found the most unusual display. There was an altar niche to the side of the señora's four-poster bed; a solid cement block filled three fourths of this niche. The block was painted with dizzying and colorful geometric patterns. On top of the altar block was a black wooden cross, before which rested a well-used pack of playing cards on one side, and a gourd-like rattle and several more bells on the other. Another row of bottles and jars was behind the black cross, deep within the curved hollow of the niche. Above, on the wall, were two posters side by side; one represented St. James in full regalia, and the other pictured St. Patrick driving snakes before him into the sea.

"And you say his name—what?—Sam? Mr. Sam what?" She wiped her hands on the dish towel hanging from the refrigerator door.

"Yes, ma'am," Martha said to her plate. "That's all. Just Mr. Sam."

Suddenly a newspaper flopped on the table under Martha's nose. "I show you something—read this—and this." Señora Blanco was bending over her shoulder; her chubby, red-nailed forefinger was scanning the columns of print.

"I don't want to."

"Then I say it. A little child raped and beaten yesterday. Another murdered by his own papa. And now a machete maniac. And *you* go out at night with this strange man." The morning *Herald* was gone, the señora was seated once more. "Martha, Martha, what bothers me most is you don't tell me all. You are not telling me the truth about this. *Dios mio,* you are foolish—don't you know?"

She was fighting hot tears. "He's coming tonight. I'll bring him to see you."

"Tonight, tonight?" The woman seemed to recoil in the baroque Spanish chair. Both were silent for a time.

The woman clutched her necklace chain. "Martha, *mi rosa,*" she finally whispered, "there is something else, not in the news, something that *Americanos* don't understand. There are things that happen—oh—there are people who know certain ways. There are crimes that take place; ones who work evil do things police can't stop."

"If it was important, the cops'd tell us." She hid her trembling hands under the table.

"No. Our people who work in the hospitals and police departments, they repeat rumors. There is a dark side to Santeria." She exhaled forcefully and bit her lower lip. "Now," she said, "you confess to me." Her tone was sure but her voice was thick and wet.

The girl lowered her chin. "I guess I'm crazy, that's all. Just like my old man says."

"Why?" Her eyes seemed black as she nailed them on Martha's blotching face.

"Because Mr. Sam is, he's, he is very powerful," she answered with great concentration.

"Oh, *sí*. Your Señor Sam is riding a fine horse."

Martha didn't understand. "He took me to Bear Cut beach last week. He flew, he turned into smoke," she insisted defensively, trying not to cry. "He made the porpoises dance!" She pulled off her glasses and pinched the bridge of her nose. "Or I think he did." She squeezed her eyes shut but to no avail. Liquid slid down her cheeks.

"Shh, shh, no more. It's all right." The señora was up, and hugging her, and passing her a napkin to blot her tears. "Quiet now. You will invite him nowhere. You will tell him to go away now? Yes?"

Martha only sobbed.

✦ ✦ ✦

Sunset honey-gold, grenadine, and lavender swirled and graded from west to east. The colors bounced from the window-plated newer buildings downtown, and wormed their way into the most sullen corners of ghettos and low-income neighborhoods. For fifteen minutes the entire metropolis indeed seemed magical, while the air quickened and the birds sang for release from the sun.

Martha walked toward the Golden Time, her gaze locked on the now magenta last vestige of heavenly glory. The buildings obscured the horizon, so purplish gray was soon all that she saw. She reached the boulevard and absently crossed against the light. A horn brayed. Someone leaned out a car window and cursed.

In the motel office, she found her father snapper-eyed and slush-mouthed. She cringed as the closing door struck the bell.

"Look who's here," her mother said in a near hysterical voice. She tried to smile at her husband, who was glowering at Martha.

The daughter held position in the center of the terrazzo floor, her pride and fear at war. It was one thing when her father was sober and drumming orders, but quite another when he was drunk like this and expected her to be his target. The danger was growing, the tightrope was vibrating.

And then she gratefully heard a ting behind her.

Mr. Sam's hands were on her shoulders, and she leaned back against him. A flood of drowsy joy swept into the hollows left by the abrupt sapping of tension. Security and trust enwrapped her.

Her father was a statue once again, and her mother also. Martha pivoted under Mr. Sam's unrestraining, cool hands. She stared up into his dark plastic-hidden eyes. "You saved me," she said with innocence and awe.

He laughed, removing his newest cigarette and fully exposing a row of sharp needle teeth. He appeared livelier.

His coffee-toned face was more lustrous and carefree. Even his clothes were more fashionable and trim.

She felt completely inadequate and ashamed as she noted his appearance. She wrenched backward and self-consciously glanced down at her own wrinkled gray dress, dusty knees, and drab sandals.

He cupped an affectionate hand behind her neck and propelled her to the door before she could say a word.

They walked through the muggy, gnatty early-evening glow and came to number 18. He brought her over the threshold and pulled the door after them. A flip of the toggle, and the dirty, buggy ceiling fixture spread light.

With wide caramel eyes she surveyed the unchanged motel room. He was striding, was at, was sitting in an opposite plastic chair. He crossed one knee over the other and observed her. "Are you looking for something?" he asked after some moments.

"Your . . . your . . ." she stammered.

"And if the police were to break in here, or anyone who had no business in here, would it matter whether one of your vampires was laid out on the bed or in a box?"

She knit her brows, uncertain of what he meant.

He was on his feet, at her side, inviting her forward. "He would end in the county morgue in either case, heh?"

"But . . ." she began.

"Oh, you young things all have vampires on the brain." He giggled.

She lowered herself on the end of the bed. "I don't understand," she whimpered.

He sank beside her and removed his dark glasses. He twirled them by one earpiece. He was hatless, but dressed in a black velvet suit. His black tie and mauve shirt were silk. "Now listen," he said matter-of-factly, "there is a difference between the *je-rouge,* that slovenly snot, and myself. I'm his boss, see? I'm the big boss." He sighed with a whistle through his teeth. "Now, my lily, what troubles you?"

The sudden intimacy of the last question caused her to stiffen and lean away. "What?" she asked shortly.

"You fear me?"

"I don't know. Senõra Blanco says that I should."

"So, the señora again." He laughed deep in his throat. "She was in the local society, you know. She was once a big mambo, a priestess they say here, for this place you call Miami."

"She's my best friend. She's afraid you're going to hurt me. If she believes you exist at all."

"Oh-ho, she believes that I exist." He giggled, folded up his glasses, and slipped them into his jacket pocket.

"We'd better go back. Suppose someone comes into the office?"

"Your parents reanimated at your exit. They have forgotten you." He paused, and with the fingertips of his left hand tickled the alabaster skin of her nearest inner arm. "Do you know who your Mr. Sam is? No? Why, he's the giver and the taker. He can tell the future. He is the king of love and life."

"You're talking crazy again," she whispered fearfully as she sighed at his touch.

He lightly, twice, stroked her neck. He drew his thin fingers down below her left collarbone and slowly began to knead one of her small, swelling breasts. He worked open the top button of her dress, and the next button, and the rest until he pulled the top half of her dress down in a heap around her hips. He was stroking her everywhere, kissing her nipples.

"What are you doing?" she asked over the roar in her

ears and the electric sensations coming from her breasts and shoulders.

He giggled and gently embraced her. He pushed, pushed insistently, saying "honey heart" and "lamb baby" until her back was on the bed and her dark blonde curls rippled out behind her over the bedspread. He rocked her flexed legs—to the left, to the right—and she felt him pull her skirt up and her panties off, whisking the latter down and up over her knees and down off the ends of her toes.

She felt his fingers between her legs, rubbing her, making her feel good. She stretched her arms out over her head. "Nice little curls," he was saying, "sweet little pink puss," and her knees were parting, falling away from one another. She strained and strained over the warm, shock-like pulses until she thought she couldn't bear it anymore; she began making small animal noises.

Then it stopped. She continued to hold her knees as far apart as she could, waiting for him to do more. She heard nothing. Then a cool and silky coffee-dark body was on top of hers, nestled between her legs and mouthing her face, her breasts. Something hard and warm was shoving at her where the fingers had just been.

"He wants in, Martha," a nasal voice whispered in her ear, "he wants in."

✦ 3 ✦

The whooping of police cars, screaming ambulances, the tumult of raging motorcycle platoons transformed the street leading from the boulevard, and the Golden Time, into a firecracker show.

Martha held Mr. Sam by the arm and intently tracked the juggernaut until the last wail stopped. She could see throbbing red, blue, and green lights reflected from upper-story windowpanes several blocks away. "That's close to the motel," she said. "Maybe I'd better go see what's going on."

"What do you care?" he asked, grinning while the bright colors reverberated in the black plastic depths of his shades.

She briefly touched her lips as if bewildered. After a minute, she hesitantly slipped her fingers into his. "No, I don't care. I don't care about that place anymore."

His face was phosphorescent as he giggled in a high-pitched tone. She felt dizzy as she gazed at him.

"Don't you trust me?" he purred with a voice of spiced honey.

"Yes, I do," she whispered.

"Don't you love me?" he breathed.

"You . . . I . . ." she stuttered. Then, "Yes, more than the whole world."

"Soul and body, you will be mine, valentine?"

"You really, really want *me?*"

"Your body, your body is a good lay so I can hatch in it and grow until I sprout wings and fly."

"What do you mean?" Her brows came together as she searched his face.

He giggled again, very softly, and with his free fingers carefully combed her tresses beneath one gold hair clip, setting her glasses awry. He straightened them for her.

The pleasurable feelings these actions aroused dissolved her doubts. "Can we see Señora Blanco now?" she asked dreamily. "I told her we would come."

"Wait," he said, holding up a finger. "You promised me."

"Promised?"

"To be mine."

She opened her mouth to speak but the words caught in her throat. She shuddered.

He waited silently, his hand like a cap on the crown of her head.

"To marry you?" she finally forced between chattering teeth.

"Sort of, sweetie." The voice was light and delicate like floating down feathers. "You do promise, right?"

"Yes." And her renewed nervousness immediately evaporated at the sound of her own acquiescence. "Yes, yes, yes," she cried. "But I can't believe it!"

"Hush, lamb heart. Now, we will visit your friend."

✦ ✦ ✦

Mr. Sam lifted palm fronds, leaves of elephant ear, croton branches. He brushed aside hibiscus bushes and banana trees to clear a passage that pointed to the grocery's rear stairway. Martha tread dewy grass that crunched underfoot; he let the lush greenery swing into place as he soundlessly reappeared by her elbow.

They moved in the darkness between apartment houses, in a web of radio soul, television hawkers, stereo hard rock, and multilingual human quarrels that spun from yellow, yawning windows.

The steep cement steps were guarded by a wrought-iron banister that wobbled as Martha clutched it. She paused and stared up, amazed at what seemed a shadow or a panther flitting to the door ahead of her. By the yellow light of the stoop, she watched the dark mass assume human proportions once more. She climbed, and came to a halt at Mr. Sam's side. She smiled with mixed pleasure and excitement. Her glasses were golden circles. He fingered the bell button. Some expression played about his lips but was gone before she could name it.

The entrance cracked a line of light, then opened wide.

The señora's stern, pale face and draped body were framed in the doorway. The voluminous silver caftan with its cowl settled on her shoulders; her strange serpentine bracelets, her cowry shell necklaces and leaden rings were an aspect of the señora that the girl had never seen. *"Buenas tardes,"* Señora Blanco said coldly, but not to Martha.

The girl's mood plummeted. She eyed the señora and stepped inside. She glanced over her shoulder to see Mr. Sam still without. He was placidly receiving the señora's bitter glare. "You may enter, Señor," the woman finally said, and took one step backward as the man walked past. She narrowed her eyes and kept her guests in view as she shut the door.

Martha's head spun; she sensed change before she absorbed the room's details.

All the mirrors were reversed on their wire loops so that only moldy wood squares and oblongs gawked senselessly from the four walls. The dining table's finish reflected several mismatched candle flames dancing in waxy depths. The odor of incense—a cloying combination of scents—made the air difficult to breathe. Two deep blue porcelain bowls rested on the coffee table and flanked a capless human skull studded with metal nibs and glass beads. In the far bowl protruded a mass of brown, in the near simmered a dark red liquid. Of the remaining furniture, only the sofa was visible.

The carpet had been taken up. Drawn in charcoal on

the floorboards was a complete circle in the center of the living room. Inside it was another circle, inside which was an elaborate design of squiggles, coils, arrows, and glyphs.

She gaped, and then touched the señora's arm half in question, half for reassurance. But the woman, her back to the entrance, was again in a standoff with Mr. Sam. From the folds of the caftan, a hand the señora had thus far kept hidden suddenly emerged clutching an ancient silver and gold Spanish sword.

"What's wrong? What are you doing?" Martha cried.

"You! You!" Señora Blanco shouted and raised the beautiful weapon like the Archangel Michael. "What you want with this child?" Her stark voice rebounded from the walls and floor. "Why choose her? Why?" She pointed the gleaming blade at the unmoving amalgam of shade, sallow skin, and human clothing.

He removed his dark glasses as he grinned. His black eyes were speckled with tiny, bright pinpoints as if they'd suddenly given birth to swimming motes of fire. He urbanely held one fist behind his back and gestured with the shades in his free hand. "The sword of Ogun, my, my. Isn't that special, now, heh," he said reasonably.

"Do you think I am like the others? Do you think I would not know you? Do you think I would not try to save her?" Her left hand twisted the strings of cowry shells.

He giggled and arched his brows, giving himself a look that was both sinister and comical. "Señora, what fun you are. Why you old dug, you old Judas mambo, what power do you think you still have? Come, come, let's be friends, okay?" He winged his arms as a sign of openness.

"You are not going to have power in here!" she bellowed as she brandished the sword and strode to the circle. She bent sideways over the two bowls. A long match was struck. With the flare she ignited the brownish material in the first bowl. She touched fire to the red liquid in the second bowl; blue-gold flames puffed into an instant, round inferno. The stench from both compact blazes was horrid.

Martha faced the combatants. Her toes turned inward, her knees touched, her elbows squeezed into her ribs. "Please stop, Señora Blanco," she whimpered. "Please."

"Rotten fruit and herbs, bones and blood. To drive me away, or call me to you, eh?" Mr. Sam's tone was congenial though his eyes were now lusterless and his features sharp. "Ah! And what little goodies do I detect hidden behind the picture frames, and over the door, yet?" He pointed.

"You think this be a joke? You think I jest?" She shook her weapon. "No mere force of world church do I call. I know that is useless. No. I know force beyond that. On the islands they know. On the ancient continent, they know."

"This isn't fair, it isn't right," she sputtered. "Mr. Sam is going to marry me. He wants me to be his bride."

Her eyes were lightning and thunderheads as she whirled and confronted the girl. "And what you say to that? WHAT DID YOU SAY?"

"She said yes, what do you think?" He twirled the dark glasses by an earpiece. "What are you going to do about it? Huh?" He smiled broadly, purposely revealing his pointed, catlike teeth.

This momentarily unbalanced Señora Blanco. When she recovered, her face darkening, she shouted, "You little clown, little death. You are not the Master. You take his name but you are little trickster. You have no power against the great gods."

"Uh-uh," he sang, "I am the big boss, you know it."

"Then why you play with this little girl?" she demanded.

"Ummm." He grinned at Martha. "Why, I've been called

here. And how many golden-haired virgins can be found these days? You know I can't stand to see a plump pink puss go to waste."

The señora blanched suddenly. Although her eyes were red-rimmed and filling with tears, they seemed helplessly locked onto the figure of Mr. Sam. "This be all a game to you and your kind," she said tightly from behind her teeth.

Meanwhile Martha seethed. She heard her own voice fly from her mouth out of control. "He loves me! He's never hurt me. How can you do this?" She wiped tears from her face. "I thought you loved me," she sniffed.

"Stupid girl, stupid me," the señora muttered. The veins pulsed in the woman's neck, her complexion was mottled by rose, purple, and white. Sweat and tears mingled on her round cheeks, in front of her ears. She seemed to sag, to loose energy and tension. The sword lowered. "There are natural laws," she said with a chilling, hopeless calm, "that govern the physical world whenever it becomes mixed with *his* other." She pointed as if her red-tipped finger could shoot bullets at Mr. Sam. "We, the poor people, are tangled in the third dimension. *He, other,* belongs to a different space and time."

He sighed and took several steps toward the drawing in the center of the room, beside which Señora Blanco seemed to shiver and cower from his approach. He studied the strange charcoal wiggles and slashes several minutes —all the while the gurgling fires and Martha's sobbing were the only sounds to be heard. Then he studiously donned his dark glasses, sliding them up his nose and into position almost with a click. The lenses writhed with small flames as he turned them to the señora.

His high-pitched giggle made the woman start. "Let me put it this way, ex-priestess, old mambo," he said with a hollow, nasal tone. "You shell throwers, you bell ringers with your sidewalk sorcery, do you think your bones and stones, your leaves and plaster saints mean anything to me? You play with hexes and headless chickens, sorcerers and signs. Where I come from the gods are jealous and demanding; our subjects live from minute to minute in holy thrall. Where I come from I am Baron La Croix and Baron of the Cemetery. The Baron, Baron Sam. My people are here too, now. And we are strong."

"Get out of here, leave me alone," the señora whispered, seeming to forget about the girl. "Get out of here."

"But I've been called," he explained, spreading his arms.

"I didn't call you," the woman shouted. She repeated in Spanish the command to leave.

Martha choked and coughed. She tried to wipe her nose on a sleeve. "I'm scared," she said to anyone.

Mr. Sam was instantly at her side, was patting her between the shoulder blades while singing "lamb lily" and "honey heart."

At that moment, as if released from her selfish fears, the señora charged. Her teeth clenched and exposed, the sweat breaking from her forehead, her eyes purple sparklers, she lunged with her desperate grip high and the glinting sword point aimed at Mr. Sam's breast.

Martha screamed.

But he easily caught the woman by both wrists as the metal tip impressed the velvet jacket over his heart. The señora's eyes were glassy and bloodshot. Her face drained of color. She groaned and tried to avoid her captor's dark plastic eyepits. Her face contorted.

The sword suddenly reddened and began smoking. It fell with a clunk to the floor, bounced once, and rested, hissing. The woman's bloody palms and swollen fingers fanned like storm-broken tree limbs from his coffee-colored hand.

"Leave her, I beg you," the woman shrilled through gritted teeth. "She is young, give her time."

"Señora Blanco, please. It's all right, really . . ." Martha began, then was stunned into silence.

He had lowered the woman's wrists. He now circled her with his left arm. Señora Blanco was absolutely still. He softly braced her chin with four fingers while his lips came down, down, and fused with the woman's lips in what seemed a sensual kiss. In seconds the señora's body was limp, her eyes dilated and unblinking.

Martha stuffed a hand in her mouth. Her mind pushed helplessly at spreading numbness. Her feet and thighs felt like lead weights, her heart slowed. She wanted to close her eyes but the lids were like broken roller blinds. Faint neighborhood noises abruptly came through the windows. This was a reality she could relate to. The scene before her was a movie she'd seen one Saturday afternoon.

✦ 4 ✦

"'Maiden arise,'" Tooney grimly quoted to himself. *Maiden arise*. "Find anything?" he called to an officer who momentarily appeared in the Golden Time's wedged-open office door.

"Nothing," was the terse reply.

A bevy of city and Metro personnel—detectives, ambulance attendants, police staff—plus a knot of spectators on the well-lighted porch outside the motel office, harried Leon as he made his way to Tooney. He stopped to chat with a city detective, finally approached his partner. "Room eighteen is empty. Completely unlived in."

"Damn . . ." Tooney mopped the carroty hair off his brow while he scowled with anger.

"Yeah." Leon sighed. He shifted to observe as the strapped, green-plastic-wrapped bodies were wheeled out from behind the counter, one after the other. "All we can do now is look for the girl, and hope."

Tooney stretched one corner of his mouth and wagged his head. A guttural grunt hung in his throat.

"So all we have is the letter left in the typewriter?"

"Yeah, a letter about a 'ghost with twinkly eyes,'" he quoted. "Would you believe it?" Tooney shook his head, sank his thumbs behind his belt, and absently watched the lab people about their business. "Old Dalston must have been one crazy, tough mother. That is," he added, "if his prints match those on the typewriter. We found the body on the floor beside the chair."

"You want to know what one of the paramedics told me?" Leon was pale and sweaty, his slicked brown hair was coming unstuck in separate arcs. He chortled self-consciously. "Says the bodies were completely healthy, not a mark on them. It's like someone pulled their plugs."

"Oh, that's fine, real fine. Did they look for needle tracks in their arms, too?" He swatted at sandflies.

"Yeah, but Hal, old chum, think about that. Those two prostitutes, the dope shipper at the Marina; their deaths could be drug related. Which isn't surprising."

Tooney's bushy brows melded, his mouth opened. "The Dalstons?" he asked rhetorically. "Shooting up?"

"Well . . ." Leon mused to himself. He once more surveyed the gold-speckled, Formica-topped counter, the machete hanging from its rusty peg, the key rack, the crucifix. "Well, let's just hope we can find the girl."

✦ ✦ ✦

Martha recognized the building that materialized from a tumbling world. It was the white, massive public library building. They were in Bayfront Park.

Mr. Sam eased her to the ground, his hands lingering at her waist and neck. "She can go to heaven, now. I pulled that stubborn woman out of her old life. I sucked out her soul like soda through a straw."

She swiveled, frightened and confused. "She didn't want to hurt you. She was protecting me." She flinched slightly as Mr. Sam snatched away her glasses. "Who are you? What are you?"

"You promised me, remember?" His right forefinger alighted briefly on the tip of her nose.

"But what she said, about gods and you being from another dimension—why do you talk crazy all the time? What are you going to do to me?"

His exploding, high-pitched giggle sounded like a wild xylophone cutting the warm night air. "I already told you," he finally answered.

She blinked and stared; his eyes seemed so round, large, and dark that she couldn't tell whether he had his glasses on or not. "I don't know anymore. I want to go home," she whimpered. "Everything's crazy. I want to go home."

"Pussy, you have no home, except with me. You have nothing now, only me." His voice was mellow.

Around them hulked shadowy banyan and ficus trees with brittle root beards that struggled for the ground. Park benches supported human bodies intoxicated and dead to the night. Others strolled, on the lookout for baited hooks.

She peered at these, projections on a screen as much as Mr. Sam was the center of gravity, a force drawing her faculties no matter how hard she tried to focus on herself. She began to cry. Her tears fell noisily, rolling into her mouth corners and salting her swallowed sobs.

"Stop that, lamb heart," he ordered, and waited until she was silent. Then, "Now why the tears? We had fun, didn't we, sweetie pie?"

"Yes," she murmured. She began to shiver.

"And now you're a lady-girl, right? Now no nasty minor demons can have you, huh?" He fingered one of her supple earlobes. He stroked the fresh skin that was pearl-white under her mane of hair. "Only the best for Martha," he said with his tangy accent.

Her hair was drawn aside like a curtain. She sighed and sobbed at once as Mr. Sam's soft, coral lips met hers, then slid to her chin, to her ear, and finally back to her inflamed mouth.

✦ ✦ ✦

Martha felt the cold leave her feet first. Her soles tingled as she gulped breath and shook her head to dislodge the fog from her sight. But the fog thickened, and as she rubbed her eyes she realized her wire-frames were missing. Her neck was stiff.

"Mr. Sam," she timorously called to the surrounding shadow-dappled darkness. She craned her head, still unwilling to move from the spot.

A wind hissed through the looming trees. The library was a miserable glint of white too far away. "Mr. Sam, are you here?" She moved a step forward and paused. She lifted her arms as if greeting someone, let them drop limply. "Please, where are you?" The childlike tremolo echoed. A new moon provided no illumination, and one of the nearby park lights was out. "Where did you go? Where are you?" Her voice sharpened. "Don't leave me here, please."

A figure was approaching from the north, a man dressed in black. She watched it expectantly, but soon she realized the hesitant, heavy tread was not that of Mr. Sam. Her legs began quivering and she couldn't move. "Oh, help me," she whispered to the moist air. The distant drone of a jet answered.

He stopped before her. Martha recognized the shiny metal blade hanging from his right hand. Her lover's final words were a roar in her mind: *only the best for Martha*.

The greasy-haired specter in front of her smiled crookedly and twanged, "And what's a nice girl like you doing here alone so late at night?"

MOTHER CALLS BUT I DO NOT ANSWER

by Rachel Cosgrove Payes

Rachel Cosgrove Payes, originally from Maryland, earned a B.S. degree from West Virginia Wesleyan College. She's worked for many years in the science fields, first as a registered medical technologist, and later as a research biologist for a large pharmaceutical house. Her forty books have been published in a wide variety of fields: sf, gothics, mysteries, historical romances, Regencies, teenage romance, contemporary romance, although she says she's never done a Western. Yet. Her first novel was *Hidden Valley of Oz*. Her latest book, *Emeralds and Jade*, a romantic suspense novel, was published by Doubleday in July. She recently moved to a town along the New Jersey shore of Barnegat Bay. She has a grown son and daughter, both married.

Misunderstood or alienated youths are a fairly common theme, but in Rachel's hands it takes on a much darker side.

✦ ✦ ✦

Mother calls but I do not answer. Soon she will come up the stairs, hand reluctant on the railing, and she will tap on my door. Gina, she will call. Gina. May I come in? But I will not answer.

I look into the mirror. It is the mirror on the old dressing table that Aunt Millie gave them when she bought her new bedroom furniture. Father enameled the dressing table white, carefully doing the frames around the triple mirror so that no paint would mar the glass. Mother made a ruffle of pink and white checked gingham to hide the rickety legs. There was no stool for it, but father painted the old wooden chair from the side porch, white with pink legs.

I sit for hours on my pink and white chair, looking into the mirror. Some days they do not come. Some days they are there when I wake in the morning. If they are in my mirror, I do not eat my breakfast. Mother calls but I do not answer. I hear her voice grow shrill with anxiety, but I do not care. I would rather watch them than eat.

Lately I have discovered that they are there at night. I woke one night two weeks ago and had to go to the bathroom. The floor was cold, because I did not put on the slippers that mother bought for me. They are fuzzy and pink, and I do not like them. The fuzzy part makes my feet itch, and I think that one of the beasts is crawling over my feet. I know this cannot be so. They cannot get through the glass; but I do not like the slippers and will not wear them.

That night mother heard me when I padded barefoot past her door on the way down the hall to the bathroom. She called but I did not answer. I heard her get up, but I hurried and was back in bed before she came into my room. She whispered, Gina, but I pretended that I was asleep.

I waited until she had gone back to bed. I could hear the springs groan as she eased in beside father. Then I got up, walked in my bare feet to the dressing table, and sat down on my chair. The room was dark. I will not let them leave on the night lamp. It is a pink and white china shepherdess with two woolly china lambs, and I hate it. The lambs watch me, and I know their teeth are sharp. I am not sure, but their lips may be split like rabbits'. The shepherdess looks at the lambs, pretending that she cannot see me; but I know better. I hate her. Someday I will accidentally smash the lamp. Mother will say, Oh, Gina, but I will not answer.

I looked into the mirror that night, and it was not night there. It was dusk, but I could see them as they moved about.

She was there. She is always there. I wish I could see her face; but she turns away, so that I am not able to see what she looks like. I think I know her, but I cannot remember who she is. I wish that she could look at me.

Next morning I was very tired, and I did not get up. Mother called but I did not answer.

I hear my parents talking when they think I am safe in my room. The sound comes up through the hot air register, but they do not know this. Mother says, She sits and looks into that mirror by the hour. Father says, Why couldn't your sister keep that damned dressing table? We aren't paupers. Just because we spent all our savings having Gina's harelip repaired doesn't make us objects of charity. Mother says, Do you think we should tell Dr. Dingman about the mirror? Father says, All young girls look at themselves in the mirror. I don't see why you worry about it, Fran. It's the most normal thing that Gina does these days. Mother says, But she used to hate looking at herself, because of her lip.

I hear the worry in father's voice, although he tries to hide it. I hear the shrill note when mother talks to him. I do not care. I have my mirror, and I cannot bother about my parents. I must watch what they do in the glass.

Today they crowd close, and I wonder if they are looking out at me. She is there, but she is far back in the field, in the shadow of the dense trees. The branches move, so I know that the wind is blowing. I can smell the alien odor, and I put my face close to the mirror, trying to decide whether it is the blood-red blossoms they crush under their feet, or whether the trees in the forest perfume the air with their long, writhing needles. The beasts crawl near me, but I am not afraid. Some of them look like monster rabbits, with long, sharp fangs showing through their split lips. I think the lips are made that way to allow their fangs to frighten their enemies. One of the rabbit monsters looks like Tom Duncan at school. I went into the girls' room and cried when I heard him tell Butch Baker, Gina sounds funny when she talks. I don't care, now, if they laugh at me. I do not go to school. I sit all day and look at them in my mirror. The beasts cannot touch me. I know, because I put my hand to the mirror, and it is cold, hard, smooth, safe. I laugh in triumph, and they turn to stare. Do they hear me?

Mother calls, Gina, what is so funny? Gina, are you reading? Gina, Gina—hopefully—but I do not answer.

Will I see her face tomorrow? She is tall and thin and moves with a willowy grace that I envy. Her hair is a cloud about her shoulders, the color of woodsmoke at dusk. I cannot see what she is wearing, but it flows to the ground in a stream of color. I know her, but I cannot think what her face is like. Are her eyes gray like mine, or blue like mother's? I do not think that they are father's brown. His eyes turn black when he is angry.

I can hear him now. His eyes must be black, because his voice is harsh. Father says, Dr. Dingman is a quack. He says that we must not worry about the mirror. He says that we should be glad that Gina has an interest, that she is no longer withdrawn. He talks in that condescending way, and I find myself frustrated to the point of speechlessness. Mother says, Do you think that Gina is frustrated? Is that why, when I call, she does not answer? Is all this trouble caused by her harelip and cleft palate? I thought, after the speech therapy, she would be happier;

but it hasn't helped. Dr. Dingman says it's intensified by the onset of puberty. Father says a bad word, and I can hear mother crying. I do not care. She is in the mirror again, and this time she walks toward me. If she comes close enough, I will recognize her.

Father says, It isn't good for Gina to look at her scarred lip all the time. It's unhealthy. No wonder she's so strange. I will break that mirror. Mother says, You mustn't, Ralph. Not without consulting Dr. Dingman. It might be just the wrong thing to do. Father swears again.

I have looked away, listening. Now they are gone, and I hate my father for driving them away. I go to bed, because there is nothing to do when they are not there. I cannot sleep because I am worried. What if Dr. Dingman tells father that I must not have my mirror? What if father takes it out behind the garage and smashes it to pieces with the sledgehammer? Will they come out? Or will it kill them? I do not know, and I worry. If she comes out, then I will be able to see her, perhaps touch her. But if she comes out, then the beasts will come, too.

Father must not do it. He must let me keep my mirror.

I hear them come upstairs. Mother taps on my door, opens it a crack, and calls, Gina, but I do not answer.

I worry all night. I get up frequently and pad over to the dressing table; but they are gone. What if they do not return? But they must! I cannot imagine life without them. It would be unbearable, here in this room, with the bed, and the shepherdess and her lambs, and the white dressing table, skirted in pink and white checks, its triple mirrors vacant and staring. Sometimes she is in one of the side panels, and I try to look at her without turning my head, sneaking peeks out of the corner of my eye. But she eludes me. I never see her face.

Finally I doze, and wake when mother calls me for

breakfast. I do not answer. I hurry to the mirror, afraid to look, afraid not to look, hoping that they have returned. I curl my bare toes down, trying to cling to the cold floor. I have my eyes tightly closed, and I hold my breath. Finally I must breathe. And as I do, I open my eyes, slowly, cautiously.

They have come back! She is there, moving toward me, hands outstretched, beckoning. But then I hear my parents talking, and she goes away.

Mother says, Ralph, let's have a surprise party for Gina's birthday. Father says, Gina has no friends. Father does not know that my friends are in the mirror. Mother says, I'll ask Mrs. Duncan for a list of the boys and girls who were in her class at school. Father says, I don't know, Fran. Maybe a party isn't such a good idea. But I know that mother will arrange it. I will not even object. I do not have to. No one will come. No one liked me at school, I had no friends; so mother's party will not happen.

I do not worry about the birthday party. I sit and look into my mirror and daydream. What would happen if my classmates did come to my party, and I invited them up to my room to look into my mirror? Would the people in the mirror be there, as they are now, moving about? Or do they show themselves only to me? It might be interesting to find out.

Mother has invited ten boys and girls to the birthday party. I peek when she thinks I am in my room looking into my mirror, and see the invitations. She has asked Tom Duncan, and that hateful Butch Baker—and Mellie Townsend, who wouldn't walk to school with me. But I do not care. They will not come.

On the day of the party, the telephone rings five times. Each time, through the hot air register, I can hear my mother, and I guess what the calls are. I am sorry to hear that, Mrs. Townsend, mother says. Oh, Butch has basketball practice? What a shame, Mrs. Baker. At dinner mother's lips are thin and tight, and father's eyes are dark. But I do not care. I knew they would not come. Now I will not have to put on the new frilly dress that mother bought for me. But mother says, Gina, why don't you put on your new dress and come downstairs so that we can see you? So I know the party has not been canceled.

Mother and father do not understand why I come up to my room and leave my guests alone in the living room. My parents do not hear the whispers. They do not see Cindy fold her upper lip between her thumb and finger to make it look like mine. They do not hear the others giggle. I do not care. I will never let Cindy look into my mirror. She is hateful and does not deserve to see them. I might have cried, but I did not. I look at the beasts, and wonder if there is any way I can release them. I would like to see them slither out of the mirror, over the dressing table, onto the floor, and down the stairs. Then, in the living room, they could slash Cindy's lip with their sharp teeth, and sink their fangs into Tom's neck. Then he would not laugh so loudly when I have trouble pronouncing certain words.

I did not show my gifts to mother and father. Each guest brought me something to mock me. Tom's gift was a book on rabbits—Cindy brought a stuffed blue bunny with long sharp teeth—the bedroom slippers have rabbit heads on them—everything to show me that they know I have a harelip. If only the monster rabbits in my mirror could escape, then I would laugh and laugh. My guests would scream for help, but I would not answer.

Mother comes to my room to see why I have come upstairs. She says, Gina, did you have to go to the bathroom? Gina, are you combing your hair? Gina, aren't you going back downstairs to be with your guests? But I do not answer.

I hear them all leave. And I hear father. He is furious that I came upstairs instead of staying at the party. He says, Fran, what is Gina doing up there? Mother says, She is looking in her mirror. Father says, This is the last straw. We'll be the talk of the town after those kids blab about how Gina acted at her own party. I am going to get that damned mirror out of her room tonight. Gina shouldn't be encouraged to look at her lip. It's not normal. She should forget her looks, not spend hours in front of that mirror. I'll get rid of the mirror right now.

He must not. She is so near, so near, and soon I will see her face. She moves toward me, and I know she is smiling. She holds out one long, slender hand, and I reach out to her. The glass is gone! She is there, inviting, fingers touching mine. Her face is lovely, her lips beautiful, soft pink and perfect. And I know her. She is Gina. She says, Come, and I answer, Yes. I step forward, drawn to her, and my bare feet feel the blood-red flowers crush beneath them, sending up the perfume in almost overpowering waves.

I hear mother tap at the door. She calls, Gina, but I do not answer. She comes into my room, and I see her frantic eyes search everywhere. Mother screams, Gina, Gina, where are you?—but I do not answer.

Instead, I smile at Gina, and she smiles back at me. Her perfect lips part, and I see her long, sharp teeth.

Mother calls. This time I will answer—but mother will not hear me.

NOBODY LIVES THERE NOW. NOTHING HAPPENS.

by Carol Orlock

Carol Orlock is a resident of Seattle, Washington, where she teaches fiction writing through the continuing education program at the University of Washington, and coordinates the writing curriculum there as well. Her fiction has appeared in *MS.*, *Calyx*, and *South Dakota Review*. Her first novel, *The Goddess Letters*, published by St. Martin's Press last year, met with very good reviews and received the Pacific Northwest Booksellers Award for a work of excellence by a Northwest writer.

Carol is a careful writer who has already received a lot of attention. This story shows why.

✦ ✦ ✦

In the spring we started finding gifts. A rose-colored scarf hung from a bush in the alley behind Ginny Worsted's. A child's scooter, battered but still useful, lay by the pond where the Jefferson kids play. In my garden, a jar of honey had rolled on its side in the tall yellow grass. It was clean and gleaming, and I pulled back just before the mower rolled over it.

Ginny Worsted tied the scarf around her neck. She wore green with it and looked wonderful. She wore it all week to the market and the PTA, probably even for spring cleaning, telling all who asked where it came from. She would gladly return it if we knew the owner.

The Jefferson parents, Paul and Lila, confiscated the scooter the minute Paulie Junior rolled it into their backyard. They canvassed our small town for a month, sure it was some other child's, and even put a note on the Forks' Market bulletin board. They are poor, you understand, and Paul knows everybody because he takes yardwork. No one knew where the scooter came from. Paul and Lila must have given in to their pride and donated it to charity, because I saw the scooter for sale at the thrift store later that summer.

As for the honey, I mentioned it to a few who passed regularly on their way from Forks' Market. It had not dropped from anyone's bag. I thought of asking the Marquettes, their house lay catty-corner from my fenced garden, but never having seen either of them, I put off walking up to their pure white front door and knocking. The last day of school I baked breakfast biscuits, buttery gold on top and creamy white inside. My seven-year-old broke through his small vocabulary to say the honey tasted scrumptious.

There were other gifts. There were toys for the families with children, a license-plate frame for seventeen-year-old Ed Windry, who has made Chevrolet a religion, an apron caught on Miss Emma Gilchrist's fence as if wind had given it. A lost hubcap rolled directly beside Mr. Wilson's '48 Studebaker, which needed one.

No one questioned the gifts. That April was cool, but the Almanac guaranteed a good growing season and it seemed a spring of good fortune. My garden shot up broccoli starts and the strawberry plants hung full as small Christmas trees. The seed rack at Forks' Market was empty before May Day.

The Marquettes had given the gifts of course. That is my theory at least. I make good biscuits, grow good gardens, have served twice as PTA secretary, so I am trusted in this town as a sensible woman. I told my guess about the Marquettes' gifts only to John, my husband, and even more sensible than I am. His reaction was enough to silence the sensible.

"And snakes sing serenades, Virginia. Only we can't hear them." He chuckled and cracked his knuckles. "In the first place, nobody actually lives in the Marquettes' house."

I will get to the snakes. First let me explain why, during that spring, John's belief in invisible Marquettes represented our town's unanimous opinion.

Drive out our way, as west as you can go without a sail and a rudder, and you will think you shifted gears into a time warp. Your twentieth-century tires will bump over nineteenth-century cobblestones, your rearview mirror will show a tin lizzie, its claxon horn harassing you at the town's one four-way stop. On Waterfront Street Victorian inns and four bakeries welcome you, plus a dress shop, one furniture dealer, and a pharmacy. We do a summer tourist trade and the antique chairs and apothecary tools and fringed dresses fill display windows all year. You have to go inside the stores to find modern clothes or bean-bag chairs or sulfa drugs. Otherwise, only the interior of your own car will reassure you that the industrial age has passed puberty and human footprints really do shape the dust on the moon.

We live in 1880, or thereabouts, and most residents find it comfortable. The few who do not move away, usually before Pioneer Days in early fall when tourist income requires women to wear granny skirts and men to slip on spats. We did it only for the Pioneer Festival the first few years, but women find the long dresses comfortable and even if men put off the spats I notice a fondness for vests with pocket watches and fobs.

Among time-warped Victorians, ghosts are hardly improbable. Popular opinion deciding that the Marquettes did not use three dimensions matched our accepted views about noisy attics on windless nights and suspicions on Emma Gilchrist's seven variegated and perfectly matched cats. The cats are all exactly alike, I swear, but do not drive out expecting to prove me wrong with your own eyes. Emma is old and difficult, and only once brought all seven out for a cat show at the high school.

Our houses are Victorians, protected from change not brought about by nature on this windy coast by fourteen pages of fine print in an Historical Preservation Act. It has been law since a state senator visited and went home with spats and good intentions. The Marquettes' house is Victorian, built by a robber baron to shelter a mail-order bride, or so the story goes. Miss Gilchrist might tell it to you, if you are patient. She insists that the young bride arrived by sailing ship slightly over a century ago. She was a pretty, tiny woman. She took one look at the fuchsia atrocity her fiancé had built, a gingerbread, turreted, cupolaed structure in four storeys with five widow's walks, and asked politely if it was safe for a lady to walk alone on the beach hereabouts. She took her walk and never came back.

The widowed, though not yet married, robber baron searched for days. He let all his workers off to help him, but finally gave up when no one came to work anymore or searched anymore or cared at all, not even out of politeness. The grieving bridegroom packed up, lock, stock, and shipping business and moved elsewhere. He left the house for sale and it stayed that way, held together by new paint every ten years for about a century. Then the Marquettes moved in.

The house still stands. It is empty now, but I remember the afternoon the Marquettes arrived. I remember it as more remarkable than it probably was.

Rumor that the monstrosity had been sold had hissed

through town for nearly a month. I believed it only when that dilapidated sign, pasted and painted over with the names of all the real estate companies a town suffers in a hundred years, came down. The lawn was cut and the shutters painted, white because only white can tolerate fuchsia. It was October, a Wednesday, and my three were safely off to school when a Bekins van with Michigan plates pulled in. Wilson Darling, who sells real estate, arrived with the key. The rest of the day every wife on Chester Street found work in her yard, wearing coats against cold wind, so we could watch the unloading.

"Unusual taste," Martha White said, passing my gate for the third time on her way to Forks' Market. The men were shifting an upright piano from the truck and behind it lay a brassy contraption that looked like a pole lamp crossbred with a chandelier.

"Last trip they took a huge TV," I said. "And an old oak gentleman's dressing cabinet, 1850s at least."

Martha bit her lower lip but added nothing. "I keep forgetting things for my lemon meringue pie," she said. "This time it's lemons." She walked backward up the street, watching all the way to Forks' Market.

I should have listed the crazy mix going through the wide white front door that day. Maybe you could believe me then. With no list I recall only the odd combinations of old and new—a microwave oven perched on an antique woodstove, an armful of fringed velvet dresser cloths obviously intended to cover the blond maple stereo cabinet. The men carried each into the house and, with my fingers and toes freezing, I stayed to marvel.

"I definitely do wonder what they'll look like," Miss Gilchrist whispered at my shoulder.

I had not heard her approach, leading one variegated

cat on a silk leash, and a wraith of a smile crossed her lips when I jumped.

"So do I," I managed, then fell silent. She seemed about to speak.

Emma Gilchrist looked more than ninety then, and still today she is our town's leading treasure of Victoriana. She never married, and aged to match her wardrobe of black linen and ivory lace. Her hair is white and her eyes impassive blue ice. She seldom speaks in human language, and only on matters of deep importance. She saves her spare asthmatic breath for cat conversation. What I got was a mixture of English and cat.

"One hundred years, true-oo, true-ooo," she crooned toward her variegated companion. "A century come and gone, gone on. And that day the bride arrived to her looove, loove. Wha sa say?"

I took this for an invitation to speak. "Whatever do you mean, Miss Gilchrist?"

"No-oo, no-oo." Miss Gilchrist knelt and chucked the cat under its chin. It nodded. "Sa wa go?" The cat tugged its leash, persuading her up the street without another word.

I wondered at Miss Gilchrist, but then so did everyone. With her I wondered what our new neighbors would look like. I wondered all October, in fact, and all that autumn. So did Ginny Worsted. So did my incurious husband John, and Bert who owns Forks' Market where the Marquettes never once shopped, as well as City Council President Wilbur Evans, who is rarely sober enough to wonder two thoughts in a row. Only the Jefferson children wondered about the Marquettes enough to investigate. They set us right on the situation at Halloween, but it was Christmas before we adults had the sense to believe them.

Paul and Lila Jefferson are poor, as I mentioned, but they are proud. Their eight children are renowned locally as highly acquisitive Halloween goblins. No other spooks, human or natural, would brave the blackberry tangle leading up the Marquettes' walk to ring the chimes by the pull cord beside that tall white door. I cannot say whether they were afraid. Jefferson kids must make Halloween candy last far into December, and they take risks to provide for themselves.

Maybe they had heard our mailman's account of once hearing a voice through the door telling him to leave a package. He found the slip the next day, signed in a baroque hand.

Maybe Miss Gilchrist spoke cat tongue to the children and they knew that each day, around noon, the Marquettes' draperies opened at the tug of an unseen hand. Then at four they closed, like nightfall. Emma Gilchrist stroked her cats long hours by her west window to learn these things, and she also told about lights going on and off at odd hours. She probably originated the rumors about glimpses of a tall stocky man, about the sounds of chiming female laughter late at night. Gossip embroidered this, of course, until we all believed in delighted shrieks and racing footsteps followed by pale windows falling dark.

Maybe the children knew these things, maybe not. In any event, Tommy Jefferson, or Paulie Junior if you believe the younger boy's contentious account, led the way up the front walk that last night of October.

The coach lantern by the front door cast a gold glow through the shadow of the rhododendron. Tommy, or Paulie depending, pulled the bell cord. While others on our street were watching, only the Jefferson children, John, and I were close enough to hear the chimes trill up the scale.

The door opened. I swear it, and my neighbors will back me up. A tall stout shadow fell over the sill. Eight kids crushed forward, their paper bags spread because Jefferson kids are even more practical than they are curious. Candy dropped into eight bags. I may have convinced myself I saw the shadow of a woman's hand move in a graceful gesture. The door closed. The children ran, shrieking and tripping back through the blackberry hedgesides. I nudged John, both our breaths fogged the window, and we drew back before the Marquettes might see us.

The Marquettes themselves, unfortunately, had stayed hidden. They stood out of sight by the side of the door and, as a later survey confirmed, only the kids got a glimpse of them. I am authorized to give their account because eight children, breathless and pale as ghosts themselves, arrived at my back door in less than a minute.

"He was huge," little Nanette whispered.

The others surrounded her, trembling and not yet able to talk.

"I really could see through her," Jeanie finally said. "Don't lie. You could too."

"Go on." Tommy regained his courage, smirking. "There was just a TV behind her, flickering."

"The TV wasn't on," Nanette disagreed, and because she was only four she looked honest.

"Then the lights flickered," Paulie explained solidly. "Remember that big yellowy light in the hall. Like an octopus."

I recalled the chandelier-pole lamp I had seen weeks before, but said nothing. John already held eight candy bags and he quickly emptied them on our kitchen table. Popcorn and apples and candycorn tumbled out.

Jefferson children know what candy they get and from

whom. The only unaccounted-for treasures in the pile were eight pieces of saltwater taffy. The wrappings were old, crisp silver tissue stamped with fine letters which said the candy was made in Atlantic City. The taffy itself was hard as stone. We did not have to urge the kids away from it, they gave in without complaint, and I still have seven pieces in an antique box on a shelf in the attic. Our dog ate the one piece I dropped. He died a natural death at age twelve, four years ago, long after the Marquettes moved out, and I have no reason to blame them.

As for Mr. and Mrs. Marquette, we learned little more than the kids had already told us. The boys claimed the man and the woman were perfectly solid, normal-looking adults. The girls, all younger, closed ranks on being able to see right through the lovely slender Mrs. Marquette, not just through her long billowy lavender dress, but through her hand as well, even the wrist and not just the fingers. Nanette whispered that Mrs. Marquette was young, so beautiful. For once the boys agreed. They told us, as well as everybody else they trick-or-treated that night, that she had tiny features and long silvery blonde hair. It was tied with a black velvet ribbon at the back of her neck.

And that is the sum of what we learned. Every bit of it. We learned no more because the Marquettes never did come out of their house. They never used the car, never happened to be seen picking up the evening paper because they took none, never went to the grocery. They never opened a window for air, or hung laundry in the backyard. All that year, Mr. and Mrs. Marquette never stirred, never peeked, never met us. I wonder now if they wanted to, if they cared or did not care, if those two mysterious presences even knew we were all around and watching. I think they must have, but only because of the gifts. That is my theory, understand, and only one way of looking. John will guarantee you that the gifts had nothing to do with that house, and my neighbors will probably back him. Nor do I credit some opinions about the cruel tricks that came afterward, making a minority of one again.

The Marquettes did not venture out at Thanksgiving for an evening walk. Many local families take these walks to work off the logy mood of too much turkey and pumpkin pie. Our family went extra slowly past the Marquettes' gate that evening and we saw figures moving inside, human shapes beyond the fuzzy unfocused net curtains. We supposed the Marquettes were having a party, but no one I asked saw even one guest go in or out.

They did not venture out at Christmas, though if they wanted to give gifts and make friends it would have been the natural time. They ordered a tree, by note from Bert at Forks' Market. He leaned it on their door with a thump on his way home Christmas Eve. Sometime during the night they must have taken it in because colored lights and tinsel shone through the net curtains the next morning.

New Year's Eve Ginny Worsted sent a card inviting the couple to her annual buffet. That year, since Ginny spread word of her note around town, absolutely everyone went. The buffet was a great success, highlighted by the presence on the centerpiece of Mrs. Marquette's handwritten RSVP. They had other plans that evening and could not attend. Her penmanship boiled with scrolls.

They did not come out in January, February, or March. It was only shortly after Easter, when predictably they did not appear walking to church with the rest of us in new pastel coats and white shoes; only shortly after Easter when the Jefferson children made up a story about finding a rotten black egg in the blackberry hedge, and eventually we came to believe them; only a few weeks after Easter;

by which time even our fairly accurate newspaper could have printed a story that no one lived in the Marquette house and, so completely did we all assume their spectral status among our many Victorian illusions, it would not have gotten one cynical letter to dispute it; only then did the small furtive gifts begin arriving.

I have listed those gifts, and their fates, elsewhere. Our family ate the honey and lived. We grew easy in the assumption that maybe ghosts did live down the street, but they were not hostile or mischievous. My three children grew taller and less unruly, confirmed in our childlike belief that our town shared nearly a year's history with a man and a woman who just happened not to exist. Such things grow ordinary inside a time warp. There is a great deal more, though, and none of it, for me anyway, is very comfortable. If others feel as I do, they keep silent. I never told anyone this part, not even John, and I may sound awkward telling you, but the Marquettes are gone many years now and I miss them.

There were other gifts, you see, and they came long before spring. There were long winter afternoons when, home alone and working at the sink on my prize-winning jellies, I watched out the window. Smoke curled up from both chimneys above that fuchsia atrocity. It spread gray transparence through the cold air, doubling and folding over itself like a dream before joining the cloud cover or snowfall.

Those afternoons I would wish that John were home from work. I would wish we were alone without the kids all afternoon, and the woodstove's sounds seeming to echo our murmuring. I wished for John. I wished for romance. I even once turned on a soap opera and cried with the newly married but lonely bride. I cannot remember why she was lonely, if it matters.

There were wistful evenings in the early spring when my oldest, twelve then and fairly responsible, held down the fort while John and I went for a beach walk. Coming back we had to pass the Marquettes' blackberry-entangled front gate, and our steps slowed when we saw the windows. John kissed me there once, on an impulse and deeply.

There was Ginny Worsted's confidence to me that she was having an affair. She and Bill had never been happy. There was the peculiar look in City Council President Wilbur Evans's eye, and the fact he stayed sober all summer. The affair did not last, but there were other events. There were twins born, and kittens saved from certain drowning by compassionate tourists, and the lightning storm that knocked the snag out of the eighty-foot fir behind Forks' Market without, miraculously, even scratching the roof. Even Paul Jefferson, Lila told me, won a hundred dollars in a junk mail contest.

There were lots of miracles, but none that I can explain. The PTA has twice certified me as sensible and I am. Only this. John was forty then, I was thirty-eight. We fell in love again. We grew young that spring, our whole town grew young all together, though now we are old all over again.

Miracles are not required to explain the summer growing season. The Almanac had promised it. The carrots spread fronds tall enough to wave in wind which came up evenings. Our corn went eight feet, but was nothing compared to Emma Gilchrist's. Strawberries ripened and ripened again until I ran out of room in the freezer. I called Bert only to find I could not rent space in his spare locker because others were there ahead of me. It seemed summer forever, July, August, September. October rolled around and suddenly fall came.

It arrived all one morning. I woke and frost had hit.

Night fog had crystallized on the trees and dashed every leaf to the ground. The sidewalk lay littered with shattered chestnuts like small broken glass balls. Suddenly winter had come and John nearly froze putting up storm windows the next Saturday.

Even before the winter came, the cruel tricks had started. They were clever and unpredictable, and as cold as that frost. Personally I blame the Jefferson boys, and recent history confirms my suspicions. Three years ago Tommy went to live with his grandmother after getting a high school girl pregnant. His grandmother pays off the stores that he steals from. Paulie is forbidden to ride in my two boys' cars after what he did to his parents' Buick. Then he went and rolled the principal's down the hill and wrecked that one too.

One October morning I found three dead snakes tangled in a knot around the handle of my screen door. It was early morning and John heard my scream over the roar of running shower water. Within a week, Ed Windry, then seventeen, got off work to find all four tires on his hopped-up Chevrolet slashed. He tried pressing charges against a rival at school, but the kid was playing football in front of the whole town that night. I think Tommy and Paulie Junior did it, and all those mean tricks, every one of them.

Whoever it was strangled all twelve kittens recently born to one of the variegated cats swarming in Miss Gilchrist's basement. She wrote the letter to the newspaper. Other cruelties had been noted, a razor-sharp scratch down the elementary school slide, a chunk of ripe cheese left in Wilbur Evans's mailbox, a skinned mouse neatly wrapped in cellophane on the freezer shelf at Forks' Market. The mouse was found the same day Emma Gilchrist's letter was printed in the newspaper, but she only put words to what the rest of us were feeling.

"Certain people," said the three-inch column on the *Courier*'s editorial page, "might like acting invisible and pulling mean pranks on their neighbors. They had better understand that this town knows the effect of kerosene and matches on blackberry bushes and dry old Victorian houses. Certain people should take note of that."

It had come to that. We agreed with Emma. The Marquettes appeared guilty, even if they were invisible. They were, to put it mildly, different. We knew nothing about them. They scared our children and frustrated all our attempts to gossip about them. That day even I paused at Forks' Market cash register to say it aloud. It was the Marquettes' own fault if people disliked them.

I echoed that opinion, you see, but I have changed my mind. Maybe others have too, and fear to say so. I knew differently on the frosty morning the Bekins van arrived, not a week after Miss Gilchrist's words were published in the newspaper. I knew it in my heart all along, but my heart's thoughts seemed far away by then. I had stopped listening to them. I knew with certainty, and my heart leapt to my throat instantly, an hour after the moving van drove away. My youngest son came home with a treasure he had found on the beach.

It is a small antique box, water-worn cherry wood with silver and abalone-shell roses inlaid on all four sides. We pried the lock but found nothing inside, unless you count a crust of salt stuck to the corners. It is in the attic now, dust collecting over the lovely letter *M* on the lid, and seven hard bits of candy inside. My son said he found it built into a sand castle. He was never a fanciful child.

I watched from the kitchen window all day. The uniformed men trundled everything out, the upright piano I once heard played late at night, the brass lamp contraption, the TV and velvet dresser cloths. I watched it all go, wishing that whole day for a glimpse of Mr. and Mrs. Marquette. I felt like a child, nose pressed to the glass, but I was kidding myself. They had already gone.

THE BAKU

by Lucy Taylor

Lucy Taylor is a full-time writer based in Fort Lauderdale, Florida. Prior to free-lancing, she taught English in Japan, worked as a licensed massage therapist at a Florida spa, acted as a special correspondent and book reviewer for the *Richmond Times-Dispatch* in Richmond, Virginia, and was on the staff of a sports magazine based in Tampa, Florida. She holds a B.A. in art history from the University of Richmond and has an insatiable love of travel that has taken her as far as Lhasa and Katmandu. Her fiction and nonfiction have appeared in *Thin Ice, Forum, Pencil Press Quarterly, Magna, Florida Parent, Caribbean Travel and Life, Cavalier, Not One of Us,* and over two hundred other publications. She is writing a novel.

Lucy drew upon her experience in Japan to fashion this tale of mythology.

✦ ✦ ✦

Sarah woke up trembling, not knowing where she was. She lay in a bed of sorts, but this "bed" was a fat cocoon of covers spread out on a matted floor; the divider behind her head was a sheer, rice-paper screen that rattled each time a gust of wind buffeted the house. The air felt cold enough for Oregon in January, but she knew, instinctively and with great dread, that her comfortable duplex in a Portland suburb was miles away and months in the past.

Japan. A tiny, bone-cold shard of land called Sado, east of Russia in the Sea of Japan.

It was at that moment of bleak realization, knowing that outside lay only terraced rice paddies and a narrow lane bisecting the shabby village, that Sarah realized that something else, something foul-smelling and feral, was hunkered down in the room's far corner, breathing thickly.

"Michael? Do you hear that?"

He was turned away from her, his back a passive, freckled wall, red hair jutting out at scruffy angles.

Whatever *it* was gave a hoarse, chuckling grunt as it scraped across the tatami mats.

Terror iced Sarah's spine. She grabbed Michael, yanking him toward her.

Leering up at her, her Siamese cat's face painted like a geisha's, her husband's lover spat at Sarah and laughed and laughed and laughed . . .

"Sarah! Sarah, wake up!"

She thrashed her way back to consciousness as Michael rushed in from the other bedroom, the guest bedroom that had become his several months earlier.

"What's wrong? Were you having another nightmare?"

At once she felt ashamed. Her tongue tasted as if it had been marinated in vodka. Had they argued again? Had she brought up the subject of Aoki? After the third vodka, anything was possible.

"I couldn't remember why we weren't in Portland. And there was something hiding over there in the corner and when I tried to wake you up—"

Enough. Leave Aoki out of it. What isn't talked about may cease to exist.

"You were drinking again," said Michael, sniffing her breath with distaste. "It's the drinking that gives you bad dreams."

"It's not the drinking, it's *you*!" She felt an exhilarating rush of rage. "Because I followed you here to the goddamned end of the earth, and now I'm losing you."

Michael grabbed the pillow next to Sarah. He drove his

fist into it twice. "I never asked you to come to Japan with me. I told you it was over before we ever left the States. And as far as losing me goes—you already have."

"I could change," pleaded Sarah. "I could stop." In her plaintive tone she heard—and despised—a much younger Sarah, a little girl placating angry parents.

"I've heard it all before," said Michael. "Jesus, give it up, won't you? Go on back to Portland. Start over. You *hate* it here."

"I can't give you up," said Sarah. *No more than I can give up drinking.*

Michael returned to his bedroom, sliding the shoji screen to with finality. Sarah padded down the hall to the tiny kitchen. For a moment she fancied she could smell the cloying, musty odor of the dream creature. Then a cockroach, standing ground insolently atop the coffeepot, distracted her. She bashed it to death with her slipper before starting to make coffee.

She and Michael had lived on Sado Island since July, after Michael accepted a position researching rural agriculture techniques on a U.S.-Japanese team funded by the University of Tokyo. At first, Sarah had tried halfheartedly to fit into this tiny, xenophobic farming community where even the dogs stared at Western faces as though they were creatures from Jupiter; she took language lessons and tried to learn the tea ceremony. Useless, foolish stuff! While Michael was making trips to Tokyo and falling in love with Aoki, a whore-eyed little student who, when she wasn't studying English lit and stealing husbands, waited tables at The Almond in Tokyo's fashionable Roppongi district.

The nightmares had begun soon after Michael confessed about Aoki. Sarah had tried to stay awake at first, listening to the babble of late-night Samurai dramas and dubbed *Kojak* reruns on the little Sony, wandering alone down the dirt road to the little grocery store, where a gaudy vending machine with flashing lights dispensed not only "Coca-Cora" but Asahi beer as well.

Sooner or later, she submitted to sleep and was hostage again to her visions of Aoki and of the unseen thing that breathed its rancid breath onto her face as she lay sleeping.

Shivering in the drafty kitchen, Sarah half filled her mug with coffee, then brimmed it from a bottle of Suntory whiskey. A hateful brew. She quaffed it. *Oh, God, let my hands stop shaking.*

She took the mug to the table and drank quickly, grimacing at the taste. Presently her head sank down onto her arms and . . .

. . . in her lap twitched Aoki's pale arm, laden with plastic bangles, severed below the elbow. A hideous vegetable broth of cartilage and blood and tissue sloshed out over Sarah's thighs. And slowly, like a bowl filling up with foul water, the air grew thick with a rancid smell and there came a guttural grunting.

"God, no!"

Her head snapped up. Had she cried out? There was no sound from Michael.

Vowing to stay awake until dawn, Sarah bundled into her parka and fled outside into the tiny rectangle of smoothly raked dirt and stones that passed, in this part of the world, for a yard. Above, a cold cheese of moon dappled the rice paddies and the red tile roofs of the houses.

Across the road, Sarah and Michael's nearest neighbors were an ancient old lady, an *obasan,* and her teenage grandson, a lover of hard-rock music and American comic books. His English was atrocious and Sarah avoided him, dreading their painfully halting, English-Japanese conversations. Now a light came on in an upstairs window and a tiny, monkey-ish little face squinted out. The old woman gazed longingly up at the moon, and the moon cast its sheen down on her, so for an instant Sarah could see every crease and knoll in that wizened, turnip-bulb face.

So intent was Sarah in staring that she was unprepared when the woman suddenly looked at her. Her black eyes seared, making Sarah feel like a trespasser in her own garden.

Shivering, utterly chilled, Sarah had the unpleasant sensation as she went back into the house that she was retreating from something.

✦ ✦ ✦

"Gaijin, gaijin!" shrieked the small boy, pointing at Sarah and giggling as he cried out the word for foreigner. Laden down with a mesh sack full of fish and vegetables and a four-dollar loaf of American bread, Sarah tried to ignore the child, who joined up with two more brats to hoot at her as she made her way home.

So annoyed was Sarah that, upon reaching her own corner, she almost collided with the hunched little obasan, on the arm of her Walkman-toting grandson. The little crone pointed a spidery finger and uttered one word, *"Baku."*

Sarah tried to go around her, but the woman hobbled nearer. She smelled stale, of garlic and fish and incredible age, of flesh alive but already decaying.

"Baku," she repeated and gestured to her grandson.

"My glandmother," said the boy, "my glandmother sees you walking garden at night. No sleep. Vely bad. Glandmother want give you something. Give you baku."

The obasan warbled a long, tangled skein of syllables.

From a pocket of her dark kimono, she brought forth an ivory figure about the size of an egg, which she pressed into Sarah's free hand.

"Baku," she croaked. Then she folded both hands together and tilted her head in a pantomime of sleeping.

"Baku is old Japanese animal," said the boy, whose teeth, Sarah noted, could have kept an orthodontist occupied for weeks. "Baku eats bad dreams. Then you sleep. You put baku under your pirrow."

Sarah examined the thing warily. It was a carving of a stump-legged little beast with a snout like an elephant or a tapir and tiny, piggish eyes glowering out from reptilian sockets. Beneath the snout, a tongue lolled out from a nest of snowy fangs, and what Sarah took at first to be a tail curled round between the back legs, turned out to be oversized genitals that tapered to a red and saberlike point, crimson as the stamen of a flower.

"Take," said the grandson. "Put pirrow. Bad dreams go, then you sleep."

"Arigato," said Sarah, avoiding the old woman's penetrating stare. "Thank you. *Arigato gozaimasu."*

✦ ✦ ✦

That evening, while a Japanese quiz show blared on TV, Sarah examined the lurid little monster in her hand. The baku grinned toothily, its expression somewhere between a snicker and a snarl. So engrossed was Sarah in imagining its tigerish fangs shredding the dream Aoki into bloody tatters that she failed to hear Michael's slippered feet on the tatami mats.

"What's this?"

He plucked the baku from Sarah's hand.

She felt suddenly foolish. "You know how nuts the Japanese are about gift-giving. The old lady from across the road says it'll help me sleep."

"How exactly is it supposed to do that?"

"Well, this is the crazy part. It's supposed to eat bad dreams."

Michael gave the baku back to Sarah. "I've seen pictures of baku in books on Japanese mythology. Supposedly, they were once real."

Like our feelings for each other, thought Sarah bitterly.

✦ ✦ ✦

As usual, Michael retired early. Sarah put the baku on the shelf next to the sake cups and downed half a glass of vodka, enough to get her woozy, but not too sleepy. For a moment she considered a raid on the beer-dispensing vending machine and started gathering up a handful of ten-yen coins. But when she opened the door, the light was on in the old obasan's house and that, more than the dark and cold, turned Sarah back. Wearily, she trudged to the bedroom, willing herself not to sleep.

She slept almost instantly.

And dreamed that Michael and Aoki shared her futon, writhing first in coital passion, then in agony as the baku, grown to huge size, descended on them with gobbling, clicking teeth. She wanted to rescue Michael and tried to fend the creature off with her own arms, but her husband's and Aoki's flesh had become indistinguishable.

The baku spit bits of Michael, slivers of Aoki into Sarah's face like grisly confetti. It slurped up entrails, crunched bones, and sucked out marrow.

Sarah woke to a scalding rush of adrenaline in her bloodstream. Had it really been a dream? Was it possible? Was Michael dead?

Outside, a light, cold rain hacked a wintry tattoo on the roof; the shoji screen rustled dismally as a roach skittered over the thin material.

Clutching her robe around her, Sarah crossed the dark hall to the guest bedroom.

"Michael? Michael, please, I need you."

The room was empty, but Sarah, emboldened by her fear, slid into the futon anyway. The covers were still cozily warm with her husband's body heat.

Moments later, she heard his slippers making shuffling sounds along the hallway. Evidently he was having no more success at sleep tonight than she.

He's lonely, too. He must be. He'll be happy when he finds me here. He'll want to make love.

She planned what she would say, how she would touch him. His sweet, familiar scent clung to the pillow. Seduced by that musky aroma, Sarah embraced the pillow. She felt something small and hard roll away.

Reaching under Michael's pillow, she pulled out the baku, its red eyes cooking evilly behind slitted lids.

But Michael wouldn't believe in such a silly thing. And Michael doesn't have nightmares.

The shoji screens began to rattle violently. The one farthest from Sarah was punctured and then ripped open in a jagged tear that sounded like a scream. Then *it* waddled in on its stumpy legs, shuffling its clawed feet across the tatami mats. Sarah, immobilized with terror, saw only the broad hull of its armadillolike back, the jut of its short, rooting snout.

As it neared, she could make out spidery whiskers and a marbled hide and tusks that curved up almost level with the squinty, recessed eyes. It filled the room with a sour, ancient odor—a smell not unlike that of the obasan's parchment skin.

Sarah tried to scream herself awake. It could not be done. She was as awake as this life would ever let her be.

The baku paused and snorted. Like a big, heat-seeking dog it climbed atop the futon. It sank its weight down crushingly on her chest and dug into her arms like a bird seizing branches in its talons. With rapt and avid gluttony it gazed at the inviting flesh of her face and neck.

In its eyes, Sarah saw unbearable hunger.

THE DEVIL'S ROSE

by Tanith Lee

Tanith Lee was born in 1947 in North London, England. She attended grammar school until the age of seventeen, then was a library assistant for four years. After that she worked at various jobs and spent a year at art college. In 1974–75 DAW Books bought her novel *The Birthgrave,* and she became a full-time writer. Almost forty books and some eighty short stories of hers have been published, and four radio plays and two tv programs have been broadcast in England. She has been awarded the British Fantasy Award and the World Fantasy Award. She has also written an enormous fiction-fact novel of the French Revolution, so far classified as "unpublishable." Her stories have appeared in a number of *Shadows, Night Visions* I, and other well-known anthologies. She lives in Kent, surrounded by one cat and half a hundred plants.

I always enjoy Tanith's dark fantasy, and this one, one of the few historical stories in this volume, is no exception.

✦ ✦ ✦

O Rose, thou art sick!
The invisible worm
That flies in the night,
In the howling storm

Has sought out thy bed
Of crimson joy:
And his dark secret love
Does thy life destroy.

—*William Blake*

✦ ✦

Because of a snowdrift on the line, the train pulled to an unscheduled stop at the little town of L——. Presently we passengers had debarked, and stood stamping and chafing our hands about the stove in the station house. It was nearly midnight, but the stationmaster's charitable housekeeper came almost at once with steaming coffee and a bottle of spirits. A boy was also roused and sent running, apparently to wake all the town on our behalf for lodgings. We should not be able to go on for three or four days, even that depending on whether or not fresh snow were to come down. Since we had entered the great pine forests outside Archaroy, we had been seeing wolves. They were thick on the ground that winter, and in the little villages and towns, we were to hear, not a carriage or sledge could go out but it would have wolf packs running after it for mile on mile, until the lights of human habitation came again in sight.

"What a prospect!" exclaimed the estate manager who had shared my compartment from Archaroy. "Besieged in the back of beyond by weather and wolves. Do you think, Mhikal Mhikalson, we shall ever get out?"

I said that we might, in the spring, perhaps, if not this year's, then next. But in fact, being my own creature, such unprecedented quirks of venture as this one neither dismayed nor displeased me. I had no family either behind or at journey's end to be impatient or in fear for me. My friends were used to my eccentricities and would look for me to arrive only when I did so. Additionally, in this instance, my destination was not one I hankered for. The manager, however, who had business dealings up ahead, was turning fractious. On the pretense of the errand for lodgings, I walked out of that hot room and went into the town of L——, to see what, as the isolated clocks of midnight struck, it might offer me.

It was a truly provincial backwater, such as you would expect, although the streets were mostly lit, and efforts had been made to clear the snow. There was an old marketplace with a bell tower, and close by some public gardens with tall locked gates. The houses of the prosperous ascended a hill, and those of the not so prosperous slunk down it. Some boulevards with shops all shut finished the prospect.

On a rise behind the rest was an old stuccoed house which I noticed for something Italianate in its outline, but mostly through one unprovincial lemon-yellow window burning brightly there. What poet or scholar worked late in that room when all the town slept? Something in me, which would have done the same if so placed, sent a salutation up to him.

After looking at the house, I made my way—perversely?—downhill, observing the degeneration of all the premises. The lower town fell into what might once have been the bed of some primeval river, which had carved out a bottom for itself before sinking away into the past. Over the area, the narrow streets sprawled and intertwined; it would be easy to be lost there, but for the constant marker of the hill hanging always above.

Needless to say, the snow had here been churned and frozen in mud heaps, and the going was heavy. I was growing jaded, when, between some boarded stables and a parade of the poorest houses, I discovered an ancient church. It was of the kind you sometimes see even in the cities, crammed between newer buildings that seem to want to press the life from it and close together in its default. A hooded well stood on the snow and the cobbles near the church door which, as may still happen in the provinces, was unlocked.

The church intrigued me, perhaps only as the house

had done with its window, for I sensed some life going on there. It was not an area for the wise to loiter; who knew what rough or other might not come from his hovel to demand money, or try by force to take it. Nevertheless something kept me there, and I was on the point of going nearer, when lo and behold the massive church door parted a crack. Out into the moonlight, which was now laving snow and town alike, slipped the slender, unmistakable form of a woman. It was the season when men go about garbed like bears, and she too was of course wrapped against the cold, her head mantled with a dark shawl. I recognized in her at once, even so, the thing I had sensed, the meaning of the church's "life," or at least a portion of it. I wondered what she would do, confronted by a stranger. In these small towns mostly anyone of any consequence knows all the others. If an alien, and a man, accosted her, what then? Yet had she not put herself, alone and after midnight, into the perfect position for such an overture?

"Excuse me, young woman," I said, as she came along the slope.

She started, quite violently. It was so very lustrous, the moon inflaming the snow, that to tell a shadow from shadows was not easy. Perhaps I had seemed to step from thin air itself.

She was so apparently startled I wondered if there were a chance I should now take her arm to steady her, tilting our faces to the moon as I did so, that she might see me, and I her. But she had already composed herself.

"What is it?" she said in a low and urgent voice.

"The hour is very late. I wondered if you were in some difficulty. Might I assist you?"

"No, no," she muttered. Rather than reveal herself, she snatched her shawl about her face with her gloved hands.

"I am a stranger to your town," I said. "Forgive my impetuosity in speaking to you."

"How are you here?" she said. She stood like a child who is being verbally chastised by the schoolmaster, longing to break free into the yard where the other children are.

"How else but the train? We are snowbound, it appears."

But who would be those other children, her companions, from whom I kept her?

Just then, far away over the edge of the town as if over a high cliff out at sea, I heard the howling of a wolf. The hair rose on my neck as it always does at the sound. The cry was too apt, it came too nicely on my cue.

But at that moment she turned up her face, as if straining to listen, and I saw her features, and her eyes.

Although the shawl hid everything but a trace of her hair, I judged it to be very dark. And her face was very white, and her eyes were so pale in that pale face they were like glass on the snow. Her mouth, in the shadow-shining moonlight, seemed dark also, damson-colored, but the lips beautifully shaped. It was not a beautiful face, but rather an almost classical one.

"Is it safe for you to go about like this, in such weather?" I said. "Have you never heard of starving wolves running into the streets?"

"It has been known," she said. Her eyes, now they had met mine, did not leave me.

"Let me," I said, "escort you wherever you are going."

"Up there," she said, "to the Italian House. But you are a stranger—"

"No, I have seen the very house. With a light burning."

"For me," she said, "my beacon."

"Will you take my arm?" I said. "Where the snow has been left lying the way is slippery."

She came with a swift half-furtive step, and put her black silk paw into my arm. She leaned close to me as we began to walk.

I would have liked to ask her at once what she had been doing, there in the old church, to give such an intensity to the night. Even the lamp in her room—the room of the beacon—had blazed with it. But I did not feel it was the time yet, to ask her that. In fact we said very little, but walked together familiarly up through the town. She assured me it was not a vast distance. I said I was sorry. She did not then flirt with me, or move away. She shivered, and when I drew her hand more securely into my arm, against me, she murmured obliquely, "It is so easy to misinterpret kindness."

"Mine in going with you, or your own in permitting me to do so?"

Then she did not answer, and we went on again in silence. All the way, we passed not a soul, but once heard a dog snarling behind a gate after wolves or the moon. Soon enough we came onto the part of the rise which ended in her house. The high walls along the street provided cover for our approach. The light still burned before us, now a huge tawdry topaz. It looked warm, but not inviting. A blind masked that upper room from curious eyes attracted to its glow.

At the foot of some steps she detached herself from me. Feeling the cold after the warmth of me, she put her hands up to her face again. Her pale eyes were steady with their question.

"As I told you, I am marooned here a day or so. May I call on you tomorrow?"

"My parents are dead. I live with my aunt. My father's sister, she is old . . . Do please call, if you wish. But—" She left a long pause, to see if I could read her thoughts. I could.

"You do not wish me to say I met you at midnight by the church."

"No, I do not."

She had given me by then her family name. I said, "As it happens, Miss Lindensouth, I know some distant relations of yours, some Lindensouths, in Archaroy. Or, at any rate, I believe they may be related to you and your aunt. It will give me an excuse to look her up."

This was a lie. If she guessed, she did not seem alarmed. Her face was without an expression of any sort. She lowered her eyes and left me suddenly, running up the icy stair with a carelessness that saved her rather than put her in the way of an accident.

I waited, briefly, across the street, to see what would happen with the light, or even if her silhouette might pass across it. But the lamp might have shone in another world mysteriously penetrating this one. Nothing disturbed it, and it did not go out.

When I reached the station house I found the party had gone off to the inn I had seen on my perambulations. Accordingly, I took myself there.

✦ ✦ ✦

At about six o'clock in the morning the town of L—— began to come to life. By ten o'clock, when I returned to the church, the lower streets were seething. On every corner were the expected braziers of smoking red charcoal; lamps burned now in countless windows against the leaden light of morning. Having negotiated the slop collectors, the carts of cabbage, and the carriage horses of some local charioteer, I gained the appropriate street, and found this scene was also changed. The well was a gossiping spot for women, who stood there in their scarves and fur hats arguing the price of butter. A wood seller was delivering farther down, and children played in the snow with little cold-bitten faces, grimly intent on their miserable game.

The church itself was active. The door stood open, and two women in black veils came out. It was plainly an hour also for business, here.

I went forward diffidently, prepared to depart again at once, but on entering the church, found it was after all now empty.

It was like the inside of a hollowed boulder, carved bare, with the half egg shell of the dome rising above. The shrine looked decently furnished, you could say no more for it. Everything that was anything was plate. A few icons were on the screen below. I paused to glance at them; they were Byzantine in influence, but rather crude, not a form I am much drawn to.

As I was turning away, a man approached me. I had not seen him either present or entering, but probably he had slipped out from some inner place. He was about forty and had the scholars' look, a high broad forehead gaining ground, and a ledge of brows and gold-rimmed spectacles beneath.

"You are one of our trapped travelers!" he cried.

My heart sank. "Just so."

He gave me a name and a gloved hand. I took, and relinquished, both.

"You are interested in churches?" His manner was quietly eager.

With caution I replied, "There is something I am a little curious about—"

"Ah," he broke in immediately, "that will be the famous window, I think."

What could I say?

"Indeed."

"Come, I will show you."

He took me into a side arm of the church, where it was very dark. Some candles burned, but then I saw shards of red, green, and mauve thrown on the plastered wall.

My scholar brought me to his prize, and directed me where to look, and unless I had been blind, I could not have missed it.

The window, small and round-headed, was like an afterthought, or perhaps (as he presently informed me) it might belong to an earlier chapel, being then the oldest thing there.

The glass itself was very old, and gave a rich heavy light. Its subject was the Garden of Eden, its color mostly of emerald, blue, and purple. Distantly the white figures of the sinners stood beneath their green apple tree, the fatal fruit in hand. They were about to eat, and God about to say to them, like every injured parent, I gave you everything! Why could you not remain as children forever? Why is it necessary that you grow up? His coming storm was indicated by the darkling sapphires of the shadows, the thunder wing of purple on the grass. But in the foreground was a rose tree, and among the wine-colored flowers, the serpent coiled itself, its commission seen to.

"Most unusual, such a treatment," said the scholar.

How was it that I knew so well that she, my Miss Lindensouth, had been frozen before this window, had come out from its contemplation as if her pale skin were steeped in the transparent dyes.

"Yes?"

He quoted a supposed date of the twelfth century.

"And of course it had a name, a window like this. Probably you know it? No? Well, it has been called 'Satan's Rose Bush,' in church records even, for two hundred years. Or they say simply, secretively, 'The Devil's Rose.' And there are all sorts of stories, to do with curses and wonders and the rest of it. The best known is the story of the 'Girl Who Danced.' You will know that one."

"I am afraid not."

"How splendid. Now I have all the pleasure of telling you. You see, supposedly, if you look long enough and hard enough at the glass, here, by the rose tree, you find another figure in the window. It is one of those freak things, the way in which angles and colors go together randomly forms another shape—or perhaps the maker of the window intended it to happen. The figure is of a dark man, Satan himself, naturally, who took a serpent's appearance to seduce Eve to wrongdoing. I must say I have looked diligently at the window quite often, but I have never been able to make it out. I am assured it is there, however. The last priest himself could see it, and even attempted to describe it for me on the glass—but it was no good. My eyes, perhaps . . . You try yourself. See, it is here and here, alongside the roses."

Staring where he showed me, I, like the scholar, could make out nothing. I knew of course that this had not been the case with the girl.

"And the story?"

"A hundred years ago, the tale has it, one of the great landowning families had one young fair daughter. She was noted as wonderfully vivacious, and how she loved to dance all night at all the balls in the area—for in those days, you understand, sleepy L——was quite a thriving, bustling town. Well, it would seem she visited the church and saw the window, and saw the figure of Satan. She found him handsome, and, in the way of some young girls she—I do hope you are broad-minded—she fell in love with him, with the Devil himself. And she made some vow, something adolescent and messy, with blood and such things. She invited him to come in that form and claim her for a dance. And when the next ball was held, about one in the morning, a great silence fell on the house. The orchestra musicians found their hands would not move, the dancers found their feet likewise seemed turned to stone. Then the doors blew open in a gust of wind. Every light in every chandelier went out—and yet there was plenty of light, even so, to see by: it was the light of Hell, shining into the ballroom. Then a dark figure, a tall dark man, entered the room. He had come as she requested, to claim his dance. It seems he brought his own orchestra with him. They were masked, everyone of them, but sitting down by the dance floor they struck up such a waltz that no one who heard it could resist its rhythm—and yet not one in the room could move! Then he came to the landowner's daughter and bowed and asked her for the honor of partnering her. And she alone of all the company was freed from the spell. She glided into his arms. He drew her away. They turned and whirled like a thing of fire, while all the rest of the room danced in their bones to the music, unable to dance in any other way, until all their shoes, and the white dresses of the women, and the fine evening clothes of the gentlemen, were dappled inside with their blood! How gruesome!" the scholar cried. He beamed on me. "But presently the Devil dashed his partner away through the floor. They vanished, and the demon musicians vanished, although no other there was able to regain motion until the cocks crowed. As for the girl, they found her skin—her *skin*, mark you, solely that—some days later on a hill. It had been danced right off her skeleton. But on her face, such as there was of it, was fixed a grin of agonized joy."

He paused, grasping his hands together. He said presently, "You see, in my modest way, I employ these old stories. I am something of a writer . . ." As if that excused him.

But I too was smiling. I was thinking of the girl, but not the girl in the story. Miss Lindensouth's strangeness and her youth, the way we had met, and the hold I had instantly obtained.

"It is a fact, young girls do sometimes," he said, "embrace such morbid fantasies—the love of death, or the Dark Angel, the Devil. Myself, I have penned a vampire fiction on this theme—"

I looked at the window again, along the rose tree. Nothing was there, except a slight reflection, thrown from the candles, of my own height and dark clothing and hair. These were out of scale and therefore did not fit.

The scholar offered me a glass of tea, but I explained to him I was already late for one. I told him where, to see if this might mean anything to him. But he was living in the past. He bade me a cheery regretful farewell.

✦ ✦ ✦

I rang the bell of the Italian House, and soon enough a maidservant ushered me in. The rooms inside were no longer remotely Italianate. They had been choked up with things, furniture, and tables of photographs of staring statue-people, bowls of petals, pianos with shut lids. The entire house-lid seemed shut. It smelled aromatically, in the crumbling way an old book does.

The aunt received me presently in an upper parlor.

"Madam Lindensouth. How very kind of you. I bring

you greetings from Archaroy, but the snow acted as Providence."

She was a stern, thin woman with a distinct look to her of the niece, the same long black brows, but these pale eyes were watery and shortsighted. She had frequent recourse to pince-nez. Her gown was proper, old-fashioned, and of good material. She wore lace mittens, too.

"And you are a Mr. Mhikalson. But we have not met."

"Until this moment."

I approached, raised a mitten, and bowed over it. Which made me remember the Devil in the story. I smiled, but had concealed it by the time I lifted my head. She was gratified, she made no bones about that. She offered me a chair and rang for the samovar. I told her of her invented cousins in the city, concocting anecdotes, waiting for her to say, perhaps sharply, But I have never heard of these people. To which I must reply, But how odd, for they seem to have heard of you, Madam Lindensouth, and of your niece. Thereby introducing a careful error which would then make all well, confirming we were at cross-purposes, these Lindensouths were not her Lindensouths. And getting us, besides, to the notion of a niece.

I wondered, too, how long it would be before that niece contrived to make an entrance. Had she not been listening on an upper landing for the twangle of the bell? Or had she given me up? I had not specified a time, but had come late for so eager a visitor.

Then the tea arrived, which Madam served up country fashion, very black, with a raspberry preserve. As we were drinking it, she still had not fathomed the cousins in Archaroy. She had simply accepted them, and we had begun to steer our conversation out upon the state of the weather, a proposed wolf hunt, literature, and the world in general.

Suddenly, however, the aunt lifted her head.

"Now that must be Mardya coming down. My niece, Mr. Mhikalson. You must meet her, she will want to question you about the city."

I felt a wave of relief—and of interest, having learned at last the phantom's familiar name.

I wondered how I should feel when she came in, but inevitably she had not the same personality *en famille* as she had had outside in the wolf-throated snow-night. Just then she had come from her trance before the window of the rose-snake. But now she had had all night to think of me, all morning pondering if I should come back.

She stole into the room. Nothing like her surefooted tread, both mercurial and wanton, of the night. She bore her hands folded on her waist before her, pearl drops in her nacre ears, her eyes fixed only on the aunt.

"Here is a gentleman from Archaroy," announced Madam. I did not correct her.

The girl Mardya dashed me off a glance. It hung scintilating in the overheated air after her eyes had once more fallen. It said, *You? You are here? You are real?*

"He has friends, Mardya, who claim to be related to us. It must be the fur connection, or perhaps the diamond connection." They were suspected of being in trade, that was it—but since she did not inquire it of me, I did not hazard. Traders, evidently, she did not pretend either to know or not to know. "Well, Mardya," she said.

Mardya inclined her head. Her hair was piled upon it, black and silken, not wholly tidy, and so revealing it was none of it false. Her cheeks were flushing now, paling again to a perfect paper-white. The earrings blinked. She was acting shy in the presence of her kin.

"Your aunt has kindly warned me," I said, "that you will want to know about the city. I must tell you at once, I am a frequenter of libraries. I read and do very little else." Behold, Madam, *I* am not in trade, but a beast of leisure and books.

Mardya, not speaking, stole on toward us. Taking the aunt's glass, she refilled it at the bubbling tea pitcher.

"But no doubt you ladies spend a great deal of time with books," I said. "The town is very quiet. Or is that only the disaster of winter?"

"Winter or summer. Such summers we have," said the aunt. "The heat is intolerable. My brother had a lodge up in the hills, but we have had to get rid of it. It is no use to *us,* it was a man's place. My niece, as you say, is something of a reader. And we have our sewing and our music."

"And do you, Miss Lindensouth," I said briskly, "never dance?"

She had given back the glass of tea, or I think she would have dropped it. Her whole slender shape locked rigid. Her white eyelids nailed down on her cheeks quivered and would not stop.

"I do not—I do not dance," she said—the first thing she *had* said in this presence.

"But I heard such a strange little story today," I began to the aunt amiably. "A man I met this morning, an authority on your local legends—"

"Will you not have another glass of tea?" said Mardya.

"No, thank you, Miss Lindensouth. But I was saying, the story has to do with a certain window—"

"Do have another glass," said Mardya.

Her voice was hard with wrath, and her eyes were on me, full of tears. She expected betrayal. To have wounded her so easily gave me the anticipated little thrill. She was so vulnerable, one must protect her. She must be put behind the iron shield, defended.

"No, thank you so much. In fact I must tear myself away

and leave you, Madam Lindensouth, in peace." I rose. "Except—I wonder if I might ask a great favor of you, Madam? Might I borrow your niece for half an hour?" The long brows went up, she adjusted the pince-nez. I smiled and said, "My sister has imposed the most wretched duty. I was to buy her a pair of gloves, and forgot in my haste of leaving. Now I shall arrive late besides, and probably will never be forgiven. But it occurred to me Miss Lindensouth, who has just those sort of hands, I see, that my sister has, might advise me. She might even do me the kindness of trying on the gloves, selecting a color. I find this sort of task most embarrassing. I have no idea of what to look for. Which, if I am honest, is why I forgot the transaction in the first place."

The aunt laughed, superior upon the failings of the fumbling male.

"Yes, go along with Mr. Mhikalson, Mardya, and assist him with these troublesome gloves. You may place my own order while you are doing so."

I bowed to her mitten once more. She sighed, and I caught the faint acidity of medicine on her breath.

"Perhaps, since you must remain here, you will dine with us tonight?" she said, with the grudging air that did not mask a lively curiosity she had begun to have about me.

"Why, Madam Lindensouth—to be sure of that I will go personally to shovel more snow onto the line."

She laughed heartily, and bade me get along. Her eyes of watery steel said, If I had been younger. And mine: Indeed, Madam, there can be no doubt. But I am too respectful now, and besides maybe I am in search of a wife, and you see what a fine coat this is, do you? But nevertheless, I know where the fount is, the sybil. We understand one another in the way no man finds it possible to understand or to be understood by any woman under forty, and surely you are not much more?

Down in the street, Mardya Lindensouth spoke to me in a strange cold hot voice.

"I trust you rested well."

"No. I could only lie there and think of seeing you again. I have thought of nothing else since our meeting."

"But something delayed you."

"Strategy. You saw how I have managed it. I am to dine."

She would not take my arm.

"There are no gloves," I said, "I have no sisters." I said, "Run her errand later. Where can we go?"

And all at once, in an arch in one of the old walls of the street, she was leaning her spine to a door, her hands on my breast. It was a daring situation, hidden, unfrequented, yet anyone might look from an upper floor, or come by and see.

I leaned against her until her back pressed the backs of my hands into the damp wood. She was, though I could only speculate how, no stranger to kisses. Presently, engorged and breathless, we pulled apart, and went on down the street. This time she took my arm.

We went to a patisserie along one of the boulevards. To my dismay, at one point, I saw three of my fellow travelers from the train, the estate manager among them, going by the window, hesitating at the door—and thank heaven passing on.

She did not eat anything, only sipped the scalding beverage, which was not so flavorsome as the samovar of Madam.

"I dreamed of you," she said, "all night. I was burning. I thought I should run out into the snow to get cool. But

I should freeze there. You would come and find me and warm me in your arms. But you would never come back. I knew you at once."

"Who am I?"

"Hush. I do not want to say your name."

"Mardya, tell me about the church."

"You know everything about me."

"The window, Mardya."

"Not here . . ."

"No one can hear, you whisper so softly, and your warm breath brushes my cheek. Tell me about the window."

"It was quite sudden," she said. Artless, she added, "Two years ago, when I was fourteen."

"Well?"

"I saw it. The same way the girl does in the story. At first, I tried not to think of it. But I began to dream—how can I tell you those dreams?—they were so terrible. I thought my heart must stop, I should die—I longed for them and I feared them."

"Pleasure."

"Such—such pleasure. I tried not to know. But it has been all I could think of. There is nothing here—in the town. I see no one. No one comes to her house but her friends, the Inspector of Works, the banker—everyone is old, and I am old too when I sit with them. I become like them. My hands get so stiff and my neck and my eyes ache and ache. I have nothing to live for. But now, you are here."

"Yes, I am here." I put my foot gently against hers under the tasseled tablecloth. Our knees almost touched, the fabric of her dress stirred against me. Her cheeks were inflamed now. All about us, human things went on with their chocolate, their tea and cake and sugar.

"Tonight she will have those two or three friends to dine with you. We will dine on chicken bones and aspic tarts. We have no money."

"Mardya, be quiet."

"I must tell you—"

"What? How to remain behind in the house after the others have left?"

She caught her breath.

I said, "I remember the lamp burning and how you go about improperly at night, and I would imagine you have fooled her, she never knows. So you are clever in such matters. Shall I hide in some cupboard?"

"Not now. How can I speak of it? I shall faint."

"If you do that, we shall attract attention."

"Secretly then. When the darkness comes. In darkness."

"One candle, perhaps. You must let me look at you. I want to see all your whiteness."

"Hush," she said again. Her eyes swam, her hands pressed on the glass of tea as if to splinter it. "I have never—" she said.

"I know."

"You will—care for me?"

"You will see how I will care for you."

Neither of us could breathe particularly well. We burned with fever, our feet pressing and our hands grasping utensils of the tea table as if to save them in a storm. But she shook so that her earrings flashed, and she could hardly hold the tea glass anymore. I took it from her, and found it difficult in turn to let go of.

Presently, I settled our account, and we left the shop and went to another, where she ordered needles for her aunt.

I escorted her up through the town, the second time, past the smoking braziers and the lamplit nothingness of other people and other things. On the rise, in the same snow-bounded stone archway, I thrust her back and crushed her to me. Her hands clutched my coat, she struggled to hold me as if drowning. We parted, and went separate ways, to scheme and wait like wolves for the night.

✦ ✦ ✦

The dinner party—for such it was to be—was to be also all I had predicted from the picture Mardya had painted.

The Inspector of Works was there, a blown man with an overblown face, and his wife, a stubborn mouse of a woman much given to a sniff, an old maid in wife's clothing. The elderly unmarried banker had also come, perhaps an ancient flame of Madam's. But we animals were of a proper number and gender, and progressed two by two.

Madam Lindensouth came to dinner in a worn black velvet gown and carbuncle locket. When Mardya entered there was some life stirred up, even in the banker. She had on a dress the color of pale fire, between soft red and softer gold, with her white throat and arms exposed. Madam did not bat an eyelash, so clearly she had not been above suggesting a choice of finery. Mardya was self-conscious, radiant. She flirted with the banker and the Inspector in a way, patently, they had never before experienced, the delicious clumsy coquetishness of an innocent and charming young girl. Only with me was she very cool and restrained. Yet as we came to the table, she did remark, "Oh, Mr. Mhikalson, I have been worrying about it. Those gloves in that particular shade of fawn. Are you quite sure that your sister will be content?"

Her daring pleased me. I said, unruffled, "I thought they were more of a yellow tone. The very thing. But then, I told you, I have no judgment in such matters."

All this required an explanation, that Miss Lindensouth had been in the town with me buying handwear for my relative. A knowing look passed between the banker and the Inspector's mouse.

Presumably not one of them had heard the latest news of my train. There had been a message at the inn on my return there. The line was expected after all to be clear by four the next morning. The train would depart one hour after, at five o'clock. Of course, I might be prepared to miss it. They might assume I would have no more pressing engagement than a wooing, now I was so evidently embarked.

All through the dessicated dinner, my fellow guests tried to wring from me, on Madam's behalf, the story of my life, my connections, my prospects. I remained cordially reticent, but here and there let fall a word for myself. I am a good liar, inventive and consistent, and quite enjoyed this part of the proceedings. As for the meal, it was a terrible event. There was not a drop of moisture in any of it, and the wine, though wet, was fit only for just such a table, and in short supply besides.

After we had dined, the ladies permitted the men to smoke, by withdrawing.

The banker lit up and coughed prodigiously.

"These winters," said he, "will be my death."

To me he added, "How I yearn for the city. I have not been in Archaroy, let alone anywhere else, since my thirty-fifth year. Is that not a fearsome admission? Finance has been my life. I still dabble. If you were to be seeking any advice, Mr. Mhikalson—"

The Inspector broke in with a merry, "Never trust this rogue. He is still in half the deals and plots of the town. But I must say, if you were thinking of remaining a week or so, there are some horses I think you should look at, with an eye to the summer. My cousin Osseb is quite an authority. Did you know it is possible to hunt wolf here all the year round? Well, there you are. Of course, Madam Lindensouth's brother, the father of Miss, had a lodge in the forest. But that was sold."

"But you are not to think," put in the banker, giving him an admonishing glance, "that the family fortune here is on the decline. Not a bit of it. I will say, my dear friend Madam is something on the careful side, but there is quite an amount stashed away . . ."

"Tut tut," said the Inspector. "Can the ladies have no secrets?"

Finally we had smoked sufficiently, and went into the next room, where Madam regaled us all with some music from the piano, which, startled to find its lid had been raised, uttered a great many wrong notes.

Mardya would not play. She said that she had a chilblain on her finger. This evoked three remedies given at once by the mouse, the banker, and the Inspector. In each case, suffering the chilblain would have been preferable.

A card game then ensued, out of which Mardya pardoned herself, and I was left also to my own devices, being besides pushed to them by smiles and nods. I joined the girl by the piano, where she was searching among the sheet music for an old tune her father had been used to play.

"Come now," I said, speaking low, "how is it to be managed?"

"Impossible," she said.

"Think of our stop on the hill."

She blushed deeply, but continued to leaf through the music.

"I am afraid."

"No. You are not afraid."

"The ace!" cried the banker. He added to us, over his shoulder, not having heard a word, "Now, now."

"Think of the apple tree," I said to her, "think of the rose."

Her hands fluttered, some of the music spilled. Her pulse raced in her throat so swiftly it looked dangerous. We bent to retrieve the music.

"Leave before the others." She spoke crisply now though scarcely above a whisper. "I will go down and open the door. Return almost at once and go into the side parlor below. The blinds are down, there is a large table with a lamp on it that is never lit. You must be patient then. Wait until the house is quiet. Wait until the clock in the hallway strikes eleven."

"Where is your room?"

She told me. She was shivering, from desire or fear, or both.

We had regained the music and arranged it together by the piano.

"There is the song my father used to play," she said. But she did not play it.

It was almost thirty minutes past nine, and I suspected the festivity would be curtailed sharp at ten o'clock. After the banker had told us again to "Now, now," and the maidservant had brought in the trusty samovar and some opaque sherry, the card game lapsed. It was a quarter to ten.

"Madam Lindensouth," I said, "I must return at once to the inn. I had not realized how late it has grown. There are some arrangements I shall need to make." I left a studied pause. She would deduce I meant to give up my seat on the train. "Thank you for your kindness and hospitality."

"If it chances you are still here tomorrow," she said. (The banker and the Inspector laughed, and the mouse primly sniffled.) "We take luncheon at three o'clock. I hope you will feel able to join us."

At the concept of another meal of sawdust and pasted aspics I almost laughed myself. Something in her eyes checked me. In holding out to me the branch of unity with her niece, a girl therefore about to taste the chance Madam had missed, there was a sudden ragged edge to her, a malevolence, which showed in a darkening of her pallid eyes, the iron smile with which she strove to underpin propriety. It was clear from this that a callous and unkind method would have sustained her treatment of Mardya from the beginning. She had never been a friend to her and never would be. Small wonder the savage innocent turned to shadows for her fata morgana of release and love. It even seemed probable in those moments that the aunt had known all along of midnight excursions to a church on the lower streets, of a flirtation with grisly legends and unsafety. Did the woman know even that this was where Mardya had met me? Did she know what plan we had ("Now, now") to meet in the night on the shores of lust, under her very roof? Yes, for a moment I beheld before me a coconspirator.

When I took her hand, she said, "Why, your hands are cold tonight, Mr. Mhikalson. You must have a care of yourself."

I uttered my farewells, got down through the house, and was shown out into the darkness and the snow.

I went down the steps, and waited where I had done so the first night, across the way, taking no particular pains over concealment.

That light was not burning in the upper—her—room.

The window was sightless, eyeless, and waiting, too. Before midnight, I should have seen the inside of that room, should have touched its objects and ornaments, invaded the air with my breath and will, my personality, perhaps a stifled cry, the heat of my sweat. I should have possessed that room, before the morning came. I did not need to see its light, now.

After about six or seven minutes, I went back. If I met anyone on the steps or in the doorway, I should say I had lost something and returned hoping it was in the house. But I met no one.

The front door was ajar, and I passed through silently, shutting it again. A muffled bickering came from above, from the dinner party.

The side parlor was as she had described, to the right of the hall, remote from the stair. It was in blackness, the table dimly shining like a pool of black water, and the unlit lamp upon it reflected vaguely, and here and there some glistening surface. I went through and seated myself on an upright chair against the wall, facing the doorway. Naturally I was quite concealed, by night, by the shapes of the furniture, best of all by being where of course I could not reasonably be.

Like the audience in the darkened theater, then, I stayed. And down the dully lighted stair they passed in due course to the hall, the banker, and the Inspector and his mouse-wife. The maid arrived with hats and sticks, and Madam waved them off from the vantage of the staircase, not descending.

All sound died away then, gradually, above. And lastly the maid came drifting along across the open door, like a ghost, to take away the final guttering lamp. Partly I was amazed she did not catch the flash of my eyes from the black interior, the eyes of the wolf in the thicket. But she did not. No one came to bother me, to make me say how I had left behind a glove, or a cigarette case, or had felt faint suddenly in the cold, and come back to find the door was open—and sat here to wait for the maid and fallen asleep. No, none of that was necessary.

At last, the clock chimed in the hall, eleven times.

Rising from my seat, I stretched myself. I walked softly from concealment to the foot of the staircase. Hardly a noise anywhere. Only the ticking of the clock, the sighing of the house itself. Beyond its carapace, snow-silence on the town of L——, and far away, so quiet were all things now, the tinny *tink-tink* of another clock finding the hour of eleven on a slightly different plane of time than that of the Italian House.

I started to go up the stairs. The treads were dumb. I climbed them all, passing the avenues of passages, and came to a landing and a heavy curtain with a mothball fringe. And then, in an utter darkness, without even the starlit snow-light of the windows, her door, also standing ready for me, ajar.

I closed it with care behind me. The room was illumined only by the aqueous snow sheen on the blind. This made a translucent mark, like ice, in turn upon the opposite wall, and between was a floating unreality, with a core of paleness.

"Ssh," she whispered, though I had not made a sound.

I went toward her and found her by the whiteness of her nightgown on the bed. The room was all bed. It could have no other objects or adornment.

Her hands were on my face, her arms were about my neck.

"Where is the candle?" I said. "Let me see you, Mardya."

"No," she pleaded. "Not yet . . ."

My vision was, anyway, full-fed on the dark. I was beginning to see her very well.

The little buttons of her nightgown irritated my fingers, to fiddle with them almost made me sick. I lifted my face from her burning face, kissing her eyes, her lips. I pulled the nightgown up in a single movement and laid her bare in the winter water of the light, the slender girlish legs folded to a shadow at the groin, the pearl of the belly, the small waist with its trinket of starlight, and the rib cage with the two cupped breasts above it, and the nipples just hiding still in the frills of the nightgown—she was laughing noiselessly and half afraid, shuddering, pushing the heavy folds from her chin, letting them lie across her shoulders and throat as I bent to her. My hands were full of her body and my mouth full of her taste. The mass of black hair stained across the pillows, shawled over her face, got into my mouth.

I threw off my coat, what I could be rid of quickly. Her skin, where it came against my skin, was cool, though her lips, ears, and forehead blazed, and the pits of her arms were also full of heat, and her hands, their hotness stopping mysteriously at the wrists. She was already dewy when my fingers sought between the fleshy folds of the rose. "No," she said. She rubbed herself against me, arching her back, shaken through every inch of her. "No—no—"

"This will hurt you."

"Hurt me," she said, "I am yours. I belong to you."

So I broke into her, and she whined and lay for a moment like a rabbit wounded in a trap under my convulsive thrusts no longer to be considered, but at the last moment, she too thrust herself up against me, crucified, with a long silent scream, a whistling of outdrawn breath, and I felt the cataclysm shake her to pieces as I was dying on her breast.

"I knew you would come to me," she murmured. "I knew it must happen. I called out to you and you heard me. Across miles of night and snow and stone.

"Sometimes," she said, "I have seen you in a dream. Never clearly. But your eyes and your hair.

"Are you the one?" she said. "Are you my love? For always?"

"Always," I said, "how else?"

"And my death," she said. "Love is death. Kill me again," she said, but not in any mannered way, though it might have been some line from some modern stage drama.

So presently, leaning over her, I "killed" her again. This time I even pinned her arms to the bed in an enactment of violence and force. Her face in ecstasy was a mask of fire, a rose mask.

Afterward her eyes were hollow, like those of a street whore starving in the cold.

When I began to put on my clothes, she said, "Where are you going?"

"It will be best, I think. We might fall asleep. How would it look if the girl came in and found me here, in the frank morning light?"

"But you will come back tomorrow?"

"Your aunt has invited me to luncheon."

"You will be here? Will you be late?"

"Of course I shall be here, of course not late."

I kissed her, for the last time, with tenderness, seemliness. It was all spent now. I could afford to be respectful.

As I reached to open the door, she was lying like a creature of the sea stranded upon a beach. Her delicate legs might have been the slim bipart tail of a mergirl, and the tangle of nightgown and hair only the seaweed she had brought with her to remind her of the deep.

I went down again through the house with the same lack of difficulty, and as well, for I could have no decent story to explain my presence now.

As I let myself out of the front door, and descended the steps, the air cut coldly in the icy deserts before dawn. It was almost four o'clock, but I had seen to my luggage beforehand. I need only go along to the station and there wait for the train which, because the allotted hour was now both extempore and ungodly, would doubtless leave on time.

✦ ✦ ✦

Two doctors attended me at the point of my destination, one the man I had arranged, a month previously, to see, the other a colleague of his, a specialist in the field. Both frowned upon me, the nonspecialist with the more compassion.

"From what you have said, I think you are not unaware of your condition."

"I had hoped to be proved wrong."

"I am afraid you are not wrong. The disease is in its primary phase. We will begin treatment at once. It is not very pleasant, as you understand, but the alternative less so. It will also take some time."

"And I believe," said the less sympathetic frowner, "you comprehend you can never be perfectly sanguine. There is, as such, no cure. I can promise to save your life, you have come to us in time. But marriage will be out of the question."

"Did I give you to suppose I intended marriage?"

"All relations," said this man, "are out of the question. This is what I am saying to you. The organisms of syphilis are readily transferable. You must abstain. Entirely. This is not what you, a young man, would wish to hear. But neither, I am sure, would you wish to inflict a terrible disease of this nature, involving deformity, insanity, and certain death where undiagnosed, on any woman for whom you cared. Indeed, I trust, upon any woman." He glared on me so long I felt obliged to congratulate his judgment.

The treatment began soon after in a narrow white room. It was, as they advised, unpleasant. The mercury, pumped through me like vitriol, induced me to scream, and after several repetitions I raved. One does not dwell on such matters. I bore it, and waited to escape the cage.

The ulcerous chancre, the nodulous sore, long-healed, which had first alerted me in Archaroy, has a name in the parlance of the streets. They call it there the Devil's Rose.

And in that way, Satan comes out of his window, unseen, and passes through the streets. All the lights go out as he dances with the girl who vowed herself to him. And in the morning they find her skin upon the hillside.

She died insane, I heard as much some years later in another city, from the lips of those who did not know I might have an interest.

The condition was never diagnosed. Probably she had never even been told of such things. They thought she had pined and grown sick and gone mad through a failed love affair, some stranger who entered her life, and also left it, by train.

She had always been of a morbid turn, Mardya Lindensouth, obsessed by dark fancies, bad things. Unrequited love had sent her to perdition. She was unrecognizable by the hour of her death. She died howling, her limbs twisted out of shape, her features decayed, a wretched travesty of human life.

Yes, that was what dreams of love had done for her, my little Mardya. Though in the streets they call it the Devil's Rose.

MIDNIGHT MADNESS

by Wendy Webb

Wendy Webb, a registered nurse, is employed at a large medical center in Atlanta, where she coordinates anything from literacy programs to professional medical education conferences. She says her first professional sale was at age five with a drawing entitled "Giraffe and Children," for which she was paid the lofty sum of two dollars. Many years later she made her first sale as a writer to *Shadows 10*, and her second story sale was to *WOD*. She has also sold to the *Greystone Bay* anthology series. She is working on a horror novel entitled *Widow's Walk*. She lives in Stone Mountain, Georgia, and collects bears of the stuffed variety.

Wendy is a fairly new writer, and one whose stories I look forward to seeing. Her mother is a well-known writer of dark fantasy, too, and it's obvious that the talent runs deep in the family.

✦ ✦ ✦

The Volkswagen Beetle coughed and sputtered as it tried to navigate the steep drive to the shopping center. Mickey Gault shifted into first and heard the transmission groan, then shriek into the low gear. She wondered how much longer the engine would hold out. Two hundred thousand miles and counting. Just a little longer, she coaxed. Then maybe she would have saved enough for the little red sedan sitting in Al's Nearly New Car Emporium. The car was a real bargain. But then everyone said that she had an uncanny knack when it came to bargains.

She reached the plateau of the parking lot and threw

the Bug into neutral. It coasted into an empty space just as the engine quit. Overheated again. But she knew that the cool night air would revive the old engine sooner or later.

Mickey wiped the window with her coat sleeve and saw that the parking lot was nearly deserted. Tonight was the annual Midnight Madness Sale, wasn't it? She reached for the dog-eared newspaper in the passenger seat and peered at the ad. Discount City, it said in big letters. Midnight to Two A.M., Tuesday the Eight, Highway 78 and Montreal Road. This was the place.

She looked at her watch, 12:15, then out at the lonely parking lot. A handful of cars, drab gray from the dimly lit parking lights, were scattered throughout the lot. It really was out of the way, she told herself. Only the most shrewd of bargain hunters would drive this far for a sale. So where were the others? A movement within the store caught her eye.

Lights flickered in the storefront, went out. On again. Dim at first, until with increasing intensity the interior glowed with light that spilled out onto the sidewalk. Light met dark, meshed, formed a haze that tumbled with the air currents like ripples on a lake. Light met dark—they were dancers moving to a rhythm known only to them. They stopped suddenly, turned to her and smiled. Their hands moved in mirror images and beckoned.

Mickey blinked against a sudden, overwhelming fatigue that covered her body like a shroud. She shook her head, squinted, and tried to focus on the light-dark cloud that surrounded the store.

The movement had stopped. It was resting now. A cat-nap sleep with retractable claws.

Condensation from the cold air, she reasoned, it had to

be. Of course. It was an illusion brought on by the weather and insomnia. Missing sleep always affected her this way. She yawned and glanced once more over the parking lot. Maybe others would be along soon. In the meantime, there would be a bigger selection for herself. Then it was home to bed. She would sleep well tonight.

She climbed out of the car and slammed the door. Then out of habit, she bumped it with her hip to insure the catch engaging. She waited for the click, heard it, and knew that she wouldn't come back to a car with the door swinging open. No one would have to know that the lock had long since been broken.

She pulled the belt to her coat tight around her waist against the piercing cold. It found the holes where buttons would have been, and oozed through past the summer cotton shirt underneath to her skin. She shivered and pulled the belt another notch. Maybe she could find some new buttons while she was here, and some thread. She trotted across the parking lot and through the heavy doors of Discount City.

The quiet roared in her ears.

She saw row after row of checkout counters. Each bore an illuminated lamp indicating that a cashier was ready to total the purchases of a shopper.

But there were no shoppers.

A phone rang. She jumped at the sound.

There were no cashiers.

Another ring.

A sudden jovial rendition of a piped Top Ten tune shattered the silence. The sound jarred. Her muscles tightened like harp strings. She shuddered at the incongruity of loud music set against an empty warehouse of a store. Cold, skeletal fingers tickled the hair on her neck, then sent an icy chill down her spine. Her eyes narrowed to tight slits against the barrage of glassy sound. She wrapped her arms across her chest as if to block the noise.

Ring.

Answer it.

Ring.

The muffled sound of an answering device caught. "... an operator will be with you momentarily. ..."

But there was no one there.

On leaden legs, she turned to the phone. It was planted firmly on a service counter. If she could just reach it before the caller hung up . . . could hear a human voice. She punched the flashing button and grabbed for the receiver. The light sparkled once, then was gone.

She was alone. Her breath escaped in a panicked whimper. But the doors to the store had been unlocked, she told herself. Every light in the place was on. And the music—that horrible jangling sound—had been turned on by someone. And yet she was alone.

Or was she?

A sickness crept into the pit of her stomach. Who would be so cruel as to play such a hoax? To scare someone all alone? Alone. Suddenly the thought of someone else wasn't reassuring anymore.

"Can I help you?"

She felt her back stiffen at the squeaky voice. It was if his vocal cords needed oiling. She toyed with the idea of bolting for the door, it was the rational thing to do, but the sound of a human voice asking if she needed help incited something else. She felt rage rumble from her chest, then lodge in her throat. Angry words stuck in her dry mouth and she could only rasp, "What the hell kind of place is this?"

"I'm sorry if I startled you," the little man said. He

tugged at the open green vest that revealed an obese abdomen. The word "Manager" was inscribed over the pocket. "We're running a bit late tonight."

"A bit late?"

"It's a skeleton crew tonight," he said. "What with the flu and all. Besides, we're so far off the beaten path even a Midnight Madness Sale doesn't attract many."

"Is there anyone else here besides us?"

"A handful or so. But you wouldn't know it by the size of this place." A look of concern crossed his pudgy baby face. "Listen, I'm really sorry about the scare."

"No, it's okay," she said. "I'll be all right."

"You're sure?"

Mickey nodded at the little man. She hoped that the scant movement on her lips looked like a smile.

"Just pick up one of the Hotlines scattered around the store if you need any assistance." The manager disappeared into the candy aisle and was gone.

It's okay, she repeated to herself, okay. The man seemed harmless enough. All five feet of him. Even if his vest was a good four sizes too small for him, he seemed nice enough. And God knew his job couldn't be a fun one. Being a manager of a store during brilliant daylight would be tough enough. Running a place in the dark, damp after hours was, well . . . spooky.

She ran a finger back and forth through the growing hole in her pocket and reprimanded herself. Get a hold of yourself, girl. You're here for the bargains. And with family birthdays coming up, you'd better get busy. She pulled her hand out of the pocket and heard the material tear. She wondered if the coat would last as long as the Bug had.

Her eyes traversed the overhead signs that hung at intervals throughout the building. Books, Toys, Men's

Clothing, Notions—Notions, now that would be the place to start. She wandered past the magazines and books. She glanced over the blue covers of the romances, the yellow of the westerns, and stopped at the lone shiny black cover.

A horror novel. It had to be. Nothing else could grab her attention like that.

She toyed with the idea of picking it up for a closer look. Changed her mind, looked again. The face on the cover was a silhouette, vague, intriguing. Why not? she thought. A light breeze brushed her hair across her cheek in a tickling motion, then passed. A shiver started deep in her muscles. She tightened, forced the feeling away. She looked for an air-conditioning vent as the culprit. Saw none. She looked back at the book.

The face had moved.

She blinked and looked again.

Another move. Small. Oscillating.

A trick of the light . . . it had to be. She swayed forward, backward, sideways, and caught a tiny change in the blurred, nondescript face on the cover. So it was the light. She reached for the book. A pang of guilt at her selfishness stopped her. She was here to buy gifts for her family, not something for herself. Her tight budget had no room for self-indulgence. The book wasn't important anyway. After all, she was halfway through one horror, and two others were waiting for a read. Still . . . there was something different about that book. Familiar in a way. Maybe on the way out she'd stop by again, just to look.

She continued through Costume Jewelry, Belts, and Hats. Her eyes checked off the items available on a mental inventory list, when she saw a shadow flicker across a counter mirror. She turned in time to see the hanging belts swaying in a tiny arc. It was as if a hand had fondled them and then moved on.

One aisle over, an atomizer was being depressed and released. Another shopper trying out the perfumes no doubt. She rounded the corner at a half run to confirm what she already knew, had to know, that someone else was here and she wasn't alone.

A cloud billowed at her feet. She blinked in confusion as the vapor traveled the length of her body and surrounded her in a shroud of sweet perfume.

No one was there.

She tried to step away but the vapor tightened itself around her. Its currents circled her. Confined her. Bound her within. She tried to breathe but felt the air sucked from her lungs as if she were in a vacuum. The fragrance became wildflowers that she had picked as a child. Soft, sweet, safe.

Then it was decay. Death dying again.

Nausea erupted in her. Acid burned her throat. She began to run. Stopped short.

The voice from just behind her was loud, resonant, male. *Take me home.*

She whirled on her heel, faced the sound. No one was there.

Something cold stroked her neck.

She turned again. Saw nothing. Who was it? Where was he?

The scent of wildflowers filled the air. She waved her hands to clear the smell and spotted a lone bottle on the countertop. *Sudden Madness,* it said on the label. She would have laughed out loud if she hadn't felt the lone thread to her own sanity loosen a notch.

A frail metallic ting punctuated by groans drifted to her

ears. She spun around and saw a peeling spindle laden with heavy costume necklaces rotate on an aluminum base. The other jewelry holders remained motionless. The hand that touched the belts moved these as well, she knew. But why? Who was doing this to her?

The music stopped. The intercom crackled, paused. A voice, his voice, was clear, crisp, and calm: "Take me home with you."

She could feel her mouth drop open, her face turn bland and colorless. Her arms hung uselessly at her sides. Her body swayed and drooped, but remained standing due to the core of terror that gripped her spine. Where was he? Who was he? The voice didn't belong to the manager, but who else would have access to the intercom?

"Pretty lady. Take me home." His message over, the music resumed in mid-chorus. The volume was up. The staccato beat of the tune marched with the rhythm of the blood rushing in her ears.

Then she saw the eyes.

They peered at her through a slit in the handbag shelf. Was that mockery she saw in the dark eyes, or curiosity? As quickly as they appeared, they were gone. Her gaze shifted intuitively to the adjoining row. The dark eyes stared at her from a new vantage point. This time they were empty of emotion, bored.

She backed away from the intruder on legs void of sensation. Her gaze was fixed on the dark eyes to detect any movement. They stared back, motionless.

A plan formed in her mind. She would run. She would run with everything that she had in her and never look back. Then the nightmare would be over. She'd just climb back into the little Bug, head home, and forget this whole thing. Home. The cramped, dark apartment didn't seem quite so bad all of a sudden.

She walked backward, slowly at first then with a quickening pace. A cold cement ceiling support housing a red Hotline jarred her stride and forced her to stop. She turned in time to see the front doors of Discount City swing with the back-and-forth motion of someone who had just left.

He had gone outside.

He was waiting for her.

Outside.

She groped for the receiver, cradled it in shaking hands, and held it to her face. The automatic ring had already started. Was he still watching her? Her eyes shifted to the front doors. There was nothing but darkness.

"Yes, ma'am." The squeaky voice of the manager sounded tinny through the receiver. "Can I help you?"

"That man," she said. "The one with the message. He's here—out there. Waiting for me."

"What man?"

"The man that talked over the intercom."

"I'm sorry, ma'am. But no one has access to the intercom except me."

She heard her voice raise an octave. "I heard him."

"There have been no announcements tonight."

"I saw him looking at me. I saw his eyes."

"Maybe you just thought you heard him. I can't stop my customers from talking to each other." She heard exasperation in his voice. "I'll look into it, okay?"

She heard the phone go dead. So that's it, she thought. One quick phone call and it was all taken care of. Suppose the man with the eyes decided not to hang around? Or worse, suppose he decided to . . . do something, before someone could get there?

The music clicked off with the announcement, "Security to aisle ten," then resumed its cheery beat.

It was the voice.

Clear, crisp, and calm.

His voice.

"My God." The words whispered through clenched teeth. She turned and ran. The coat flapped wildly around her knees and calves; pulling; slowing. She clawed at it, tried to free her legs. The heel of her shoe made contact with linoleum and slid. She thrust her arms forward to break the fall. Her purse flew away from her, spilling its contents. She saw her car keys slide out of reach.

"No." The word was uttered as a terrified command. She pulled herself across the floor, reaching for the keys. Home. Please. Just let me go home.

Yes. Home.

It was a whisper spoken softly in her ear.

She groped, strained, to reach the keys, and saw them slide away, inches from her grasp.

I'll be with you.

The words were quiet, menacing. Spoken from within her.

The keys. Her muscles cramped then trembled with the effort. She saw them move again.

A leather-clad foot, shoe missing laces, stepped on the keys. "These yours?" the squeaky voice asked.

She looked up to see the fat manager staring at her. His eyes were blank, expressionless. He stood quietly with no offer of help.

She pulled herself up on shaking legs and pointed to the keys still planted under his foot. With a wheeze, and strain on his too-small vest, he leaned over to pick up the keys then handed them to her. She tried to form the word "thanks," but knew it wouldn't get past the dry knot in her throat. She turned to leave.

"You forgot something."

She saw the shiny, black-cover book in his hand.

"It fell out of your purse."

Her purse? But how? She grabbed the book and stopped when she saw the face on the cover.

It was moving. A metamorphosis started from her touch.

She smelled wildflowers, death, wildflowers again. She knew he was there, dark eyes, watching.

The portrait oscillated from vague to clear. Clearer. The face was recognizable now.

Her face.

The touch of her hand had made it happen. The rest of the picture shimmered, came into focus.

She heard the scream and knew that it had come from herself. Yet it seemed so far away. As if it were someone else. She knew she was running. Why couldn't she feel the floor, her feet?

Through the front doors of Discount City. Across the parking lot. Whose breath was that, so even, so deep?

To the lonely little Bug, with its door swinging open. To its inside sanctity where it was safe. Familiar.

But he was here with her.

She looked toward the store and saw the manager wave, then beckon. The lights inside flickered off, on. Then finally, permanently off. Light turned to dark.

She was tired. Tired to the bone, as her grandfather would say. There would be no more running tonight. She cocked her head for a look at the rearview mirror and saw him.

The eyes. Dark. Smiling. The eyes on the black shiny cover.

She knew about his hands too. The ones that brushed against her face, turned spindles, depressed atomizers. The ones in the cover picture. It was more than she had ever bargained for.

A sad smile crossed her lips as the cold, skeletal fingers caressed her neck, then ever so slowly tightened their grip.

MONSTER McGILL

by Cary G. Osborne

Cary G. Osborne is a native of Tennessee who moved to Virginia after graduating from high school in Texas. With her father in the army, she moved a lot, living in seven states and one foreign country. At various times she's been a carhop in a drive-in restaurant, sales clerk, waitress, secretary, editor/reporter/photographer for a small-town newspaper and plant paper. She started college when she was thirty-one and working full-time, graduating five years later with a B.A. in history and communications. Her first novel, *Beyond the Void,* is currently making the rounds; she now resides in Waynesboro, Virginia, and is heading back to school to complete an M.A. in history. She received honorable mention for her story in the Writers of the Future Contest.

Wrestling is a popular spectator sport right now, and Cary provides us with a look—almost on the humorous side, if your taste runs to the black—that might not please Hulk Hogan or any of the others in the squared circle.

✦ ✦ ✦

Mave and Ralph edged between the rows of chairs to their seats. It was a chore moving along without spilling the popcorn or tripping over people or metal chair legs. People were really pouring into the Garden this week, fans already filling the arena with the noise of their voices and with tobacco smoke which later on would be thick enough to burn everyone's eyes.

The Tuesday-night ritual. She and Ralph had to be here and in their seats before eight o'clock. That's when the matches began, when the Eastern Wrestling Federation presented an evening of "wrestling excitement." Wrestling excitement, that is, for Ralph. Oh, Mave admitted to occasionally yelling at the sweating men in the squared circle, adding her voice to the roar of the thousands of others, especially when one of the combatants was someone she liked a lot. She had heard once that nearly everyone got excited by wrestling, especially if they watched it live for a while in an arena like this one.

She *told* everyone she came because it was one of the few things she and Ralph still did together. And she didn't mind the violence since it was all fake anyway; and it was funnier than the comedies on TV.

Mave often wondered, though, if Ralph didn't take it too seriously sometimes. He could get so upset, yelling at the good guys for being stupid, the referees for being dishonest, at the bad guys for breaking the rules, and at her if he got real excited.

This evening started quietly enough, and remained so for the first hour and a half. As usual the program began with preliminary matches, no big stars, and no surprises as to who won or who lost. There were a couple of tag teams, the others being single matches. Of course, Ralph and Mave knew all the wrestlers by name and reputation, as did the rest of the crowd whose shouted approval and disapproval nearly deafened her. Every once in a while she could hear the voices of the television commentators seated near the ring itself. Ralph had already made himself hoarse, and the best was yet to come.

✦ ✦ ✦

He lumbered into the arena slowly, deliberately, moving along the wide aisle as thousands of people shouted at him from both sides. They reached out to hit him, prevented only by the arena guards who flanked him. They pelted him with trash. One drink cup was full. She saw the ice shimmer as it got caught in the tangle of hair on his torso. A few pieces meandered downward, mixing with droplets of sweat to collect at the waist of his long black tights. When he got close enough Mave threw her smashed-together popcorn box, but it fell short.

"You never could throw worth a damn," Ralph shouted in her ear.

She stuck out her tongue at him.

McGill swung his arms wildly at the fans. They backed up a step as a single being, then yelled even louder. Being the bad guy, who in a few minutes would take on one of the most popular good guys in the business, probably was not very pleasant at the moment.

The ring announcer tapped the microphone and informed them that this was the feature match. He then introduced the second wrestler, already in the ring.

"In this corner, weighing three hundred twenty-five pounds, from Bristol, Tennessee, the former heavyweight champion of the world, the Masked Avenger."

Thousands of voices exploded in approval as the masked wrestler bowed to the crowd, threw kisses, then made the "I love you" sign with his hands. Mave grinned, feeling the excitement deep in her stomach. Her heart raced. Her palms were sweaty and beads of sweat popped out over her upper lip. She was sorry they hadn't found seats on the other side so she could have seen Avenger when he entered. But you never knew which side to sit on since they entered the arena from different dressing rooms each week.

Then it was *his* turn.

"And about to enter the ring, at three hundred sixty-eight pounds, from parts unknown, Monster McGill."

Spotlights focused on him, still making his way up the aisle. Mave always said the name suited him, with his hairy body, and by almost any standard he was ugly. When they tried to interview him on TV he could hardly talk.

He raised both arms threateningly and ran the last few feet.

Boos and threats from the crowd grew in volume as he bent his six-feet-six-inch frame, stepped through the ropes, let out a fearful howl, and immediately began chasing his opponent around the ring. More trash flew through the air, striking bad guy, good guy, and mat indiscriminately. The referee finally backed McGill into a neutral corner, waved for the bell to sound, and stepped out of the way.

The match began at a furious pace. Avenger, although the smaller of the two, gained the initial advantage with a hammerlock. McGill broke that hold and several more in succession, until Avenger missed a drop kick, knocking the breath out of himself.

"Look at what he's doing," Mave yelled to the referee as McGill threw himself into mauling Avenger.

"He's biting!" she yelled a moment later.

"Oh, no," she moaned several times as McGill gouged at Avenger's right eye, then kicked the masked man when he fell to the mat.

McGill pulled Avenger to his feet, then threw him into the ropes for an Irish whip, intending to execute a back drop. But as the masked man flew to the center of the ring, he brought his knee up, catching McGill under the chin and knocking him to the mat.

"Go get him," Mave yelled as she jumped to her feet in unison with the fans around her. She reached over and slapped Ralph's shoulder as he stood beside her.

"Kill him," she said, although she could not hear her own voice anymore.

McGill staggered around the center of the ring from a well-placed forearm smash. Avenger climbed to the top rope in one corner, jumped down with his right elbow to the top of McGill's head. McGill sprawled face down. Mave howled and clapped her hands as Avenger turned the Monster onto his back and covered him for the count. The referee reached two, had his hand raised for the third count, when McGill tossed Avenger up into the air and on top of the referee.

"No! You dumb referee. Don't count so slow." Mave waved her fist in the direction of the official, who ignored the abuse of thousands, some of whom loudly expressed doubts about his honesty.

For twenty minutes the match went back and forth, first one had the advantage then the other. The crowd roared approval each time Avenger hurt McGill or got the upper hand. Mave cheered his punching and eye gouging as McGill's brutality maddened him beyond caring about the rules. Fight fire with fire, she always said.

Avenger got McGill in a headlock, popped him on the forehead with his right fist. McGill, straightened by the blow, swung wildly at his opponent, who easily dodged away. Avenger lunged, two fingers aimed at McGill's eyes. Blinded, McGill was whipped into the ropes. He hit hard and, off balance, flipped over the top rope and slid off the ring apron, hitting his head hard on the sharp edge. Avenger stood in the middle of the ring, poised for a back drop which never came.

Mave clapped her hands and jumped up and down in approval. She strained to see McGill lying on the concrete floor. In a moment he got to his feet, staggered around with arms flailing. The crowd's screams were right in his ears. She caught a glimpse of his face through the crowd now and then, confusion lining every feature. He blundered into the fans at ringside. They were knocked to one side and another. One voice of rage from hundreds of throats rose to a crescendo.

We'll get him, Mave thought.

She struggled to move forward, deliberately pushing around those in front of her.

Another roar and she strained to see.

"What happened?" she shouted to those around her.

No one answered, their attention and voices focused on the action between them and the ring.

The crowd swept to the right. Mave pummeled those bodies pressed against her. The shirts were wet, the smell of sweaty bodies filled her nostrils. She could not move forward. The crowd flowed to the left, taking her with them. She shook her fist over the shoulder of the man in front of her.

Just a few more steps. To be so close to getting her share.

Those closest to the spot where McGill had stood became quiet. The silence spread outward like a ripple in a pond. A general movement for the exits began. It was over and Mave stood still as the people moved around her like a stream flowing past a rock. It was over and she had not made it. Her share was gone.

She took one step forward, wondering where to go, where Ralph was, when she stepped on something. She held her foot on it until the press of people eased and it was safe to stoop down. It felt cold in her hand. The fingernail was nearly pure white. The bloody end still moist. The souvenir went carefully into her jacket pocket before anyone else could see.

Someone grabbed her elbow, steering her toward the exit. Ralph smiled down at her. She smiled back in anticipation of showing him her prize.

✦ ✦ ✦

The people were nearly clear of the arena. At the end of the line, Mave looked back just before passing through the exit. She patted Ralph's shoulder so he would look back too. The ringside commentators stood with the Masked Avenger and the referee in the center of the ring. They stood very still, a look of horror frozen on each face, staring out at the arena as it emptied.

The policemen and arena guards pushed through the overturned chairs. Occasionally one would holler, "Here's some," then stoop down to gingerly place something in a plastic garbage bag.

She smiled one last time and patted her pocket. They could search all night if they wanted but they would never find all of Monster McGill.

ASPEN GRAFFITI

by Melanie Tem

Melanie Tem, a social worker, has worked with abused and neglected children in foster and adoptive homes, and with disabled adults. Previously she's published in numerous little magazines, and collaborations with her husband, Steve Rasnic Tem, have appeared in *Isaac Asimov's Science Fiction Magazine* and *SF International*. Novels just completed are a dark fantasy and a mystery, first of a planned series featuring an elderly and disabled sleuth. And she's also finished a novel written with Steve. She has also published numerous articles in professional journals. A native of rural Pennsylvania, she lives in an nineteenth-century Victorian house in old North Denver with her husband, children, two dogs, and two cats.

I received many stories about husbands and wives and their disintegrating relationships. This was by far the best—and most frightening—of them.

✦ ✦ ✦

He shrugged, a peculiar stiff hunching of the shoulders that looked as if it hurt.

He said my name. It sounded brittle, like paper crumpled across his lips.

He looked at me because he had to, then looked hastily away as though he couldn't stand what he was seeing. His eyes were crowded with shadows like gossipy strangers.

He smiled, a smile so quick and sure of itself and so out of place that I barely caught it behind the beard and moustache he'd painstakingly grown that winter. They'd turned out to be a deep red. His hair had always been blond; it hung over his collar now and was further lightened by streaks and strands of gray, which had surprised us both and openly distressed him, even though I have plenty of gray in my hair, too.

The beard and moustache and the longer hair really did make him look younger. Not much; a few years, maybe. I'd told him so, repeatedly, thinking he'd like that. But, for some reason, he'd never seemed especially pleased to hear it from me.

"I don't love you anymore," he said.

Stinging little memories swarmed at me then, so precious and painful that I didn't dare speak them aloud. I remembered dancing in the kitchen. I remembered the double-lemon pie he'd wanted instead of a cake for his thirty-eighth birthday, how the candles kept slipping into the yellow meringue so that we never could get all of them lit at once. He had seemed a trifle disappointed that night, as though wishing he'd stuck with chocolate cake and fudge icing after all.

I remembered the aspen, papery-white bark carved and peeled as high as a tall man could reach, all around the mountain grove. One graffito in particular had caught my eye: two sets of initials, enclosed by a heart and pierced by an arrow, a good fifteen feet high and so deep that the frayed bark hung down like thinning hair. CM + DF, it said.

I played with possibilities: Claudia Moore and David Fernandez. Charles Mueller and Diana Feldman. Carl Masters and Darryl Floyd. I stared up at the carving until I was finally a little giddy from tipping my head back so far in the thin mountain air.

How had David or Diana or Carl reached so high? I created scenes, some sillier than others. An extension ladder, lashed under somebody's backpack and clumsily carried in. One stretching, knife-wielding lover on the shoulders of another. Neither that tree nor any of its neighbors had branches low enough or strong enough for climbing.

In the middle of a bitter night last February or March, I had awakened suddenly and been badly startled by the sight of Adrian, sleeping beside me as always, his face turned in my direction, his neck exposed in the blue-white glimmer of the streetlight on snow through our bedroom window. With the patchy whiskers on his skin, the hollows under those high cheekbones that I'd always admired, and the sinewy pulsing of his long throat, he looked ancient.

I was drenched with sweat. I'd been dreaming vague dreams of captivity and loneliness. Irritably, I realized that my sleep had been disturbed because it was so stuffy in the room; since early in the fall, Adrian had constantly complained of the cold, and he wouldn't let me open a window even a crack to let in fresh air.

I threw off my side of the electric blanket, taking care to keep his side tucked in around his shoulders and hips. Without really looking at him again, trying to keep myself from waking up so thoroughly that I wouldn't be able to get back to sleep, I turned over and snuggled against him, even though I knew it would be too hot.

I couldn't sleep. I kept fighting the urge to turn over and stare at him as he slept. I pushed the soles of my feet along his thighs and calves, trying to get a feel for his contours, his substance. He stirred and moved a little, moved away. His breath made my shoulder blades itch.

We had been together a long time. We'd slept together uncounted nights. But, half-asleep and sweating, I had now become infested with the idea that I was sleeping with someone I didn't know, someone who looked like Adrian but did not, who could have been Adrian but was not.

Finally, exasperated, I roused myself. I got up and went to the bathroom. The whole house was lit by the thin lovely light off the snow, and, although every window was shut tight, the sounds inside were different, too—muted, blurred. When I came back to bed, Adrian was sleeping on his back, and the cold blue light edged his profile, made his skin look silver and lined. He had rolled up in the covers, so that there were hardly any at all on my side of the bed; that was an old, familiar habit. I smiled and tugged gently at the sheet. He didn't move.

I bent and passed my hand over his face, brushed my palm across the prickly ends of his hair and beard, touched his eyelids. His face twitched and he turned his head, but he didn't wake up. I traced the tip of my index finger in the air above his profile, maybe a centimeter away from his skin, as though sketching his aura; I had always loved to touch him like this. I slid my hand under the wrapped covers at his neck and very lightly massaged his chest, the hollow at his throat, the hard plate of his sternum. My fingertips traced loops, scallops, the letter *B* on every part of his body that I could reach.

He jerked into consciousness and opened his eyes. "What are you doing, Bonnie?" His voice was still thick with sleep.

"Shhh. Nothing. You've got all the covers again."

He brought his hand up and brushed peevishly at my fingers. "Stop that. I don't like that. What are you doing?"

"Nothing," I told him again, soothingly. "Just playing. Just touching you."

After that, I'd noticed a change in him. He'd been more

and more irritable and jumpy. If I touched his arm in passing, he'd scowl and pull away. When I kissed him good-bye in the mornings, he'd hold his breath. It had seemed to me that he was feverish much of the time, and he often complained of a spreading ache behind his eyes. He'd refused to go to the doctor, made jokes, ignored my nagging. He'd begun to spend days in bed.

Now he said to me, "I don't love you anymore. I guess that's what it comes down to. I just don't love you anymore."

He spread his hands and curled his fingers in a gesture unfamiliar to me. We'd been married almost seventeen years, and now, as he left me, Adrian was using a gesture I'd never seen him use before; of course, I had no idea what it meant, what he was trying to convey to me. I think now that that gesture was a missed clue, a symptom masked until then by bogus symptoms of health and normalcy, a warning too early or too late.

Seventeen years. Closer to twenty, actually; we'd made sure to take our time, to understand each other's moods and layers and idiosyncracies, before we got married. It wasn't fashionable in those days, but both of us had insisted on regarding marriage as a permanent commitment. We kept no secrets from each other. I knew everything there was to know about Adrian; he knew me better than anyone ever had or ever will. And still, I hadn't seen this coming at all.

"But why, Adrian? Why are you doing this? Why are you willing to give up everything we've worked for—"

"I don't know why. I can't help it."

"Surely we can work this out, together, whatever it is."

"There's nothing to work out."

"Then let's just—give it some time."

"I don't have time. I'm losing myself. I can't tell anymore what's you and the kids and what's me. I feel invaded. If I don't get away now, I never will."

Although the things he said were desperate in their meaning, his voice was almost without emotion, and the words and syllables came out measured, even, one by one.

"I'll die, Bonnie," he said, and my name was another wound.

Adrian had lifted me against the aspen tree. I'd wanted to feel it, like Braille. He's never been a big man or especially strong, so I couldn't stand on his shoulders. I'd braced myself against the scaly trunk and stretched, but couldn't reach the letters. The bark had peeled away like dead skin under my palms and clung to the cuffs of my sweatshirt as I'd slid down out of his arms.

"What about the kids? This will scar them for life."

"I'll be there for them. I'll take them places on weekends. To games and things. Eric is starting to like wrestling."

"They need a father."

"They'll have one. I haven't stopped loving them."

"I need you, too!" I was crying.

"I'm sorry, Bonnie. I don't mean to hurt you."

He left. I couldn't stop him. The boys couldn't stop him, although Glenn put his fist through the closet door and Eric sobbed.

For a while he did show up every weekend. He took Eric to the zoo and to a pro wrestling exhibition, Glenn to a football game, both of them out to dinner a few times and to a movie or two. Then he started missing. He'd call to say he was sick or he had to work. Sometimes he just didn't come.

When I complained to him about it—the boys never would; I think they were afraid of losing him altogether

—Adrian's face didn't change expression, as if I hadn't spoken or he couldn't hear me, as if I weren't there. By then I couldn't get him to engage with me at all; he had become smoothed, featureless, without toeholds for me to grab onto. Glenn told me that the last time they'd gone out to dinner his father hadn't eaten a thing, hadn't even ordered.

I was a mess. I couldn't sleep. I ate constantly. I went to work every day, but I couldn't tell whether I was accomplishing anything; I'd burst into tears in a sales meeting or into hysterical laughter during a long-distance conference call. I couldn't read; words frayed off the page, and their meanings were insubstantial and pointless. I couldn't watch television; the sappiest sitcoms, the most gratuitously violent cop shows, even the news had story lines about relationships. I couldn't stand for my sons to touch me and I couldn't stand for them not to.

My friends gathered round me, as women will. They pointed out other women this had happened to, other men who, at a certain age, had deserted wives and children and careers—though not so often careers. Patrice's husband, John, had run off with his twenty-year-old secretary. Marge's husband, Walter, had started racing everything he could get his hands and their money on: stock cars, thoroughbreds, boats, planes; he didn't like Marge to go with him to the races, said it was a man's world, and so she hardly saw him anymore except when he needed her signature to withdraw more money from their joint account. The day Ted had moved out, after living with Susan for six years, he'd said earnestly to her, "I don't know what kind of relationship you thought we had here. I hope there hasn't been some sort of misunderstanding."

John had come back; it hadn't taken him long. "I don't know what she did to him," Patrice said, tossing her head, "but it looked to me like he was hollowed out. There was nothing of him left, nothing of the man I married. He came skulking back home with his tail between his legs, and I was supposed to take care of him. I threw him out."

Marge had stared at her, unbelieving. She expected Walter to come back any day, having run out of money or friends or energy. Whatever he'd done, she said, her face almost radiant, she'd welcome him home with open arms.

When my grandfather Jan was a boy in the old country, his father Pavel had abandoned his family—the young hardworking wife, the half dozen small children, the enormous stone house that had once sheltered the whole village after a fire. He ran a long way: to America. There is no evidence that anyone in the old country ever heard from him again, although he lived out a whole life well away from them.

He settled, we think, in a little Pennsylvania mill town in the Monongahela Valley, not fifty miles from where my grandfather Jan was to settle a few years later. But as far as we know, the two of them never saw or spoke to each other once they came to America.

My father doesn't know many details of this old story. He doesn't like to talk about it, and when he does the veins in his temples throb. His disgust for men who in any way abandon their families borders on the obsessive. For my father, there is not much difference between love and obligation. He told me once that he never wanted to get married, he never wanted to have children.

I think about Pavel, my great-grandfather, and about my great-grandmother, whose name I've never known, abandoned in her big stone house that could shelter all the people in the village but could not shelter her. She lost her eldest son, too; though my grandfather Jan wrote and sent money, he never went home.

I wonder what she would have made of that aspen grove, where lovers' initials had been cut—for eternity, I thought—into the layered bark. I had liked that grove. It had made a sudden, sweet little space in the high woods. I had gazed at the fuzzy white lines the trunks made against the denser dark green of the juniper and fir, the kind of green that people mean when they say forest-green. Each yellow-green heart-shaped leaf was suspended from its branch by a long slender stem, so that the leaves flickered like old-fashioned motion pictures even when I could feel no breeze. I fancied I could see images in them, poetry, meaning.

I liked the feeling of enclosure, of community. I felt safe there, and understood. I was with Adrian, and we were in love. The aspens stood like fellows in an approximate circle around us. Heart-shaped leaves flickered like pretty words. At night, when we lay holding hands from adjoining sleeping bags, there was the companionable rustling of small life in the woods, very close by. I'd pretended they were communicating something about love and symbiosis, and that I could understand.

"I saw Dad today," Glenn said.

"Where?"

"In the mall."

"Did he say anything? Did you talk to him?"

"No. He didn't see me."

"Well, how did he look?"

"He looked really good."

The admiration in my son's voice was so strong that I looked at him to see if he was mocking. He did not seem to be. "What do you mean?" I asked cautiously.

"He looked cool. His hair's longer, and he's got it dyed so it isn't gray anymore. He was wearing an earring, and great clothes."

"An earring?"

"He was playing, sort of."

"Playing?" I felt like a fool, repeating his words, but I couldn't imagine Adrian like this.

"He was running around the edge of one of those fountains in the mall, you know? And dancing. Like this."

Glenn stood up to demonstrate, and I saw that in the past few months, since his father had left, he'd grown to be taller than I was. Now he made his lanky, healthy adolescent body move spastically, as though propelled by an erratic energy he couldn't predict or control. His mouth was contorted into a grin like rictus. He flung out his hands in playful, frightening gestures.

I shivered and told him, "Don't do that!" But he kept it up anyway, as if there were a perverse pleasure in pretending to be diseased.

His back to me, Glenn said more loudly than necessary, "He was with somebody. A girl I know."

"Who?"

"She graduated last year or dropped out. A real airhead, you know? A real bimbo. Likes to party. Likes to get high and stay that way. Sleeps around." He cleared his throat. "Likes flash, you know? Flashy clothes, flashy cars, flashy guys."

I laughed painfully and wiped at my eyes with the back of my hand. I was already tired of crying over Adrian, and it had barely begun. "I never thought of your father as flashy."

"He is now," Glenn said. "Had on purple pants."

"I guess that means he won't be wanting the rest of his clothes out of the closet."

"He was loud, too. You could hear him all over the mall. Everybody was looking at him, you know? She had on earphones, so I guess he was trying to talk to her over the music."

"What was he saying?"

He hesitated, scuffed his feet.

"Glenn," I said.

"I hate this," he said. "I hate this place. No wonder he split."

"Tell me."

"Shit!" My son stormed out of the room, shouting over his shoulder at me. "He said he loved her, okay? He kept saying he loved her!"

Not long after that, I saw Adrian myself. Eric and I were shopping for school clothes, and we'd been arguing all afternoon about the seventy-five-dollar Reeboks he insisted he needed. Both of us irritable, we were leaving the crowded shoe department of K-Mart where I'd been trying to show him that a cheaper brand would do just as well, when suddenly I saw Adrian in the stream of shoppers moving toward and past us along the aisle. "Eric, look, there's your father!" I cried, and then wished I hadn't.

Eric didn't even pause. He was ahead of me, so I couldn't see his face, but his fists clenched at his sides. "That's not my father," he declared. "My father is dead."

Adrian was still there. His body moved as if he were moving with the flow of the crowd, but he hadn't passed us. He was staring at me, his face rigid. He was so close I could have touched him, but of course I didn't. This was not the animated man Glenn had described; there was almost no energy about him. In the fluorescent light he looked sallow, and under the ragged beard I saw great pocks in his cheeks, as though the flesh of his face were collapsing inward.

"Here," I said hastily to my son, and fumbled in my

wallet for some bills. "This is the money I set aside for your school clothes. Spend it however you want. I'm tired of arguing."

His eyes widened. "Are you serious? I can buy the Reeboks?"

I waved him off impatiently, afraid I'd lose sight of Adrian as carts wheeled around him, children raced and shrieked, shoppers absentmindedly pushed past. Adrian, the love of my life, was close to me and standing still, but I had no sense of his presence other than that I could see him there: I could not feel his body heat, or hear him breathing. "Go finish your shopping," I told Eric, "and then go on home. You know which bus to take. Tell Glenn I'll be there when I can."

"Where are you going?"

"I have to talk to your dad."

"My dad is dead," he insisted again, flatly. He held the money in both hands like a bouquet of limp flowers, and he looked much younger than he was.

"Just go!" But he was already gone; head down and shoulders squared, he tunneled through the crowd as though he were headed for the end zone. I took a deep breath and turned back to my husband. "Adrian," I said.

He said nothing. His eyes were dull and didn't focus. I saw now that his hair—badly dyed an odd sandy blond—had receded at both temples so that his forehead was high and very pale. He started to move away.

"Oh, wait."

He led me along the center aisle, past the lavender and turquoise shoulder bag display, through Domestics where towels and washcloths made colorful rolled-edge towers. A man with a cartful of toddlers got between us once, but Adrian waited for me to catch up. He went out the back door of the store, which was marked Emergency Exit Only.

I hesitated only slightly before I followed him. No one stopped us and no alarms went off.

He led me across the parking lot that spread around the store like a shroud come loose. The pavement was heavy gray with rain; the sky was a lighter gray, and gray mist rose between the two. Adrian was a wraith. I worked hard to keep up with him, my feet slipping, my shoes wet; I was afraid I'd lose him altogether among the grays, and I was equally afraid of where I might be letting him lead me.

At the far edge of the parking lot was a row of trees, and beyond the trees was the channelized river that flowed through the city. Adrian vanished over the edge of the embankment. I started to run after him, slipped on the wet grass, fell, got to my knees. From there I could see down to the silver-brown river and the careful green ribbon of park on either side. I thought I saw Adrian. The man standing directly below me had the stiff bearing, the slightly gaping mouth that I had come to associate with the man I loved.

Then I thought I really had lost him forever, for I saw that the banks of the river, the entire greenway, were dotted with men just like him. There must have been hundreds of them: gray, almost fluid in their teeming, and absolutely silent.

I lowered myself flat onto my stomach and slid as close to the very edge of the embankment as I dared. The longer I watched, the more of these men I recognized, the lovers and husbands of my friends.

John was there, looking like a wooden caricature of the man I'd seen with Patrice at company parties for the last ten years. The lines in his face were so deep now that they looked to have been carved; his jowls hung down like scaling bark.

Walter lay on the grass between me and the river. At first his flesh looked stippled, and then I realized that I was seeing blades of grass, motes of dust through his body. His torso was bare, and even from this distance I could see him shivering. Across his chest was a network of angry red scars, like knife wounds, many of them not yet healed.

Under a spindly planted tree, holding on to it with both hands, crouched an old, old man with a face like a wooden doll's. He looked so much like my father and grandfather that I knew who he was even though of course I'd never met him before.

Suddenly Adrian was standing before me. He didn't speak. He didn't touch me. He made no gesture or movement of his thin, rigid body. But clearly I knew what he wanted me to do. I was to leave him. I was to leave him there.

I raised my hand and lowered it again, aching to touch his skin with my fingerprints, thinking that with hardly any pressure I would be able to leave my fingerprints there. "Adrian," I said hopelessly. "Come home with me."

He spread his thin, shaking hands in the gesture that had by now become familiar to me; I gave it my own interpretations, though I didn't want to.

"You can't just stay here."

He opened his mouth, and after a moment the thin ribbon of his voice reached me. "This is only a gathering place. We'll be leaving as soon as everybody gets here."

"Where are you going? Oh, Adrian, don't leave."

He shook his head and backed away. The outlines of his body shimmered like the mists. The noise and motion of the river current flowed through him. He raised his hand to his lips and blew me a kiss; that was the last I saw of him, that jaunty, affectionate, bone-chilling gesture.

When I got home, Eric met me at the door. His new shoes looked very large and white on his feet, making his ankles look frail. "Glenn says he's gonna run away," he told me, and then went to watch television, leaving it to me.

Heavily I climbed the stairs to Glenn's room. I knocked. He didn't answer. I knocked again, and went in anyway. He was lying on his bed with his back to the door, and he didn't acknowledge me. "Glenn," I said. "What's going on?"

He rolled over. His face was strained, long shadows into the eyes. In a low voice he said, "I gotta get out of here."

"Why?"

"I can't stand it. I can't stand Eric and I can't stand you." He looked at me hastily because he had to and then looked away. "I'm sorry, Mom. Nothing personal. I don't want to hurt you. I just want to go live with Dad."

I thought of that crowded, misty valley. I shuddered, gripped my son's shoulder, and said, "You can't."

He pulled away. He was trembling. He was shouting at me, although his voice was very quiet. "Someday I will. You can't tell me what to do forever. Someday I'll go find him, and I'll be just like him. You just wait."

In the mountain clearing, long enough ago that it seemed a lifetime, I had especially liked the graffiti carved carefully, joyously, playfully into the bark of the aspen trees, which had been soft and pliable enough to accept the cuts of the knives. I'd fancied I could hear the murmurs of all those people, could in turn tell them how happy Adrian and I were, could feel the comings and goings, the passing through, of all our love and whimsy.

Until Adrian, who used to know about trees, had told me: "It kills them. When you enter the bark like that, get under its skin, break its seal, you make a point of entry for a certain type of fungus, and that fungus kills the tree. The rangers up here have to rotate campsites, to let the aspen recover. If they can catch it in time and get the people away, sometimes the bark will grow back over the graffiti and the tree will heal itself."

It had made me feel guilty. "I guess I won't carve our initials then," I'd promised, and snuggled closer to him.

But after we'd made love again and I was sure he was asleep, I did anyway. AR + BY, cut with the tip of a paring knife about waist-high into the bark of a sturdy tree on the side facing away from the clearing, where I hoped Adrian wouldn't notice. He didn't. We were in love. I couldn't bear to leave that beautiful place without leaving some small record of us.

Now I wonder whether that tree died, or whether it was able to heal itself, grew its bark back over our initials and over the deadly fungus our love allowed inside.

SISTER

by Wennicke Eide Cox

Wennicke Eide Cox was born in Norway during the German occupation. She says her first memory is of hiding in the basement during an air raid. After high school she studied art in Oslo for three years before quitting to work at a youth club as a ticket seller, bouncer, and disc jockey. In 1970 she moved to Copenhagen. She has lived in New Mexico and West Virginia, and has recently returned to Norway.

There seems to be an unusually large number of stories in this anthology centered around family members. Does this mean that most families that seem quite happy upon the surface probably aren't, after all? This is Wennicke's first published short story, and it proves that she's definitely a writer of Southern Gothic.

✦ ✦ ✦

In wintertime she waits beneath the ice; I see her hand, a distant movement far below: she tries to greet me. Her voice is faint and I can barely hear her through the wind. I feel alone.

But spring arrives: she thaws; she rises. The pond is cold, I visit from the bank. We speak. She sings to me.

The summer is the golden time: I swim, I wade, I float; she moves with me. We are together. I laugh my joy with her, and cry my tears. She listens: she would cry with me if she had tears; she cannot jump and run, pick flowers, hug me.

When she is sad, I cannot comfort her. I search for words

but I am clumsy, and the words, the right ones, words to touch her heart and still her sorrow will not come; I need to touch, hug, kiss, my warm arms holding her, I am too young to use another language.

How terrible to have no tears. I ache for her, I don't know what to do; I love her. She's my sister.

✦ ✦ ✦

I love to read, to lose myself in foreign places, new emotions, learn what other people feel; most all my friends live within books. I wish that I could go to school more. But Mama needs my help. I understand that. We are alone now, just the two of us.

Once we were five. I don't remember; I was just a baby then. Augusta told me. Augusta's my sister.

Daddy died when I was one. Sometimes I remember but I know I'm only seeing what Augusta tells me; she was five, she knew him.

Augusta says he loved us.

Before Mr. Emrick we were four: Mama, Eliza, Augusta, and I. Mr. Emrick made five, but he did not belong with us. Mama wanted us to call him Uncle Ben, but Eliza and Augusta and I always called him Mr. Emrick.

Mama brought him. When we saw her coming up the hill, the tall man walking with her, Augusta took two steps forward, opening her mouth to shout, "Daddy," but Liza grabbed her, pulled her back, and shook her head. Eliza was eleven when our daddy died.

Smiling, Mama held his hand and said to us, "Girls, this is Uncle Ben."

I knew at once that Mr. Emrick wasn't like my daddy.

Mama reached for me and I stepped back; I would not have Mr. Emrick touch me. Liza pulled me close, hand resting on my shoulder, put her arm around Augusta.

Mama liked him, couldn't keep from touching him; she touched his hand, his arm, she touched his back; when he sat down she touched his cheek. He was a large man. When he rolled his sleeves back, muscles moved beneath the skin; his hair was curly black, his teeth were white. But there was something wrong inside his eyes: he looked at me and smiled and all I wanted was to run, hide in the woods till he was gone. Augusta looked at me, she felt it too.

But Mama's face restrained us. We stood still. Our mama's face was shining.

I stayed out of his way. And I was only six, he didn't want me. But he wanted Liza near him, always. Liza's eyes changed; her face closed in on itself; her body hunched, shoulders bent, hands clenching together.

Eliza ran away that winter. I asked Augusta why but Augusta looked at me and wouldn't talk about it.

Mama's face changed too; she looked a little puzzled, sad, and hurt, and there was something in her face, something that wasn't quite anger, or guilt, or shame; an emotion that was not ready to live in Mama's face but wouldn't go away.

Mr. Emrick never changed. His smile made me freeze inside and want to go hide. I didn't have to, though; Mr. Emrick's smile was for Augusta. During the thaw, and through the greening, and later, as the summer covered us, thick, hot, and heavy, Mr. Emrick's smile was for Augusta.

In school I caught the late summer flu; I was in bed, on

the screened-in porch, so hot that the thin sheet burned me, too hot to sweat, or cry. Mama dipped cool well water and sponged me down, she sat by me all day and evening, changing the cool cloth on my forehead.

Mr. Emrick came at nightfall but Augusta didn't come. Mama was afraid to leave me; she was afraid for Augusta. Mr. Emrick offered to go look. When he came back, alone, it was full dark. Mama cried. She called to Augusta, over and over, she walked to the edge of our clearing, her voice rang out like a soaring night bird. She returned to me, to lift the warm cloth from my forehead, dip it once again in cool well water.

Mountain people keep to themselves, but when somebody has troubles they all share, and help.

They searched the hills for my sister but they never found her. Mr. Cross's coon dog found her dress, dirty and torn. Some said the dog did it. But when they found her underwear it, too, was torn, and there was blood on it. They searched the woods for strangers but they didn't find a tramp, or escaped convict, or a maniac; they didn't find Augusta either.

There was talk that fall: people talked about John Hurst who was in custody for smoking grass, they talked about Mike Kelly who was drinking more than ever, mumbling about crazed dopeheads and senseless drunks, but the talk died down soon. After all, most people drink; and many tend strange weeds in hidden clearings in the woods. But for a long time, people eyed each other. No children walked alone.

Mr. Emrick left that winter. He did not come back. Mama's face was older; she did not sing anymore, or even hum, and when she spoke to me it was to do with work. I didn't tell her I was glad.

✦ ✦ ✦

The woods stretch endlessly above our place, steep hillsides overgrown with thick green, honeysuckle twining, joining lesser trees with moss-grown forest giants in one sweet-smelling embrace. Pale seedlings push between the ferns and leafy mayapple-umbrellas, seeking light.

I love the woods. I walk there always, climbing hills to rest atop a ridge, catching a breeze, surveying never-ending waves of green; I run and slide the steep slopes, down, loose soil a tiny avalache beneath my feet. I walk; I watch; I listen; I explore.

The pond lies in a hollow deep within the hills. It's too far from the road; the hillsides are too steep to farm; nobody comes there. Only me. I came sometimes to swim, or hide, when Mr. Emrick lived with us; I come there every day now, stealing a few minutes even though I have a lot of work to do.

Augusta is in there. She is still ten years old.

She looks so very small, and young; her braids are all undone, her hair is long, it ripples round her head beneath the water. I can only see her when the light is right: no direct sunlight, and no wind to ruffle the surface of the pond.

I have come to meet my sister every day for three years. She cannot leave the pond; she has to stay below the surface and I cannot touch her. But she will listen to me, she hears everything I say. I tell her about school when there is time for me to go; I tell her about work. I talk to her about the things I see, and think, and feel. She likes to listen, but she talks to me too. Sometimes she comforts me, or gives advice; sometimes she teases me, or we play games; sometimes we talk about the past, remembering together.

But she will not tell me what happened to her. I don't know how she died, or how she lives here, in the pond.

✦ ✦ ✦

This spring I'm ten years old. I am my sister's twin. Next year I'll be the older.

It worries me. I'm growing fast this year; I'm tall, my arms and legs are long, my hands and feet are large. My chest is flat still but my nipples changed, they itch sometimes, and rub against my T-shirt so I want to take it off. I want to cut my braids but Mama will not let me. At night I brush my hair out; I would like it haloing around my face the way Augusta's does, beneath the water, hers a darker auburn than my rusty red.

Sometimes I wake, too hot, although the night is cold; my sweat smells different. I touch myself then and my skin is smooth as silk, so soft; I chew my hair and cry, I don't know why. It worries me.

Augusta doesn't want to hear me when I try to talk of these things. I see her face closed, pale, still, listening, not answering, and she looks like a younger version of myself. I feel like I'm the older, then; I feel alone, and scared.

In bed at night I read; the school library is my friend. So great a planet Earth; so many places, peoples, pleasures, wonders; such misery, and cruelty, and pain. I want it all; I want to see it, feel it, be it, I want it filling me, I want to be set free; and yet I am afraid.

My teacher speaks to me: she wants me there, in class, each day. I think she likes me. She encourages my reading, lets me borrow all the books the school library owns. Sometimes I wish she would be angry, insist I stay in school. She doesn't, though; she knows the mountains.

✦ ✦ ✦

It's summer, school is out; it's hot but I am cold, cold to my bones. I tremble on the porch steps. Mama's laugh rings out, in joy. She touches him. He smiles. But not at her. He smiles at me. He's back; he smiles at me.

I leave before first light, I run, run to my sister. Augusta rises through the water; I touch my fingertips to hers, a tiny surface ripple: the most she will permit. I cry.

Through my sister's eyes I see the deep pond bottom-green; my tears distort her image. I stop. I hear my sister's voice.

"Janey, sisterlil, what happened, love, why do you cry?"

I tremble once again, I meet her eyes, I stare into them, down, I sense the icy bottom slime, my feet are cold, the sun touches my brow but cannot touch my fear. Augusta's face is older once again, it's spare and sober, cold; her anger glints but not at me: before I speak, she knows what I will say. She is my older sister.

"He's back, Augusta, and he smiles at me!"

She speaks his name; I do not have to say it, she can see it in my face: the pond goes dark and ripples with it: Mr. Emrick.

All day I visit with my sister. We do not speak of him again, we talk of summer, and of school, the books I read; we swim, I doze; she guards me.

Mama, happy, does not notice I am late; he does. His eyes touch me, notice stains of mud and greenslime, my damp hair. Suddenly I feel the cotton of my shirt against my nipples, I look down: they show. Over Mama's greying head he smiles at me.

Midsummer's past; blackberries ripen, clustered purple-juicy on the stem: they stain my mouth. My legs are brown and full of hair-thin scratches.

I do my chores, I read, I help when Mama cleans the house or weeds the garden. If Mama doesn't need me I am gone; I flee, I slip away, a shadow through the greenery, a noiseless footstep, unheard and unseen. Augusta waits for me.

I do not like him looking at me. When Mama isn't near he touches: he nips my braid, or puts a finger on my neck; he passes, brushes close, his hand rests on my shoulder. And when I meet his eyes he smiles.

I'm frightened.

✦ ✦ ✦

He wanted to go fishing but I wouldn't. Mama laughed and shrugged; he smiled. My sister didn't smile.

The pond was still. The sun was hazy. Augusta came to meet me, saw my face. We stared a long time at each other. I had not before thought of Augusta dead: she was my friend, she was my sister. But now I saw the green-cast skin stretched tightly on her cranium; her too-large teeth; her hair, dark auburn halo, slimy reptile-tangle. Her speech shaped tiny bubbles on the water's surface.

"He doesn't stop. He will not stop. Eliza, and myself, and now my baby sister. He did it, Jane, he did it all; it was because of him that Liza ran away, but that was not enough: he put me here."

I stared. I knew, had sensed, that Mr. Emrick had some

knowledge of my sister's fate, had been a presence in the woods that day, had seen, heard, had, perhaps, touched; his touch perhaps the agent which had sent my sister headlong to her death. But my mind had not made the leap from accidental death to murder.

"I was getting out of Mr. Emrick's way. I had planned a long day in the woods, I had corn muffins and tomatoes and an apple; I ate blackberries.

"I did not see him come. He grabbed me from behind; I choked on blackberries and couldn't scream, I couldn't breathe, he had me on the ground before I even knew what happened. It hurt; it hurt; he hurt me terribly inside: I bled, I tore, I broke. I felt my blood run, faster; and still he did not stop.

"He finished and I couldn't move; I saw his face at last, all stained with blood and blackberries, and white teeth smiling at me.

"He told me to get up. I couldn't. He lifted me and the blood welled; I saw it in his eyes then, just a moment's fear and then determination. He knew well he couldn't bring me home, pretend that nothing had happened.

"It hurt me being carried. He stumbled, limping, cursing: the woods were hostile, hating him. The pond hated, too, but it welcomed me with open arms. The water cooled and soothed me, and cleansed my wound; its bottom grass was soft, a green and gentle bed. I saw the murderer's hands above, washing off my blood, but I was too weak to move.

"But don't you worry, sisterlil; I'm stronger now. Much stronger."

I saw my sister's body, the length of bony limbs, a look of strength in spite of insubstantial flesh. Thin toes and fingers tipped by pearly claw-length nails. Her eyes cold, hard, green bottom stones.

✦ ✦ ✦

Late summer's heat oppresses us; we rock, and fan, drink cool liquids. Mr. Emrick sleeps on the porch swing. At night I hear how Mama tosses in her bed.

A late-night fire; a neighbor's life in ruins. We go to him, our being there a silent statement of our sympathy, an offer of support. We children search for strayed chickens and pig survivors. The men go through the smoking rubble, to see if anything is salvageable; they drink, and smoke, their callused hands are gentle on the widower's bent shoulders. The women try to clean what's left, they serve their home-cooked food. I notice how the women move away from Mr. Emrick's hands, their sympathetic eyes avoiding Mama's.

Sunset: the children are sent home, along with older siblings to keep watch. I'm ten; I don't need supervision.

As I walk through the hot dusk I am calm. It is the time; I've known for months the time would come. An hour from now, or two, he'll slip away. He'll come for me. I fan myself on the porch swing. I wait for him.

Augusta is my sister. I trust my sister. She will not let him harm me. Over and over, she has told me what to do.

The night is moonless. There is no wind. Even the mosquitoes are too hot to bite. My foot is dangling from the porch swing, the only motion in the night.

He is here. He is standing in the yard, looking at me. Though it is too dark to see, he knows my presence, as I know his. His voice is soft.

"Want to go fishing, Janey?"

I get up. My feet are hot and sweaty in my sneakers; my jeans cling. I'm dressed for walking. He takes a forward step, and I move back. We are both accustomed to the dark; though my feet are silent, he will find me. When I head into the woods I can feel his smile, stirring the tiny hairs on the nape of my neck.

I am small; he's large. I slip through honeysuckle, under brambles; low-hanging branches do not slap me. I can hear his progress, and his curses.

The ground is slick with dew. And there are sounds: small rustlings, sighs, a plaintive nightbird cry. Each of my steps produces different odors, intensifying thick miasma damply rich with crushed green life and heat-bloated decay; I'm glad my feet are sneaker-covered, and that I can't see what they touch. My sweat smells differently, tainted by the sodden air which saves each hint of rot and overripeness, a musky reek of den and death, as if the woods themselves were one great swollen trap, lair and stalker both.

I'm born here; my home is in the woods. It seems fitting, all the same, their sudden alienness: the safety of my home has disappeared beyond the stranger's smile, and my fear has turned to anger; I feel the woods echoing my resentment at his presence, my rage is amplified; I know each twig will lash him, and each thorn will rip. Can fury be revoked?

Thickly grown vines touch lightly, I crawl beneath their stiff embrace, my hands grip damp and rotting leaves. I scramble steeply up, loose soil moving beneath my caked knees. Hidden rocks shift loosely, evasive fish in water; I hear the muted rattle of their flight, a curse below.

Dead trees, moss-clad, outline the ridge. I touch soft, horrid growths which crumble wetly in my hand; I slip, and fall. Harsh breathing just below me, a heavy body struggling with the shifting hillside: a hand touches my foot, grabs hold, lets go again as treacherous dirt gives way beneath him. My breathing harsh as well, now, I must run; I hear his heavy steps, the sound of brambles tearing cloth but no more curses: he is listening.

High on the grass-grown ridge I am still small, and he is large, his legs take giant strides, his fury stronger than my own. Augusta, sister, help me!

Black shadow swoops, mute night wings close enough to move the air beside my cheek, another just behind; I hear his stride break, heavy body thud against the ground, voice raised in a yell of shock. Against the stars I see bats, black on black, soundless; I never saw them flock before. They swoop, smoke-swift, are gone.

He is up, but the fury of his stride is tinged with caution as he follows me once more down through the woods, both of us enfolded in its hot and putrid breath. I feel as if I'm in a mouth, feet slipping on the furry tongue, among moss-grown, cavity-riddled fangs; I'm moving down, down, down, toward the maw.

No windbreath stirs the pond. The darkness glows above it, faintly luminescent, the water pale patina, soft green ice. I fear my foot will break it.

Once more, he's near. Green-tinged, we pause among the cattails, both breathing choppily. His bulk towers above me. He extends one hand, as to a skittish dog; the other scratches at his crotch, and lingers there. I move back warily, sideways, I do not take my eyes from him; I edge toward the curve of soft moss where I always meet my sister.

"You fish here often, Janey?"

I nod. My eyes are on him as I slowly pull my shirt out of my jeans, undo two buttons, bend my head to blow softly between my breasts, to cool the sweat there. I feel very young, and very old; I am performing as Augusta told me but there is suddenly a woman inside me, an ageless female who directs my hands, my eyes, my body's movements: timeless signals. I know exactly what I'm doing.

"And is the fishing good?"

"Always."

I let my eyes speak to him, knowing that the pond is mirrored there, within them, deep and green.

Inside me, a small girl trembles as I finish undoing my buttons, pulling off my shirt; I shake my sweat-dark hair loose, it flows to my waist, cradling my nipples: two small, pale peaks.

He is breathing hard, his unconscious hands are restless, touching this and that part of him as he stalks me softly round the pond. I match each step of his with one of mine.

My jeans are open, but my sweaty sneakers hug my feet, laces wet and dirt-encrusted; I need time, and space.

"Stop," I say. "I want to swim. I'm hot. I'm dirty. Aren't you? Want to swim with me?"

He stops, uncertainly, intrigued as well as snubbed by my defiant words, the nuances of my behavior: he looks at me, sees Jane, the child, but sees as well a woman, self-aware, seductive, ripe; a match for him. His momentary hesitation is enough. I'm nude; the water, warm, laps at my naked feet. He stands still. In his eyes I see a memory, a picture from another summer: the body of another child of ten with long, red hair has been superimposed on mine; my sister Augusta. Her blood, black in the night, pours down her legs, hot on the ground.

I feel a movement from the pond, a faint ripple of water at my ankles. It is not my voice that calls to him but only I can hear the difference. He sheds his clothes, at her command; his large white body shines with sweat, faintly green-lit. It is the first time I have seen the naked body of a man: the child within me trembles.

My sister beckons him with my hand, as she spoke

through my mouth; she shakes my head to free my hair, which flows behind me now, exposing me. He comes toward me.

Taking a step backward, I slip, but my flat, graceless fall becomes, somehow, a water-jeweled arc of beauty: I'm swimming, and I hear his strokes behind me.

The night is moonless and yet much too bright; I want to close my eyes but I must look. We are no longer two, but three. I see his face change as she touches him, his momentary pleasure, then confusion when he sees me treading water well beyond his reach. With fear already in his eyes, he cannot help himself, his mouth goes softly brutal, sighing as he reaches for the pleasure-giving hand.

Does he know her? She rises momentarily, my sister; her large teeth grin through long, wet hair, she nips his earlobe playfully and presses close. She is my size, though thinner: her body, outlined against his, a darker shade of pale, her bone-limbed strength twines round him, small enveloping large. He stares at me, his mouth an opening scream; her kiss steals sound and breath, he chokes, his stark eyes begging me.

I tread water. I cannot look: I cannot look away. My sister, Augusta, is ten; who is this miniwoman coiling pond-green round his body in a dreadful parody of passion, hungry mouth devouring murderer's lips?

Cold now, water-logged, I tremble, scared to move. His head is disappearing, shiny wet-white skin beneath the undulating surface. One hand reaches, grasps for air.

I am alone.

I tremble, and the water trembles with me. I cannot move. Cool hands: my sister's. My chilled body meets the shore. I crawl. I retch. I cry. The earth is damp; the air is fetid, thick with fear and greenreek. I find my shirt and hug it close. My jeans. My shoes. My way home.

✦ ✦ ✦

I've cut my hair short. And I never want to touch a man for love. The world is cold; I hide beneath the covers of my bed; I will not read, or dream.

The pond is still. I watch it sometimes from the ridge. At times I ache with missing her: Augusta; sister.

But she is not alone; she plays with Mr. Emrick. And I'm afraid: if he should rise, and smile at me?

SAMBA SENTADO

by Karen Haber

Karen Haber was born in Bronxville, New York, grew up in the suburbs of New York City and has lived in Pennsylvania, Missouri, Texas, Paraguay, and Brazil. She planned to be a poet until she perceived the inequities between aesthetic and economic compensation in the field. She received a B.A. in journalism and worked as a nonfiction writer and editor, lately concentrating on artists and art-related subjects for *American Artist, Southwest Art*, and other magazines. She began writing fiction, especially science fiction and fantasy in 1986. This is the fourth short story she's written but the third she's sold; other stories have sold to *F & SF, Heroes in Hell*, and *The Fleet*. She is under contract to Bantam/Doubleday (Foundation/Spectra) for a series of science fiction novels entitled "The Mutant Season," and, with her husband, is editing the "Universe" anthology, also for Spectra. She lives with her husband, writer Robert Silverberg, in the San Francisco Bay area, collects primitive and modern art, and enjoys bonsai and rose gardening.

The title means "Dance of the Initiates," and with this tale Karen shows her fine mastery of the dark side of us.

✦ ✦ ✦

I was sitting on the beach at Ipanema four days after New Year's when my husband's body washed up. I was just finishing my third caipirinha and watching the sweat glisten on my knees and the breakers roll in from the turquoise Atlantic when the translucent arc of a green wave deposited Jim on the wet sand.

Around me, lithe, bronzed Cariocas cavorted on the sand, hugging, preening, reading fashion magazines, rubbing oil into glowing arms and legs. None of them seemed to notice the body, face down, freckled shoulders bobbing gently each time the waves washed under it. But I knew it was Jim. It was the fourth time I'd seen his corpse this week.

My stomach tightened into painful cramps. But I made myself get up and casually stroll down toward the water. Nudge the body with my toe. It felt rubbery. Real. But two children frisking with their pet spaniel splashed right through Jim's knees as if they weren't there.

I returned to my blanket. Sat down. Nursed my drink and counted the heat waves rising from the sand until my heart rate slowed. I began to wish I'd never gone to see that fortune-teller.

✦ ✦ ✦

The last time I talked to Jim, he'd been in Scarsdale. With Gwen. His former accountant. Damn artistic imagination—it was too easy to imagine them together in her tidy bedroom, wrinkling the peach percale beneath them in their passion. Exactly when they had moved from balance sheets to bedsheets, I could only guess. Probably while I'd been preparing for my last show. Up late painting, all night, all day. I was honed. Focused. The red dots beside each painting on opening night merely confirmed what I already knew.

"You're the rage of SoHo," Sandy, my agent, said, kissing me on the cheek and spilling his champagne along the white pleats of his tuxedo shirt. "They're calling your work contemporary primitivism; pictographs for the eighties!"

"So those painting lessons finally paid off," my father said over the hissing phone connection from San Diego.

"At least you're good at something," my husband said,

as he slowly closed the door behind him, leaving me alone with my triumph.

I did what every humiliated, abandoned wife does. Badgered Jim's friends and co-workers for advice. Stopped sleeping. Cried. Stopped eating. Forged and betrayed confidences. I even went to see my mother-in-law in Bronxville, who told me all about the need for sacrifice in a marriage. Finally, every ritual exhausted, I surrendered and fled.

December in New York is cold and lonely. I decided to melt the ice.

✦ ✦ ✦

I flew south, seeking heat and light, new sensation to erase old experience, like naphtha on a bloodstain. I've always hated crowds—I prefer to be alone, where I can maintain control over everything—but my plan was to let go, immersing myself in ten million people, all in furious motion; dancing, eating, drinking, making love, murdering, begging, and stealing. Isolated among the celebrants, I would move at half speed, a somnambulist annealed by the noise, the heat, my pain, and the rum.

Alice, my sister, lives in Rio with her husband, Peter, a loyal employee of Royal Dutch Shell. Together, they run a little exporting business on the side. She is many things I am not: patient, cheerful, and tolerant of others' excesses, especially those of her older sister. She was a convenient hideout, located in a semitropical paradise, or so I thought.

What I discovered is that Rio is a terrific place to hide if you're a war criminal, tax dodger, or having an illicit affair. If you're suffering from unrequited love, it's purgatory.

I hid in my own skin, shedding my jeans for a tonga

bikini two sizes too small. I browned myself on the white crescent beach, dark, wiry hair gilding in the sunlight, hazel eyes hidden behind dark glasses. I watched all the sleek, glossy lovers frolicking on the beach, holding hands, kissing long and loudly, and tried hard not to think. The paint flaked from my hands. I waited for the ache to fade from my heart.

The day after I arrived, Alice suggested a visit to her favorite fortune-teller. I tried to be polite, but I've never had much patience for mumbo jumbo.

"You really believe that stuff, Allie?"

She nodded, then giggled, pink cheeks blushing pinker. Where had my sister gotten that delicate coloring, nothing like my own? Nordic gypsies?

"Of course. How else did I know to dump that shipment of tablecloths? Don't look at me like that, Jo. Everybody I know here goes to one fortune-teller or another."

"Why?"

She shrugged. "Maybe they don't have anything better to do. How should I know? Anyway, I like going to Madame Bruna. She's helped me a lot. You should come with me after lunch."

"Maybe you're right," I said. The afternoon stretched like a desert into the distance, with only the promise of rum to break my long trek across it. "Let's go."

An hour later, we were in Botafogo, beyond the Rio Sul shopping mall, bumping along a muddy road toward a small cluster of brick houses. We stopped outside a gate with a blue door and got out of the Peugeot. Alice clapped her hands twice.

The door swung open—a small child with a dirty nose and bare feet beamed up at my sister. She handed him a piece of hard candy and he ran off chortling in Portuguese. Dusty hens herded by a green-feathered rooster scooted across the yard, complaining loudly. We joined several other clients on a breezy patio and waited our turn.

Alice went first, then stayed around to translate for me. Madame Bruna was fiftyish, fleshy, pale, with red hair and tired eyes. She looked at me, nodded, and made a quick observation to Alice, placing the cards on the table before me.

"She says you've been crying a lot. Cut the cards."

I did and waited. She laid out four rows of four cards in front of me. Most of them were hearts. She frowned, tapped two of them, and spoke again.

"She says that you are in pain. Someone far away is very angry and confused. You have been hurt."

"So far, so good."

The medium replaced the cards with a row of four others; mostly diamonds this time.

"She says that you have artistic vision. Beware of what that vision may show you. Revenge is tempting. Be careful. She wants to know if you will go to the beach at New Year's."

"Why?" Despite the humid heat, gooseflesh prickled up my arms.

The medium reshuffled the cards, had me cut them again and again, laid out four rows: clubs and diamonds. She stared at me in a peculiar, penetrating way, made a quick observation to Alice, shrugged, gathered the cards together. This felt less and less like a diversion.

"She says that the beach is a prominent symbol, the waters. The turning of the year is significant for you. But under no condition attend the *macumba* ceremony."

The words sent a chill through me, right up the back of my neck. Macumba ceremony?

Madame Bruna was repinning her shawls around her shoulders—the audience was obviously over.

"That's it?" I turned to Allie, but she shook her head and gestured toward the exit. We made our way out through the deserted yard, stepping over the chicken shit.

Back in the car, I was confused, dissatisfied.

"What did she mean about going to the beach?"

Allie shrugged. "At midnight on New Year's Eve. Everybody dresses in white and goes to the beach, to throw white roses into the waves. If the sea carries the roses away, their wishes for the next year will come true."

"That seems simple enough. And symbolic, to boot. But what's this macumba thing I should beware of?"

"The local voodoo. The slaves brought it over from Africa. To Bahia. It permeates religious life in Brazil. Those ladies with the white turbans that you noticed last week at the gypsy market? They're macumba priestesses."

"I thought this was supposed to be a Catholic country!"

"Only on the outside. Oh, come on, Joanna. Don't look so skeptical. So the church serves double duty here. The priests just wink. Everybody here practices it."

"Even you?"

"No. It's forbidden to foreigners."

"Sounds interesting in an anthropological way."

"I'd stay away from it if I were you, Jo."

"Fine. I'd just as soon stay away from this entire New Year's thing. You know how I feel about crowds. Not to mention voodoo."

"Well, going to the beach on New Year's can't hurt, can it? Honestly, Jo, it's not like I'm trying to make you do something bad! I think it sounds like fun. Do what you want. You always do." She sounded disgusted.

I didn't blame her. She'd been wonderfully patient with me since I cast myself on her doorstep with twenty-four hours' notice. I put on my best wheedling voice. The one

I'd used when we were kids and I wanted her forgiveness after taking the biggest slice of cake.

"Come on, Allie. I'm sorry. It's a good idea. You were good to think of it. Of course we'll go to the beach on New Year's. I can't wait."

✦ ✦ ✦

Dinner was late. No self-respecting Carioca would think of eating before nine at night. By eleven-thirty, we'd finished up at the bustling *churrascaria*. The steaming plates of grilled fish and meat and potatoes had vanished. The toasts to the coming year had been made. It was a party of Shell employees, with the boss picking up the bill. I wasn't hungry. I drank out of boredom. After all, it was New Year's Eve.

I wore a white skirt, blouse, and sandals. I hated white—it was a boring color. Virginal and ridiculous. But appropriate for a reluctant pilgrimage. My hair, pinned back in a twist with large, sharp hairpins, sent shooting pains across the back of my neck each time I moved my head. Cheap white plastic earrings dangled from my earlobes—I knew better than to wear anything worth stealing on the streets of Rio. My money and house key were pinned in my bra. In my right hand, I clutched a white rose.

We left the restaurant and crossed Avenida Atlantica to Copacabana Beach, already packed with white-garbed Cariocas. A cool breeze, ocean-driven, bounced fine particles of sand off my cheeks. Fireworks burst above the mob, leaving spectral flashes behind my eyelids. A shower of golden sparks cascaded from the top of the Hotel Caesar Park. Music from a hundred outdoor speakers and throats pulsed and rumbled.

A crowd had gathered around a circle of large black women who were wearing lacy white gowns; their puffed sleeves and wide hoop skirts glowed in the light of candles and beach fires. Each proud head bore an immaculate turban—the mark of the macumba priestess? Sweat beaded their cheeks. Their eyes rolled back in their heads in private ecstasy. As they circled together in their noble, hip-swaying dance, the crowd shouted approval, a high, wild keening sound. The skin on the back of my neck felt rigid and cold.

They danced around a shallow, hand-dug crater in the sand. It was filled with candles, playing cards, facial powders, and wine bottles. Boring, familiar offerings. Where were the goats' intestines? The bread soaked in menstrual blood? All those exotic, creepy voodoo things I'd watched on the Late Show? Then I saw them. Neither entrails nor animal sacrifices, but oddly carved bits of soldered, burnished metal reflecting the firelight. Junkyard scraps? Abstract sculpture? Tribal artwork? I couldn't get close enough to tell.

The women moved to their own eerie rhythm, oblivious to the spectators, lost in private reveries. A tall man swaying next to me offered a sticky brown glass bottle. The liquid it contained was fruity and rich, almost too sweet, but my throat was dry. I swallowed gratefully, and swallowed again. Handed it back and he melted away into the crowd.

"I'm going to get a closer look," I told Alice, and pushed forward through the thronged bodies. The glow of the candles compelled me with a hypnotic warmth. All warnings were forgotten now. Hadn't I come to Brazil seeking warmth? New experience?

I began to sway to the beat that came pulsing up through the sand, through my feet. All around me, people were nodding and dancing. I was one with them. With the sand and the circle. The priestesses welcomed me into their procession. I joined their dance eagerly, seemed to know the steps instinctively.

I don't know how long we writhed together before the women to my right and left took my hands and led me away from the circle, down the beach, toward the waves. They pantomimed a tossing gesture, and I complied, throwing my rose far overhead, away, into the opaque waves. As it was carried out to sea, I realized that I'd forgotten to make a wish. But I had no time to think about it. My companions seized me by either arm and led me away, behind some rocks. A passage had been carved between the two rocks—by the surf?

We moved along the passageway, sloping downward—the noise from the beach faded. The beach sand gave way to solid rock, carved into narrow stairs. Each priestess held a candle in her free hand to guide our way. The passage gradually widened into a larger chamber. We stopped here and my companions gestured impatiently for me to remove my shoes. Each of them put a hand under my elbows and propelled me roughly into a massive amphitheater carved from stone beneath the beach—how long ago? By renegade slaves and voodoo worshipers? I trembled with excitement, breathing quickly in shallow gulps.

A turbaned, lace-garbed congregation was gathered here, humming a hypnotic melody, nodding and swaying side to side, eyes closed. They faced an altar. My two companions shoved me toward it and melted into the crowd. I turned to look back toward the way we'd come. A sea of impassive, almost hostile faces blocked my view. My excitement segued into fright. I gasped for air, parched. My tongue felt like leather. What was I doing here? Why had I left the warmth of the beach? Why hadn't I listened to the fortune-teller?

The altarpiece was massive, yet intricate, decorated by strange hieroglyphics engraved in the burnished metal or bone. Candles punctuated its golden expanse, winking from carved recesses. My knees buckled at the sense of age emanating from it; what perversely ancient civilization steeped in bloody ritual had forged this masterpiece? I wanted to study the thing. To paint it. I wanted to turn and run. But the way was blocked by a thousand swaying bodies and opaque eyes.

A statuesque black woman in golden, beaded robes moved forward, and a strange parody of high mass began. The celebrants gathered before her to receive communion, each raising a hand before her face, then sipping from a burnished cup. Each swallowed, smiled, and then closed her eyes in some private reverie, moving aside to nod and hum. I joined them, glancing up into the head priestess's remarkable golden eyes. She could have been carved from the same golden stuff as the altarpiece. She looked down upon me as a god views a fly.

I lowered my head to the cup and, in the surface of the liquor, saw a reflection, burning like a candle flame.

The cup held the image of a ship of odd design, carved in harsh angles and spiny points ending in enraged faces; mouths open, shouting defiance. It was caught in a horrific gale, slammed by harsh winds and high seas, tossing from wave to wave like a tin cup. The crew, desperate, raced about the deck like ants, frantically bailing water, reknotting rigging, only to have the ropes torn from their hands and the raging water swamp the deck, washing the hapless sailors into the ravenous waves. And I was on that tossing deck, golden-skinned, long-legged, running, bailing the brackish water in frantic spurts, crying out in a liquid, husky tongue to my brothers and sisters to bring the buckets, bring more buckets, quickly.

The ship's hull broke open like a cracked egg, spewing forth a cargo of exotic men and women, strange pieces of metal, and precious objects. Our tribal heritage. I could hear the cries of those drowning; desperate screams in our strange, fluting language. I paddled feebly, legs entangled by my skirts. I was drowning, mouth and throat filling with salt seawater. The ship disappeared beneath the waves with a dreadful groan. In its wake, corpses floated beside bales of cloth, casks. A piece of bulkhead floated by. I grabbed it, clung.

I was not alone. Nearby, a male and female were clinging to a wooden barrel, also afloat in the rocky sea. They could have been the priestess's brother and sister, so strong was the resemblance. We paddled ashore. Once safe, we opened the cask, which formed a series of asymmetrical walls; shelters. And altars.

Time passed. The male shared his seed with us both. Many times we accepted his ritual offering, eyes rolling back in trance state. We bore a generation of children, saw them grow straight and tall. From them, other generations emerged, to farm, to dance, circling in strange patterns about the ritual structure that I should know . . . did know . . . how to worship. As they added to it, I saw that it was an altarpiece of human bone, burnished to a fine, golden gloss like antique ivory, incised with the same rippling, geometric patterns that we cut into our flesh as ritual scarification. Words floated before me: *candomblé, yalorixa, exu* . . . words with many meanings. Voodoo meanings.

The vision rippled, wind across water. I was back in the stone chamber. Unchanged. Before I could speak, the priestess seized my hand and drew a golden knife across my right forefinger in a clean, crescent cut. She held it to drip into the chalice. I gasped in surprise, but there was no pain. Each celebrant in turn had contributed her precious essence to the cup. We were commingled there. We were community. It was The Way.

I looked up at the priestess. Our eyes met. She nodded and smiled. I lowered my head to the cup. Numbly, I closed my eyes and drank. The taste was not unpleasant, musky and rich, with that same fruity essence. I opened my eyes.

The vision changed. I was looking in a mirror. My face was moving, changing shape. First square, then oblong. Green, then red, auras flickered along my jawline, around my eyeballs. Color complements, a tiny voice, ever the artist, noted giddily somewhere in my cerebrum. My forehead broadened, sloped, eyes squinting shut from the weight of my brow. My teeth elongated, became sharp and pointed; I smiled a carnivore's smile. I was bestial. Ferocious. I would tear out men's souls with my claws and teeth. *Quibungo!*

The vision changed yet again, moved away from my face to a photograph pinned on a corkboard; the wedding picture I kept in my studio. But something was wrong with it. One half of it seemed to be crumpling inward, burning. Obliterating that portion of the photo—the part with Jim's image. The flames licked around my face but didn't touch me. Dizzy with the heat, I rent the fabric of my skirt, my blouse—anything to cool off. Sweat streamed from me. My hair was soaked. I stripped away my underwear. Stripped away layers. I was white-hot, transparent. I kept carving away, knowing that when I reached the core there would be only a howling, molten emptiness. I stumbled toward the high priestess. Yalorixa, help me,

I whispered as I fell, clutching at the beaded hem of her gown. She did not look down.

"Jo? Joanna? Are you all right?"

Someone was shaking my arm.

"Joanna, answer me!" The sting of a palm against my cheek, slapping, then slapping again, distracted me.

I was no longer in the chamber. The *semba*—celebrants—were gone. A pale, blonde woman in a white dress was slapping my face. I remembered that she was my sister. That I was on the beach in Rio. At New Year's. I looked down at my bare feet in confusion. Where were my shoes?

"Joanna, what's wrong?"

I took a deep breath. The vision of the cup, the blood, the shipwreck, and the *sentados,* the initiates, wavered before me, ghosts seen through grey smoke. An image of myself as seen in a dark mirror, misshapen and monstrous. How could I tell Alice what had happened? How could she believe me?

"Whew. Some party," I mumbled, wiping my forehead. "I guess I've just had a little too much to drink. Made me dizzy." I smiled sheepishly.

Behind Alice, Peter smiled back, obviously relieved that his crazy sister-in-law was not going to ruin the evening.

"Better watch out for that Brazilian rum," he said. "It'll get you every time."

Alice watched me closely.

"Do you want to go back to the apartment, Jo?"

I shook my head. "No, it's New Year's. I feel like kicking up my heels," I lied. "Let's go dancing."

As we moved off the beach I felt something clenched tightly in my palm. It was a golden bead, carved with strangely familiar crescent-shaped hieroglyphics. I tucked it into my bra, above my pounding heart.

✦ ✦ ✦

We all slept late the next day, then headed for the beach. I felt light-headed, reflexes displaced by a hangover and too little sleep. The sun melted me into the sand. I lay there like an offering. I wanted to become a beach rock. To be wise and ages old. To never drink again.

I opened one eye and peered out toward the water. What was that dark object interrupting the sun's reflected glitter? A raft? A log? As I watched, it resolved into a body. A drowned body. A big wave carried it onto the sand. Left it lying on its back, dark hair strewn with seaweed, mouth gaping open like a surprised fish, sightless eyes staring into the the sun. It was Jim. I didn't breathe for a full minute.

"It can't be," I whispered. My head felt like it was going to explode.

It was Jim. Face bloated, features blackening, but I recognized him all the same. I jammed the scream back into my throat, jumped up, pointed at him, gasping. Peter looked up, alarmed.

"Jo, what is it?"

"The b-b-body!" I stammered.

"What body? There's nothing there."

I stared at my brother-in-law. He was obviously telling the truth. I looked down the beach. Jim's body was gone. I sank down on the sand, holding my head.

"I'm sorry, Peter. I was just thinking that my body feels like it's made of sand. This awful hangover is making me punchy." I tried to look sheepish.

"Don't worry about it." He laughed. "Everybody feels that way on New Year's Day."

I settled back onto my blanket and hoped that I would

never feel this way again. I ventured a look toward water's edge. Jim's corpse was back. He never moved.

✦ ✦ ✦

Over the next three days, I learned to stay calm, not to betray my horror and disbelief each time Jim's body washed up. It was always the same thing. I would notice a dark, immobile shape in the surf, and sure enough, he would come floating in. Again, and again. And no one but me ever saw him, as far as I could tell. I began to wear the golden bead I'd found on New Year's Eve. Somehow, I felt better having it bounce against my collarbone as I walked, suspended on a golden cord. It gave me courage.

So the fourth time Jim's body came washing up onto Ipanema Beach, I poked at it idly with my foot, went back to my blanket, and took another sip of my drink.

"I'm going in for a quick dip before lunch. Want to come?" Alice's voice sounded loud in my ears.

I squinted up at her and shook my head, then watched her dive into the surf, right next to her brother-in-law's body. If her aim had been any less certain, she would have landed right on him. I touched the bead at my throat. Jim vanished. My chest felt less constricted.

In the taxi on the way back to the apartment, Jim's corpse appeared in the back seat. My gasp made Alice turn in alarm to peer at me. All she saw was her crazy sister. All I could see were Jim's eyes, wide open, mottled yellow like aging linoleum. As the taxi slowed down for a light, I jumped out the door.

Allie hurriedly paid the cabbie and followed me. We were a block from the apartment. She ran to catch up with me.

"I felt a little carsick," I muttered. "Just thought a walk might help."

"You could at least have said something." I shrugged an apology as the doorman admitted us into the cool lobby. There was a telex waiting for me by the mailbox. A fire in Scarsdale. Jim's body hadn't been found. Nothing left.

A very small, calm voice in my head said that at least it hadn't been me—my suburban studio was safe. I crumpled the message. Waited for it to vanish like my visions. It stayed crumpled in my fist. This hadn't been part of my plans at all. Jim dead? I'd left the vision of his corpse in the taxi. Wasn't this just a game I was playing in Rio, on the beach? The scream that had been lying dormant since my arrival began to build, surging toward my throat.

I turned toward Alice, but she was gone. The macumba priestess, the yalorixa from last evening, stood in the lobby, watching me impassively. Slowly, she raised her right hand, extended it, palm up, toward me. Her hand was empty.

"You may keep your heart's desire," she said, voice vibrant and deep. "There are many ways to smooth your path, *ekedi pequena*. Or to revenge. Look to *mãe d'água*—the mother of water. You will choose."

I closed my eyes. When I opened them, I was lying on the beach and Allie was shaking the saltwater out of her hair.

"Well, you certainly were fast asleep," she said. "Feel like some lunch?"

I sighed in relief. A dream. No telex. No fire. I took a deep breath and nodded quickly. Gathering up my blanket, I looked down at my hand and saw the fingers turn golden, slim, impossibly elongated. The scar where the yalorixa had made her ritual incision, a crescent pattern, throbbed slowly. I reached for the bead at my throat. Felt my heartbeat slowing, fingers shortening. What was happening to me? Somewhere, I found my voice.

"Let's go back to the apartment, okay? I feel like changing before lunch. Maybe I'll do a little sightseeing." I wanted to get off the beach and away from drowned visions.

✦ ✦ ✦

The trolley slid along the almost perpendicular rail bed to Corcovado, complaining occasionally as the brakes were applied. I was anxious to arrive, to touch the concrete Christo. That streamlined icon, arms outstretched in forgiveness above the sinning, glistening city.

Singing schoolchildren and tourists weighed down with cyclopean cameras filled the compartment. It was not a cool ride, and we made a sodden group, straggling up the stairs, past the concession stands and souvenir shops, professional photographers snapping "candid" photos which they transferred to souvenir dishes and tried to sell. I wondered idly about their inventory—who wanted to eat off a plate with their own face on it?

I lumbered up the remaining steps toward the statue. Sitting in his benevolent shade, I sketched a few flowering aloes. I hadn't done such realistic stuff in years. It felt good. Then my drawings took on a more abstract look, filled with rounded shapes, inscribed symbols, skulls and bones. I couldn't stop—it felt like automatic writing. My heart was beating out the rhythm of the sentado dance; the pulse of macumba initiates. I reached for the golden bead. The beat only intensified.

With great effort, I closed the sketchbook. Lowered my head to my knees and felt my pulse calming. I waited until the crowd near the entrance to the statue had diminished. Reached up, slid the necklace with the golden bead over my head and tucked it into a corner at the statue's base, below the Christo's big toe. Maybe he would know what to do with it. Relieved, I left the statue, feeling a refreshing breeze lift my hair off my neck. The ride back down the mountain was pleasant.

Leaving the tram station after my descent, I felt my stomach rumble. When had I last eaten? I stopped in Ipanema and bought an empanada and a Cuba Libre at a sidewalk cafe. The coconut-milk-flavored turnover was delicious—I tried not to gulp it down. As I munched, my back began to itch. I felt like someone was staring at me. I looked around quickly. Three tables away, a fleshy woman with red hair and tired eyes sat watching me. It was Madame Bruna, my fortune-teller. She smiled sadly and shook her head. I began to greet her, then remembered that she spoke no English. To me, Portuguese was still a confusing, sexy jumble of sounds, not quite Spanish. I shrugged at her sheepishly, took another bite of empanada, and when I looked up again, she was gone.

✦ ✦ ✦

When I got back to the apartment, it was empty. The percussion of traffic bounced up twelve stories, off the elegant white high-rise facades as if climbing canyon walls into the cool, bronze-carpeted rooms. Otherwise, the place was as silent as a cave.

I went into my bedroom to change for the beach. When I opened my lingerie drawer, I saw a flash of gold. The engraved bead I had left at Corcovado glinted up at me from a tiny bowl. I felt a vein throbbing in my throat. I had left the bead at the statue, hadn't I?

I slammed the drawer shut. At the beach, I swam hard, forcing all thoughts of beads, visions, strangeness from my mind, reveling in the pure joy of physical exertion.

Afterward, I lay panting on my blanket, seawater trickling down my legs. A vendor sold me an ice bar, and I sat up, sucking on it, dripping raspberry juice down my chin. My gaze wandered down toward the water. I nearly choked on the ice as I saw Jim's body wash up again.

I heard the yalorixa's voice in my ear.

"*Filha de santo,* daughter of the gods, you will choose."

A bass rumble like a hundred heartbeats vibrated in my skull, punctuated by the slap of bare feet moving over stone in a rhythmic dance, of ritual words incanted to the *pandeiro*'s drumbeat: *acheche,* the funeral rite. And *opele,* revenge.

I jumped up, turned my back on Jim's corpse, and began walking down the beach. As I moved, I heard men clicking their tongues in appreciation; the sign of a Carioca's approval. I didn't care. I just wanted to put space between me and my visions. But Jim was relentless. He washed up again and again, between the young mothers and their toddlers, the students playing paddle ball at water's edge, the elderly men with sagging bellies dunking themselves to wash away sweat. Soon I was running. I would have run all the way to Cabo Frio but I ran out of breath instead. Finally, I went back to the apartment.

Allie was there, needlepointing a pillow.

"Have a good afternoon?" she asked cheerfully.

I nodded. Walked into my bedroom, opened the drawer of my dresser. The bead was still there. I slipped it back over my head. Felt calmer. Walked back out into the living room.

"Jim called," my sister said, a little too casually. "He sounded kind of strange. Nervous, I guess. Anyway, he asked to talk to you."

"What'd you say?"

"Well, not much, although I'd love to give him a good kick in the ass, Jo. Honestly, what do you see in him? He's such a rat."

I couldn't tell her about the sense of humor, the playful tenderness, the way he'd touched me in bed. How I'd loved to stroke the downy hair on his forearms. To me, he was art in motion.

I shrugged, touched the bead at my throat. My voice sounded tight.

"I dunno. I'll call him later."

"Whatever you want. You also got a telex from your agent. He wants to know when you're coming back."

Back to New York? It seemed impossible; a foreign place now, filled with ice and snow, filled with cold strangers. I shrugged the thought off.

✦ ✦ ✦

I phoned Jim at ten o'clock that night. He answered on the second ring.

"Jo?" His voice sounded warm. Nervous.

"Yeah. How are you?" My throat felt tight.

"Okay. I miss you, Jo."

"Where's Gwen?"

"Gone. It was a mistake, Jo. I swear it. I want to see you. Come home."

I touched the bead at my throat.

The phone rang for the eighth time. Finally, the answering machine came on. The message was in Gwen's voice: "You have reached 555-1320. Please leave your message at the sound of the beep."

Wordlessly, I hung up. Leaned my head against the wall. Yalorixa, show me the way, I prayed. I don't know what to do. I thought of the beach at night. Of cool breezes. Put on my jacket. A flower vendor stood outside the apartment—unusual after dark. She had golden eyes and skin. I purchased a white rose, crossed the street dodging a hell-bent motorcyclist and roaring Mercedes truck; Rio's ubiquitous night animals. I hailed a cab easily.

The beach was deserted save for a small fire where two figures were huddled. A persistent wind lifted my skirt. Blew my hair into my eyes.

It took me a full minute to reach the water's edge. White foam lace trailed each receding wave down the beach in the moonlight. I watched the triangular reflection of the moon on the bay. Took aim. Cast my flower far out over the black water, upward, toward the moon. It seemed to float suspended for a moment before descending. The waves carried it away into the night.

"The heart gives up its dead," I said, watching the flower recede. A dark shape appeared in the moon's light trail, pushed slowly ashore by the waves. It was a dead body. Gwen. The moonlight leached any remaining color from her face. She could have been a drowned porcelain doll, pale red hair floating in a tidal pool like seaweed. I could picture crabs dancing in that hair. Her blue eyes, sightless, stared up at me.

I touched the bead at my throat. The corpse remained. I bent down and touched her arm. Solid. Resilient flesh. Cool from the water, but not the flesh of a dead woman. Not yet.

I plucked a hair from her head. Turned toward the fire on the beach. I was not surprised to see the priestess waiting for me. She reached into her cloak, brought forth a small, pale object that squirmed in her grasp. A toad. When the mottled thing opened its eyes, they were pale blue. Like Gwen's.

Without hesitation, I stretched out my hand. Into it, the yalorixa placed the toad and a needle.

I threaded the strand of Gwen's hair through the needle's eye, knotted one end, and sewed the toad's mouth shut. The blue eyes watched me, unmoving. A corpse's eyes. I turned and cast the animal into the flames.

"Exu, she is yours," I cried.

An explosion of golden sparks cascaded into the air. The priestess nodded and smiled at me. She took my hand, and then our sisters appeared to join us in a stately dance around the fire pit. When I looked over my shoulder, the corpse was gone. At daybreak, the circle parted. I walked up the beach, happy, cleansed, tired. The beach was deserted.

✦ ✦ ✦

Allie was sitting in the living room wearing her robe and slippers when I walked in. She looked exhausted and furious.

"We called the police! The consulate! Where have you been?"

"Dancing."

"Well, I'm glad you've been having fun. We've been frantic."

"I'm sorry, Allie."

"I'm tired of hearing about how sorry you are, Jo! You're forever apologizing for your behavior as if you think that makes it okay. Then you just go and do something else irresponsible."

As she spoke, my irritation grew. I began to hear the drums pulsing again. I tried to breathe slowly.

"I think you're going native," she continued. "That's not a good idea here. It's dangerous. I know you wanted to get away from New York and all that, but maybe it's time for you to go home and get your life together."

Home? Where was home? Here, on the beach, with my filha de santo sisters. I began to imagine a vision of us all dancing together in white gowns at water's edge. But as I watched, another body floated into view. A body with long blonde hair and Nordic coloring. I took a deep breath, shook my head, and threw off the vision. I would have to be very careful. I didn't want to see my sister's corpse float by me as I sipped a rum and coke from my chair on Copacabana. She was right. It was time to leave. To stay away from people whom it would hurt me to hurt.

"I'll try to get plane reservations tomorrow, Allie. I'm sorry for all the trouble I've caused. You've been terrific." I hugged her, and was relieved when she hugged me back.

"I hope things work out for you, Jo."

I smiled. "I have a feeling my path will be smoother now. And if nothing else, I've got some great ideas for a series of paintings on ritual objects and patterns."

I walked toward my room, thinking about a warm shower before sleep. Allie called after me.

"Jim called again, at one in the morning. I told him you were out. He didn't sound happy. Why don't you try to reach him before you leave?"

I shrugged, smiled. "Maybe I will."

I touched the bead at my throat. I thought of the toad with the blue eyes. I was ready for the cold.

WHEN THUNDER WALKS

by Conda V. Douglas

Conda V. Douglas is a documentary film editor. Since 1979 she's worked in different locations on documentaries of cultures threatened by the incursion of modern Western technology and economics. She divides her time between Tucson, where her company is based, and Boise, Idaho, her home, and wherever the filmmaking is going on. Her first independent production was a short film entitled *Writ in Sand: The Art of Luther A. Douglas,* which showed her father's efforts to preserve the tradition of Navajo sandpainting. It won honors at several film festivals and is now being distributed to cable TV. Last year she was elected a Fellow of the International Explorers Club, one of very few women members, for her work with film and the Navajo. She sold her first article to *Seventeen* when she was fourteen.

Conda's father grew up among the Navajos, and his respect for their culture was passed on to her, as evidenced in the following.

✦ ✦ ✦

"Where is Coyote Tail?"

"I know of no man such named."

"Where is your grandfather?"

"There is no grandfather."

"The old man owns this place?"

"I own this place, Anglo woman."

"He was here yesterday. You know, the old man who always sits there?" I said, pointing to a battered kitchen chair behind the counter. Four times. Four times I'd asked and now he would have to tell me the truth. That's the Navajo way. It's not the first time I've used those endless

Navajo taboos to my advantage. Most of Navajo life is tied to their complex beliefs. The "rules and regs of the Navajo rip-off business" is how I think of it.

The sweat ran down the back of my neck and I could feel the heat rising off the wood floorboards. October and it feels like August. Crazy Navajo weather, I've had enough of this damn reservation.

I watched the young Navajo's face while I waited for him to answer me. He wore a traditional red velveteen shirt, the ubiquitous blue jeans, and a cheap belt with pieces of blue plastic as fake turquoise. I took one look at the belt and dismissed it. Made in Japan. Thirty years ago his belt would have been handmade with real turquoise and sold for a song. Now the Navajo hold degrees in business administration, use pocket calculators, and sales tax numbers. I've never seen this young Navajo before, must be the old man's grandson, or even great-grandson.

"Is Coyote Tail dead?" That ought to do it. The Navajo hate speaking of death. Might call up ghosts.

"No, ma'am. There's never been any old man here," he said. He glanced at the side of my face and turned his attention to some tourists. There was a time when he would not have looked away. That was before the accident tore my face apart. I looked good, once. They'd pieced me together until the insurance money ran out, then left the rest. Left the seams that distort the left side of my face, making me sneer always.

I waited while he served the tourists. I've waited over a year for this, I can wait a little longer. I felt the upbuilding of pressure that precedes a thunderstorm, the heavy heat.

The young Navajo returned and echoed my thoughts. "You going someplace you better hurry." He gestured at the open door of the trading post. In the distance thunderheads built up over the mesas. "This is Coyote's month and his kind of weather."

"What makes you think I'm in a hurry to get someplace?" Did he know where I was going? Had the old man told him?

"Anglos are always in a hurry." He handed me an amulet. "For you, to keep safe."

"What? Why—"

"Walk in beauty," he said, the Navajo equivalent of "have a nice day." As if walking in beauty were possible with my marred face.

I waited until I was outside in my jeep before I examined the amulet. A stick with buckskin wrapped tight around it, the amulet's charms included pieces of abalone shell and turquoise, a jet bead, two buttons, and a baby's blue diaper pin. I never understand why the Navajo mix trash with sacred objects on these things. According to Navajo belief each piece contains protective value, but a diaper pin? I tossed the amulet into the glove compartment. I know a dealer who'll take it, junk and all.

Ripping off the Navajo, I thought, as I headed the jeep down the highway, a time-honored tradition. It figured the old man, today of all days, wouldn't be at the trading post. Crazy Navajo, as unpredictable as the weather. But I no longer need Coyote Tail. I'll find the death hogan without him. I drove slowly, looking for the turnoff he had described to me.

I'd met the old man about a year ago. First time I saw him, he sat tipped back in his kitchen chair, like he'd been sitting there forever. He was one of those antique Indians that like to tell the tourists, "I'm over a hundred." He sure looked over a hundred, with his white hair, streaked yellow, his face so creviced it was tough telling whether he smiled or frowned. Set up as a draw for the tourists, I had no doubt.

He tipped the chair forward when I laid my jewelry out on the counter. He looked at the array of silver for long moments. Neither of us spoke. It's considered Navajo bad manners to speak when first meeting until some time has passed. I looked around the one-room combination grocery store, jewelry store, and tourist stop. Just like every other trading post I had visited in the six long weeks I had been trying to sell my jewelry on the reservation.

I learned silversmithing in the hospital while waiting for my face to heal. Good therapy, they said. The old woman who taught the class used to talk about her early life as the wife of a trader.

"They don't know what they've got—most of 'em hardly speak any English. You can get those rugs and jewelry for nothing and sell for plenty," she had said. I'd discovered in those long six weeks that maybe that was true decades ago, but now the Navajo spoke English, could figure percentages in their heads, and made rugs to order.

Finally the old man had picked up one silver freeform piece and said, "This looks like a coyote's tail."

I thought it looked like a feather, but said nothing. This was the first time any Navajo had shown interest in my wares.

"My name is Coyote Tail. Shall I tell you the tale of Coyote Tail?" He laughed at his pun. "It begins with the way of Creation." He leaned forward on the counter. He smelled as if he slept on old sheepskins, which he probably did, a heavy, oily odor. "When the sexes were separated by order of the gods Coyote managed to get in among the women and—" He reached out and touched the scarred side of my face. I jerked away.

"I know the story of Coyote's tail," I said. It unsettled

the Navajo when an Anglo knew something about their beliefs. "Once the gods grew so angry with Coyote that they destroyed him. But they missed one hair of his tail and he rebuilt himself from that one hair. Isn't that right, Coyote Tail?"

He nodded. "You must be the woman I've heard of, the one who has been trying to pass herself off as a Navajo silversmith."

I grimaced. "That was six weeks ago, you're my last chance." I hated confessing that to the old man, but what did it matter?

"You found you could not pass. Whatever made you think you could?"

"I thought I looked like an Indian," I said. Another of my bad ideas, coming onto the reservation, thinking I could make enough to get the scars wiped off my face.

"Because you got black straight hair and a tan? Maybe you look like an Indian to other Anglos but—" he said, and shrugged.

I looked away from the old man's black watching eyes. On the wall hung a cradleboard, modern, used, and maybe not for tourists. A few Navajo still used those practical devices for their babies. A small Snoopy doll hung from the board by a leather thong. Funny how the Navajo jumble two worlds together. They'll go to a sing, as their ceremonies are called, in a truck, with a thermos of coffee and a pouch of sacred corn pollen.

"You want the cradleboard? For yourself?"

"What would I do with it?" I said, without thinking. I could always sell it.

"You are marked by the gods. Like me." He pointed down at his foot. He wore a built-up boot.

"You a Singer?" I asked, using the Navajo name for medicine man. Often cripples were chosen to be so. "Or are you a Navajo wolf?" I teased. "Wolves" were the Navajo version of witches. "You are a large coyote, after all," I punned, for the literal translation of "wolf" is large coyote.

He laughed at my pun, showing teeth stained yellow by cigarettes. "Now I bargain and trade," he said, "but what are you doing, Anglo woman, on the reservation alone?"

"No one bothers me," I said, touching the scars for emphasis.

"Yes, but a coyote charm? You'll never sell this here."

Tell me something I don't already know, old man, I thought as I gathered up my jewelry.

"Wait. I know a dealer, Anglo woman, in Taos, who will take this and take you to be Navajo, too. What is your tourist name?"

"I—First Woman," I stammered.

"Of course," he said, catching the irony of naming myself for the one known for her beauty, "but now you are Coyote Dawn, my granddaughter. I will call this man and tell him you are coming."

"What's your commission?" I could hardly believe my luck. This is what I needed, a connection.

"Ten percent gross of all sales." He grinned his feral yellow smile.

"Why help me?"

"I am good at giving people what they ask for." He took down the cradleboard and gave it to me. "To seal our bargain."

Over the year that followed he put me in contact with dealers in Taos, Albuquerque and Phoenix. Now "Coyote Dawn's" line of "Navajo" jewelry was known all over the Southwest. This was my last day on the reservation. As soon as I loot that death hogan, I'm out of here, I—

I spotted the turnoff. This was going to be easy. I maneuvered the jeep onto a deeply rutted track. The thunderheads, black as pitch, built fantastic shapes over the mesas and brought hot wind in front of them, making my eyes sting. Thunderstorms turn everything but the major roads into mudbaths. With luck, I'd beat the storm.

Death hogans had almost disappeared with the incursion of Anglo ways. Still, some Navajo left their distinctive octagonal one room homes when somebody died in the structure, abandoning the body and its worldly goods. Of all the Navajo feared, they feared most the ghosts that walked about such a hogan. Only Navajo wolves visited death hogans. And me.

I pulled my gun out from under the seat. My .22 kept trouble away better than any of the superstitious junk the Navajo lugged around. Just as well Coyote Tail didn't meet me. Why split the profits?

Up ahead I saw the hogan. The eight-sided home clung to a small indent in the side of a mesa. Built of weathered logs, it blended into the cliff wall so well that if the trail had not led up to it, I never would have found it. I scanned the surrounding countryside. Nothing, not even a sheep pen. Trust the Navajo to build as far away from their neighbors as possible.

The hogan huddled half in shadow under the overhang of the cliff. The thunderclouds gathered around the mesa, crowding, as if holding the hogan in a loving embrace. I wiped the sweat from my forehead, feeling the weight of the clouds.

When I shut off the ignition I heard the yelping of a coyote. Next to the hogan, on the north side, deep in shadow, I saw a fluttering, like a dust devil kicked up by the wind. Then the movement stopped and a coyote stood watching me. If I were Navajo, I'd turn back, bad luck having a coyote cross your path. Coyotes often hung around death hogans. The Navajo say the coyote searches for the spirits of the dead, but I figure it's just because there's something for them to gnaw on.

It surprised me that the hogan still stood. Most death hogans collapse soon after being abandoned. The door, facing east according to Navajo tradition, leaned open. I slipped through, feeling dirty cobwebs brush at my face. I felt for my gun in its holster. Rattlers sometimes infested these places.

But this hogan was infested with something else. The mud once caked between the cracks of the logs had long since washed away so that light streaked into the hogan. Sitting on the dirt floor of the hogan was a young man.

"How the hell did you get in here?"

"Through there," he said, pointing to a hole in the north wall. When the Navajo originally abandoned the hogan they had breached that wall because evil enters from the north. The young man bent over a fresh sandpainting on the floor. He picked up a piece of white sandstone and crushed it in his hand. A thin precise white line poured between the second and third fingers of his hand. Then I saw it.

In the center of the sandpainting lay a fetish. Unflawed, carved out of a single chunk of high grade turquoise, a coyote slept, its head laid on its flanks, the tail curled round so the fetish made a complete circle. Like nothing I'd ever seen before. I knew a West German collector who'd pay top dollar for such an item, no questions asked.

I watched the young Navajo as he laid down a white line, only his hand moving over the painting. No doubt he was one of Coyote Tail's grandsons come to collect a percentage.

"What ceremony is done in a death hogan?" I asked. I

could think of none, yet the sandpaintings, drawn loose on the floor, were intrinsic to ceremonies, a method of calling up the gods.

"The Coyote Sing," he answered, without looking up. He wore a breechclout and buckskin moccasins. His long black hair was tied back and wrapped in the Navajo manner and he possessed the typical flat features and high cheekbones of his race. Where the light touched him he glowed deep bronze.

"You're striped, bad luck for you," I said, reaching out and touching him where the light from the cracks in the walls banded his skin. Why let this character spook me with his antique clothes and scribblings in the sand? "Besides, no one knows how to do the Coyote Sing anymore, it's been lost." I tried to remember the story of that sing, but it slipped away from me. Through the breach in the wall I saw the thunderclouds blacken. They hung so heavy it seemed impossible they should not give up their rain.

"The sing is nearly over. You shall have what you came for, Coyote Dawn." He finished the painting by sprinkling corn pollen over it. The pollen settled over the fetish, dusting it with gold.

"You've come to strike a bargain?"

"Of course," the man said, then drank from a chipped enamelware cup. He held the cup out to me, in approved ceremonial fashion.

I accepted it and sipped at the contents, following along with the bogus ceremony. The tea tasted bitter and acrid, yet washed away the desert dust in my throat. I drank the tea and handed him back the cup. The bitter taste lingered in my mouth. It felt like I tasted the rain in the thunderclouds hovering above.

"What's your name?" I looked at the man again and saw that the bands across his flesh were not only shadows, but heavy muscles moving under the skin. His hairless chest, smooth and Indian, showed no sweat, despite the suffocating heat. I wished the storm would break. He arched his head back and stretched, as if he knew how I looked at him.

"Which name do you want, Coyote Dawn?" he said. "I have many names, like a good Navajo I am called many things." He pulled a medicine pouch from his belt and sprinkled some of the contents into the cup. He rubbed his forefinger and thumb over the material in the cup and it came alight with fire then smoldered. In the flash of light I saw his fingernails curved over the pads of his fingers.

"Good trick for the tourists," I said. "You have the match concealed in your palm?"

"Trickster is one of my names, or Mischief Maker, either serves me well." He looked at me through the smoke rising from the bowl. The smoke tickled the back of my throat and smelled sweet, tinged with sage and juniper, inviting.

"Or would you like my clan name? My secret name? Or do you know that already?"

"I will have the fetish."

"I will give you what you ask for," he said, and reached out and stroked the scars along my face. His touch felt cool and soothing, his hand soft. He leaned forward and kissed me. Outside the wind died down and the smoke eddied about the hogan, trapped. Thunder rumbled. He tasted of the desert wild, of wet earth.

He began to chant. I'd heard chanting before at a staged Navajo sing for the tourists. Even then the Navajo could not disguise the quality of that sound. His voice thrummed high, then low, filling the hogan with sound. His breath burned upon my face. He held me and his chanting rhythm thundered in my mind, moved with the beat of my blood. The heat of his body blanketed over me and the smoke swirled about our moving bodies. I felt his skin rippling under my hands as if a great weight of dust shifted over me, burying me beneath. I dreamt of a turquoise child, nestled within me, a jewel of a sleeping infant. The child opened eyes of obsidian and I awoke.

The young man had gone and Coyote Tail sat in his place. The thunderheads broke and rain roared around the hogan, as if the thunderstorm might tear through the crumbling walls.

"Where is the fetish?" It was gone from the center of the sandpainting.

"You have what you asked for," the old man said.

I took out my gun. "Give it to me, old man, or I'll kill you." Why not kill him? What better place for him to die than where no one ever dared look?

"Don't you remember, Coyote Dawn? You know our ways so well." He gestured at the sandpainting and I saw that it was covered with a heavy layer of dust. "It is time for thunder to walk upon the earth. Don't you remember when Coyote made the women mad with lust and—"

I shot him through the chest, emptying the gun in a burst. He laughed, a hard baying laugh as he fell, ending in a lightning crack that blinded me.

When my vision cleared the dead man lay still in the center of the sandpainting, destroying it. Little remained of him, dry bones wrapped in rotting cloth. He wore his shirt, pants, and shoes on the wrong way to keep his ghost from walking. One shoe had a built-up heel. He had lain in the death hogan a long time.

Bright blue glinted among the folds of the shirt. I reached out and pulled the fetish away from the filthy cloth. It was mine; I had earned it. The skeleton shifted at my touch and the skull rolled away from the body, its jaws gaping wide, as if Coyote Tail laughed at me still.

The fetish felt warm as if taken from living flesh. Within the palm of my hand the coyote woke, its jaws grinning, its eyes opening wide, filled with black obsidian. I knew those eyes. As thunder walked around me I remembered . . .

. . . Coyote copulated with the women
. . . deep within me it stirred, new, alive, awakening
. . . and the women
. . . I heard the coyote laughing
. . . gave birth to monsters.

SLIDE NUMBER SEVEN

by Sharon Epperson

Sharon Epperson says she's a self-taught writer who was born and raised in Wichita, Kansas. She is also a competent artist, specializing in pencil portraits. Her writing career began when she won a fiction contest in the Spring '86 issue of *The Horror Show*. Since then she's sold a number of short stories and is presently awaiting word of the sale of her first novel.

Sharon has written a tale that is not only exceedingly timely, it's a hell of a good story. And provides one of my favorite subgenres—the horror medical story.

✦ ✦ ✦

"Move, will you? I'm not into necrophilia."

How appropriate, Elaine thought. I am dead. He's buried himself in a human grave.

"I'm going out later, Todd."

"Going out?" He groaned in disgust and pulled away from her. "Is that what you're thinking about while I'm trying to make love to you?"

"Yes," she said. "I need a drink."

Todd wiped at his groin with the sheet. "You women make me sick. Your detachment is—"

"Todd?" she interrupted.

"What?"

"Do you know what CEBV, or HBLV, is?"

"What?"

"How about Epstein-Barr virus? Ever hear of that?"

"No. What are you talking about?"

Elaine sat up and pushed the damp tendrils of her dark hair away from her neck. "Got a cigarette?"

"You know I don't smoke in bed."

I know, she thought.

"Are you going to tell me what you're—Elaine, what are you doing?"

"Getting dressed to go out." She turned her back on him and stepped into her panties. "I need a drink and a cigarette."

"Cold-eyed bitch," he muttered as she fastened the hooks on her bra. "Running out to meet the rest of your egghead buddies from the lab?"

"Yes," she said.

On the way out she took a copy of the latest *Rolling Stone* from her bag and placed it on the kitchen table. Inside was an article on the Epstein-Barr virus, also known as CEBV, or the "yuppie flu." There was mention of HBLV, and the possible connection, as well. Todd would need to know about it sooner or later. Slide number seven had seen to that.

Only two of her egghead buddies were at the club. Marti and Carlos were fellow research assistants with Elaine during the day. Right now they were drunk. Carlos sang along with the music videos on the big screen above the dance floor; Marti eyed the new bartender with lascivious intent.

"Look who's here," she said at seeing Elaine. "Fresh from the bed of Todd the Luscious Bod, no doubt."

Elaine tossed her bag on the table and walked to the bar for a drink. The new bartender winked at her.

"When can I get you? Ooops, I mean what."

"Gin and tonic."

He eyed her as he prepared the drink. "I hope you come in here often. Do you?"

She studied the pink line of the paper cut on her right

index finger. The ungloved finger that had rushed to intercept slide number seven's fall to the lab floor.

"Yes," she said.

"Great. I'm Andy. I get off at two."

Elaine laid a five on the bar and took her drink back to the table.

"What did he say?" Marti demanded.

"His name is Andy."

"Andy what?"

"I don't know. I don't care."

"Well, aren't we cheerful."

Carlos stopped singing and looked at Marti. "Don't get bitchy because he talked to her and not you."

Marti sniffed at him and flipped the short tails of her bleached hair. "I'm not." To Elaine she said, "I hate you."

"Really." Elaine sipped her drink and watched the singer on the video screen. "Who's that?"

"The man we have tickets to see in exactly one hour," Carlos informed her.

"We?"

"I have four," he explained. "I was going to scalp two at the door, but now you're here you can have one."

Elaine looked at the screen again. "Thanks, Carlos."

"You're welcome. He's got a voice, doesn't he?"

"He's beautiful," Marti said.

"Anyone have a cigarette?" Elaine asked.

Carlos held out a Carlton.

"I'm going for another round," Marti announced. She looked pointedly at Elaine. "Can I get you one?"

"Yes. Thanks."

When Marti was gone Carlos snickered. "It just kills her to be snubbed. Did you see the way she scrambled to get out of the lab and see that CDC guy in from Atlanta today?"

Elaine nodded. Oh yes, she thought. I saw myself ready to go to lunch. I saw myself forget my badge and walk back into the lab unprotected. I saw Marti knock everything over trying to get out and be noticed. I saw my hands reach out instinctively to catch . . .

"Andy Powell," Marti said triumphantly.

"I have to pee," Elaine said.

In the bathroom she sat on the toilet and stared at the tops of her thighs. After a moment she peered between them, half expecting to see the virus clouding the bowl along with her urine.

Like AIDS, the Human B-Lymphotropic Virus could wreak Friday night horror flick havoc on the immune system. Combine HBLV with Epstein-Barr, another herpes virus capable of creating cancer cells, and you get—guess what, boys and girls?—slow death from a fresh paper cut.

Shabby business, she told herself. Shoddy practice. Ten years of being careful. Ten years of being Lysol-clean and having that Windex shine of protection.

Her first impulse, a stupid one, had been to cut off her finger.

Useless. Utterly useless.

She snagged the toilet paper roll and suddenly thought of a movie she'd seen called *Letter to Brezhnev*. In one scene two women were in a bathroom stall talking and taking turns peeing. Neither had wiped.

That disturbed Elaine.

✦ ✦ ✦

"Drink up," Carlos urged. "I want to find a decent parking space this time."

Her nod was perfunctory. She downed half the drink,

asked for another cigarette, then stared at the print of her lips on the rim of the glass.

Passed through blood . . . and saliva.

"C'mon, Elaine." Marti picked up the glass.

Elaine didn't stop her.

"This doesn't taste right, does it?" Marti said with a feral grin. "I'll just have to go up and tell Andy he has room for improvement."

Elaine didn't stop her. She watched Marti take the glass to the bar and shove it at the new bartender. Andy raised a brow and took a sip. He passed it back to Marti, who made a show of placing her lips where his had been.

"Slut," Carlos said when Marti returned.

Her lip curled. "Let's get out of here. The guy has a band of white a mile wide on his ring finger."

In the car she turned to Elaine. "Did you and Todd have a fight? You've been unusually quiet tonight."

Elaine said nothing. She was thinking how much she would miss going fishing with her father on hot and lazy Sunday afternoons.

Then she thought of a picture she'd seen in *National Geographic:* a large bullhead with fleshy red tumors decorating its helpless mouth; carcinogens courtesy of industrial dumping finding its way into the Great Lakes.

She wouldn't miss fishing after all, she decided. But she would miss her father.

"Look who's being bitchy now," Marti complained. "What did I do to deserve the silent treatment?"

"Leave her alone," Carlos said. "Get out some money to pay for parking, would you?"

"Let Elaine pay. She's getting a free ticket."

Aren't we all, Elaine thought. She dug into her bag and handed Carlos a ten.

"Is that all you have?"

No, she thought. "Yes," she said.

✦ ✦ ✦

"Damn," Carlos murmured. "I thought our seats would be better than this."

Elaine looked at the stage. They sat near the center of the arena, but the features of the man checking the microphone were a pale blur.

"It's hot out here," Marti said, eyeing a dark-haired man three seats to the left. She unbuttoned the first two buttons on her blouse and fanned herself with a program. The fabric at her breast fluttered and rose with each pass.

The sky above their heads held Elaine's attention. She gazed at the first stars and tried to think of every poem she'd ever read about dying. None came. She remembered instead the words of Saint Augustine in *The City of God:* "The way by which minds cling to bodies cannot be understood by men; nevertheless, this is man."

When she looked down again people were standing up around her. She stood with them and looked at the stage as a steady rhythm of bass notes filled her ears. The heavy thrumming tingled in her toes and traveled up through her legs to rest somewhere around her center. It throbbed there, a sexual thing. Voices began to cheer.

She was lost again. Contemplation of the traitor that was her body sank merciless fangs into her reality. The venom traveled swift, sure, to her heart.

No right, she thought. We have no right to become so attached to our bodies. No right to thrill at the simple thrumming of a bass guitar just because we can feel it as well as hear. *We are not gods, after all*. We are corporeal.

We do, and we die. Oh, but the things we do before we . . . I'm losing it, she thought.

"Isn't he beautiful?" Marti crowed.

Elaine focused her eyes on the stage. She saw what there was to see of him: a bright halo of golden hair; baggy white pants and a faded jean jacket. She heard his voice, crystalline. But she couldn't see his face. She wanted to, because the faces all around hers were filled with light, shining with adoration. Just the way one would look at a god, she thought angrily.

She ached to look into his eyes and see how the power of being this god each night for an hour and a half affected him; to know what the adulation of the masses looked like when reflected in a man's eye. Just a man after all, with washed-out skin, hair, a faded jean jacket that looked far too warm, and a voice that broke once, oh yes, twice—not even gods were perfect, were they?

She begged to see his face, because she saw the rows of worshipers rising and falling like waves at his feet, their faces upturned, arms lifting at command . . . and she wondered if they saw something she didn't.

A spirit, perhaps?

Her head pounded with the music, her racing pulse keeping perfect time.

He's real! she wanted to scream at them.

They were all straining to reach him, thrusting their bones, blood, and tissue at his unreachable form. But they were held at bay by their own bodies; their yearning souls inescapably trapped in dirty, sweating, traitorous flesh.

I could help them, she thought.

"Elaine, tell that guy to sit down!" Marti commanded. "I can't see!"

I could free them, she thought. I could make women

start wiping and . . . losing it . . . help fish breathe clean water again. I could help them all gain the ultimate form of notice. I could . . .

"Elaine, where are you going?" Carlos called.

"I've lost it," she said.

The first man she kissed jumped and looked at her with a startled expression.

"You're free," Elaine told him. "Courtesy of slide number seven."

THE UNLOVED

by Melissa Mia Hall

Melissa Mia Hall has dabbled in photography and filmmaking, singing, and used to do a little acting, as well as writing poetry. She's published book criticism for the past eight years and is a member of the National Book Critics Circle. Her short stories have been published in numerous anthologies, among them *Shadows* 6, 7, and 10, *New Frontiers: Best of the West 2, Things That Go Bump in the Night*, *Greystone Bay*, and *Doom City (Greystone Bay* 2). Her short fiction has also appeared in *Twilight Zone Magazine*, and the *American Voice*. She lives in Fort Worth, Texas, where she's just completed her first novel.

Melissa hasn't been published all that long, but already her stories have been widely received. And there's always a singular bent to them—and I won't say it's because she's from Texas. However . . .

✦ ✦ ✦

The sisters are alike and they are unlike, although looking at them, it is very difficult telling them apart. When they sing, as they sing now, their voices blend in cool harmony. Rachel and Celia, identical twins, watching each other's eyes as the song spins out over the trees and into the cloudless sky. " 'He'll be coming 'round the mountain when he comes . . .' " Celia strains a little on the low notes. Rachel comes down hard on "when he comes." Her voice is the stronger one. Pretty soon, though, they tire of the old song and fall in effortless unison into a clump of spring grass. Laughter rises from the tangle of their bodies and streams throughout the well-kept garden. Flat on their backs, their rainwater eyes intensify the blue morning sky. Their fingertips touch lightly and their tinkling laughter gives way to comfortable conversation.

"Do you think he's really gonna come?" Celia asks.

"Let's go look at the apartment again," Rachel says and they jump up with renewed energy. They're going to rent the garage apartment to a man, someone who'll do the stuff that Daddy used to do around the house and lawn. In many spots, the white paint peels away from the wood frame, and most of the window screens need fixing. Celia groans as she stoops to pick a wildflower. "I don't know, Rachel; it's awful ugly. I'd never want to live here."

"Well, you're not going to, he is. But, hey, if you want to forget the whole thing, I'm willing. I mean, we don't need him *that* much. It's not something that has to be done, you know." She turns, picks a pebble from the ground, and pitches it into the cracked birdbath. She lowers her voice confidentially. "It being so cheap and all will make it look pretty good to someone trying to save money." She can sense Celia's determination returning and isn't about to lose it.

"Yeah, I guess. Well, let's go back inside now. The wind's getting cold." She looks down at her jean cutoffs that expose too much skin for March.

"I know, I'm all goose pimples." Rachel laughs and they run back through the garden, racing to see who'll reach the back porch first. It's a triumphant tie.

The back door slams behind them and they start rummaging in the refrigerator simultaneously. From the living room, Joni Mitchell's *Ladies of the Canyon* begins its third revolution on the record player.

"You want to hear 'Willy' again—'he is my child, he is my father'—" Rachel sings, holding an egg aloft, an egg unusually narrow and pointed, as if the chicken had had a hard time laying it. She squints at the cruelly tapered point and wonders what kind of baby chick it would've been, probably skinny, scrawny, maybe deformed.

Celia puts a package of pork chops down on the counter. "I don't care."

Before Rachel can move, they hear the doorbell ring. They catch in each other a sudden breathlessness and fear. Maybe it's him. And they can't help getting excited. He'll be the first man on the premises since Daddy died. They each have a flash of what it might be like and they each tense with suppressed feelings. Rachel goes past Celia, turns down the volume on the stereo. Celia, after taking a deep, steadying breath, beats Rachel to the front door. She swings it open with one fluid and most emphatic motion.

He has come. The man. He looks like Jesus or James Taylor. Maybe both. "Fire and Rain"'s melody comes to mind. She sways a little. "Rachel?" Celia says over her shoulder, pleadingly. It's 1974 and she's supposed to be an emancipated, securely smooth woman, but Rachel handles these sort of things better. Men. Like Daddy.

His voice rushes over. He's there like he said he'd be over the phone, in response to the notecard posted on the board in the student center.

Rachel's arm comes around Celia's reassuringly. She smiles at the man. His long black hair is parted in the middle. He is tall and very thin. His teeth glare whitely underneath his black moustache. He's much older than they are, with mauve circles underneath his green leaf eyes, fine lines across his forehead. Probably a Vietnam vet, out to start his life over.

Their gazes widen and their nostrils embrace his male scent, slightly unclean from walking out in the sun, slightly fragrant of woodsy plants and trees, tall and spreading wide into some distant sunshine. Celia whispers in Rachel's ear, "Let him in." Rachel undoes the latch, shivering under her thin Mexican shirt. The first official date for spring is weeks away. It's really still winter now. She'd like a fire in the fireplace and mugs of hot, steaming coffee. He walks past them into the living room like he's been there before.

"My name's Denny."

"I'm Rachel. I talked to you on the phone, and she's Celia, my sister."

He wears that incredulous grin that keeps starting and stopping that everyone wears when first confronted with the twins. "Man, it's incredible. I can't help it," he apologizes, rubbing his shoulders, freed of the backpack now sprawling by the sofa. "You look like mirror images of each other—mirror children."

"We do look alike," Celia says with a straight face.

"And all that hair, like wheatfield, cornfield, gold. I just came from Kansas, working in the wheat."

Rachel checks out his large bony hands. The calluses are still there, from the plow or from a gun? It didn't much matter. He is a man.

"Our dad was a policeman after he was in the army. Then he got into insurance. What'd your dad do? Are you good with your hands? Our dad was, I mean, a real handyman," babbles Celia before Rachel can stop her. Denny's eyes sharpen into black green pinpoints. "You alone here?"

"Daddy's gone, yeah, he's gone now. Dead, like our poor momma. She died giving birth to me an' Rachel. Isn't that sad? But that's all over and you're here, now," Celia says. Rachel glares at her. She starts sucking a tip of blond hair. Her eyes dart toward the record player. She can hardly hear Joni's voice.

"Things need doing around here. It's part of the rent. That's *why* it's part of the rent."

"I understand. I am pretty good with my hands." He smiles at Celia. Botticelli women both, but she's the sweetest, childlike, gentle. He likes her. The other one, though, she bothers him. She's powerful, strong, and in control.

"You'll have to clean up the place you're going to live in. We haven't had time, see. We just posted the notice last week."

"I don't mind. I'd like to move in right away, if I can. I don't have a place to stay in, nothing decent. Just got into town a couple of days ago. I'm really beat."

"You said you were from Kansas?"

"Montana."

"That's a long way away," Rachel says. "Do you have a car?"

He shakes his head, holding her eyes. Rachel's body trembles, his glance shooting holes in her skin. Maybe it's not a good thing to do, renting to a man who looks like Jesus. He walks around the room now, having unleashed her glance. He walks, hands easy in the pockets of his green fatigue jacket. He picks up the photograph of Daddy in his World War II clothes. "You miss him a lot?"

Rachel's color rises. Denny notes the two spots of fire in her cheeks. Celia rushes to his side, alarmed by his bony fingers spread out across her daddy's face leaving dirty fingerprints. Embarrassed, he puts the frame down, wipes his hands on his jeans. "I didn't mean to offend you. Well, can I see the apartment?"

Celia and Rachel exchange strangling glances. When he sees it, he probably won't like it. But they want him to stay; he has to stay. They want him so and it's frightening, to want him.

They go out the back way through the kitchen and they notice him staring at the pink pork chops on the counter. His obvious hunger is amusing and reassures them that there might be a chance that he might just stay. For a while. Out the door, the young women quicken their pace and the man has to hurry to keep up. Celia takes the stairs two at a time. She opens the door to the apartment. It's unlocked, the key has been lost for ages. Daddy probably lost it, or one of his army friends that used to come visit, that they had to entertain so long ago. "It leaks some, when it rains," she says, blushing. Rachel looks at her until the blush recedes. Celia couldn't help it. He was staring at her breasts, the stare spreading out, like fingers.

They huddle, three on the landing, looking into the dim apartment, at the bed sinking in the middle, at the grimy windows, the greasy hotplate, the curling linoleum floor.

"One hundred fifty bills paid, no phone, though. You'll have to take care of that yourself. One fan."

The fan in question looks to have one blade broken, but he's thinking of the girls with their Rapunzel hair. His heart starts to sink but his tired feet refuse to move. He hasn't been around women in a long time and their sexuality is like honey, natural, golden, sweet. Still, there are bells pealing in his head, telling him something's not right, that the flat's too horrible to bear, too cheap to be real. Still, she's looking at him kindly, the one called Celia.

"Do you have a job? We don't want a bum out here," Rachel says shortly.

"I can manage a hundred. How'd that be?" he hears himself saying. The honey is underneath his feet, sticky, positive he won't leave.

"Rachel—" Celia says, jabbing her sister in the ribs.

"Where do you work?" Denny asks suddenly, pushing his hair behind his ears.

"I work at a museum. I'm receptionist," Rachel says proudly.

"And you?" he asks the nicer one. She sways a bit, rocking gently to some secret tune. "*Me?* I keep the house and garden for Rachel. I grow flowers and things," Celia replies weakly, pushing her hair behind her ears, echoing his gesture with complimentary aplomb. "I'm not very good out among people like Rachel is."

"I don't believe it," Denny says, staring at Celia closely, thinking this is the one I'll take to bed and how can I tell her apart from the other one? Is her nose longer? Is there a freckle or a beauty mark on her face? Is her hair slightly darker? Is her waist wider, one breast larger?

"I did go to the university for a while. I took botany and volleyball."

He smiles. "I think that I might do that—go to school for a while."

Rachel frowns.

"Of course, just part-time. I'll be working, too. I promise to pay my rent on time."

"Then you'll take it?" Celia steps back in a faint swoon of shock. Rachel holds out her hand, not very surprised. They're lucky to get a hundred a month for that dump. He pulls out his billfold and crosses her palm with a wad of green.

"But you can't stay here tonight. Why don't you stay in Daddy's room, till this place is fit? I think it's gonna rain tonight."

Rachel looks away, clutching the money. Celia slips out of control sometimes; that's nothing to worry about.

"It's time for lunch. I bet you're starved. I cook some mean pork chops. I dip 'em in flour and fry 'em, then I pour a can of mushroom soup over 'em. Real fine, delicious. 'Course it's important to drain off the grease before you put the soup on 'em. You know?" Brazenly obvious, Celia links her arm with his and they go down the steps. Rachel watches them, speechless. So it was done. Like that. So quickly. Another man in Daddy's bed.

✦ ✦ ✦

He'd gotten the place in pretty decent order before nightfall, but the rainstorm Celia had predicted came on in a broad and nasty fury, strewing marble-sized hail and mutilating the trees, especially the flowering redbuds. It even blew out the remaining windowpanes in the garage apartment. He had to stay in the house with them. He had to stay in Daddy's bedroom. There wasn't a choice and it was more convenient anyway. Still, Rachel kept the gun in the nightstand by her bed and told Celia to keep a knife under her pillow (sheathed, of course). She wished they had the same room, even considered asking Celia to sleep with her tonight. When he was taking his shower, she accidently opened the door and saw his naked body diffused by the glass door. She left swiftly, mumbling "I'm sorry" like some kind of child. She sits in her bed, now, trying to calm down, but the idea that the man had come and is there, just down the hallway, unnerves her. They can't lock their bedroom doors because those keys had been lost, too. Daddy wasn't one for locks on the inside of the house. She hears Celia talking to him out in the hallway.

"See you in the morning." Celia is openly flirting, out in her nightgown, for God's sake. Rachel sinks under the covers and feels her heart beating fast and furious like she's just run a race. How's she going to sleep tonight and she's got to be at work early? She'll have to leave them alone and she's just going to have to accept it. Nothing else to do.

He's a drifter. No relatives, no friends—maybe. She'd kind of like that. Makes it all simpler. They don't have any relatives, not to speak of—none in Texas. And Daddy's unspeakable friends are all gone. But is it possible he could be one of their sons? Rachel's teeth chatter. It's not something to think about while trying to get to sleep.

✦ ✦ ✦

Celia buries her face in a clutch of roses. Early May roses. Denny helps Celia cut roses to put in vases around the house. The neighbors probably think he's her boyfriend. Denny does odd jobs around the neighborhood, cutting yards with the lawn mower that belonged to old man Sanders. She goes with him, often, armed with the edger and a pair of large green gardening gloves. Her skin's growing darker than Rachel's just a little, but enough to inspire Denny with the belief that he'll eventually have no trouble telling them apart. He's getting more and more convinced he'll be taking her away soon. He doesn't like being tied down. They could travel about on the motorcycle he got just last week. They'd get back to the country, go down those damn country roads. He dreams of walking across America, ditching the bike, but keeping the lady. All by themselves.

"You're fun, you know that? God, I like you," Celia says. Denny puts down the flower cutters and holds out his arms. She laughs and says that Rachel will be home soon and dinner's not ready.

"You really like Rachel."

"Of course, I do, dummy, she's my sister!" she says, heading inside.

They stand side by side at the sink, while Celia fills the last vase with water. Denny arranges the flowers, occasionally pricking his skin with thorns. "Do you think you could ever go away with me, I mean, leave Rachel?" He can't look at her directly. He's afraid to.

Celia holds on to the edge of the sink and looks down. Her hair conceals her features. Denny has a sharp, wild longing to cut that hair. He has begun to tire of the loose strands caught on doorknobs, others found in his soup or even in the branches of the hedge by the fence. Everywhere. He's tired of it. His own hair does that, sometimes, falls in his soup, but his hair is not so long that it goes past his knees. That sort of long hair seems freakish and reminds him of old sepia-tinted photographs of women before the turn of the century, but at least they had the decency to keep it pinned up most of the time. What is he saying? He loves it, loves it. He grabs a long lock and twists it around his hand.

Celia grimaces, pulls back. Her eyes are the color of a ripening bruise, angry, bewildered. "I can't leave Rachel. Not ever, and don't you be asking me that again. Do you hear me?" She yanks her hair away from him. "Let go!"

"But Celia—I thought, well, I thought I was special. You love me. You know I love you. I didn't stay here because of Rachel, I stayed because of you, of what we have together."

"What's that?"

"You know," he says, thinking of their secret nights, of how the other one wasn't to know of how the skins matched, theirs scents mingling, their animal couplings made silent out of some desperate need.

"Get out of here; I've got to cook. Gee, you sure are silly sometimes."

He shakes his head; his hands flail out to his sides. This

is a dream he lives in—the light pouring into the kitchen from the laced-over windows shimmers with dust motes or tears. He can't cry. He won't cry. He feels very young and foolish.

✦ ✦ ✦

The middle of the night, the torso. She comes again, as she has done for several weeks now. She is an angel in his arms, violet-scented tonight, so silent it breaks his heart. When they finish their rite of love, almost obscenely silent, he whispers he can no longer stand it. She slips from the sheets, pulls her nightgown down. She stands for a moment, her body white in the moonlight.

"Celia, don't go."

She shakes her head. The street lamp on the corner touches one side of her head. She won't make love to him in the daytime. He suggested it once and she pretended not to understand what he meant. When he pressed her, she gazed at him with such thinly veiled disgust that he knew he wouldn't suggest it again for fear he'd lose even the nightly visits. But he can't go on like this much longer. The other one is ruining everything. Her presence looms over Celia. It has even begun to bother him, that she looks so much like Celia. He feels like their resemblance is a chain between them. If that chain is broken, just one link severed, surely that would enable Celia to become more independent. Eventually, he'd be able to cajole her away from Rachel, so she wouldn't need her so much.

✦ ✦ ✦

They sit in the large tub with the old-fashioned claw feet, facing each other. The bubble bath steams. The bathroom is like a sauna. The June sun shines in through the open window, but there isn't a breeze. Rachel and Celia admire themselves, their legs touching, knee to knee. They like taking baths together, even if their long legs often get in the way. It's reassuring, and in the privacy they can talk about almost anything.

The herb-scented soap slips out of Rachel's hand. "I'll find it—" Celia says. "No, here it is, I've found it," Rachel says. "You know what, Celia?" Rachel soaps her washrag while Celia uses a sponge to keep sending hot water down the curve of her breasts. "Yeah?"

"When Denny comes back from the store, let's tell him he has to go. I think it's done."

"Do you know for sure?"

"No."

"Then he can't go, he just can't. He's not any better than Daddy. We have to do it right."

"He hasn't hurt us." Rachel drops the washrag. She's cold now, very. Celia stares at her with that obstinate blankness she's grown to fear. The bathwater has grown tepid and milky with melted soap.

"You want him. He doesn't want you. He wants me."

Rachel stands, pulls her sister up. They get out of the tub. Rachel tries to think of something to say, something to convince herself and Celia that she doesn't want him, not at all. She dries herself then starts drying Celia gently. Celia's eyes have become distracted by the mirror over the sink.

"If he stays here a while longer, will you promise to be good?" Rachel asks her. "Celia, look at me when I'm talking to you. This is serious."

"I am."

"He's not like Daddy."

"All men are like Daddy."

"That can't be true," Rachel says, her voice pinched and metallic.

"Rachel, will you comb my hair? It's all tangled."

Sighing, Rachel finds the big-toothed comb and blinks away a few hot tears. Celia's smooth back faces her. Dark spots on the silky kimono indicate wet places Rachel's towel rubbing has missed. She looks too vulnerable. She remembers when they were twelve and the bath they shared the morning after Daddy hurt her the first time. She kept thinking, Why wasn't it me, why did he want Celia all the time to do those things? Later, when his buddies started coming and he made her do things with them—have sex, she reminds herself—they were all pretty nice to her, if creeps could be nice, none of them hurt her—they paid Daddy, after all—he still didn't want her, Daddy didn't. But he hurt Celia, he hurt her badly, and that time when she was fifteen and she got pregnant, he beat her up, the next day she miscarried. When she went to the doctor (a man doctor) he told her she couldn't have a baby. She felt Celia's rage, she shared it—it was like a fire spreading from one to the other. Next time Daddy wanted Celia, Lord knows Celia would do something. Rachel had to protect her afterward. She understood. But since the commotion Celia had never been the same, the years kept making the wound wider and her head younger.

"Be still now," Rachel whispers.

"I'm home!" Denny's voice blasts through the house.

Celia jerks away from her, ignoring the painful tangle of hair she leaves in Rachel's comb. "But I just started—" Rachel cries, except Celia has already fled the room. Her voice welcomes Denny with a confusion of questions about what he's bought for supper. Rachel stands by the edge of the bed and studies the damp places where Celia has sat. In her mind she keeps thinking of how he said "home" as if he belonged here. The frightening thing is how maybe he does and she doesn't anymore.

✦ ✦ ✦

The scissors were sharp and new. They cut her hair out in the open, out in the August sunshine. Celia trembled throughout the whole event, gripping the sides of the kitchen chair they'd brought out into the garden. Across the street, the neighbors kept flitting back and forth on obscure jobs, like moving geranium pots around and watering the hanging baskets half a dozen times, just so they could watch. Denny imagined he could hear their murmured disapproval.

He'd looked at some beauty magazines before he cut it, reassuring her she'd like herself much better once he got through, that she had the perfect bone structure for a cool, close style. He'd never thought it would take so long. When he was through, she covered her face for a few minutes.

"Don't you want to see?" he says, and he thrusts the mirror into her trembling hands.

She looks in the glass, her large eyes huge with surprise and disbelief. "But where is she?"

"Who?"

"Rachel. Will I still look like Rachel?"

Denny flushes. Somehow, the debris of golden strands on the dusty green grass disturbs him more than he thought it would. His hands feel gritty. He keeps wiping them on his worn jeans. "Sure."

"Then you're going to cut her hair, too?"

"Don't be a baby! Don't be a baby! Don't you want to be different from her? Can't you grow up?"

Rachel's Toyota turns a corner two blocks down. Closer

and closer. Denny's hands sweat an ungodly amount of moisture. Celia's standing and now she's twirling a child's impression of a ballerina. "I feel like a feather: I'm so light. I can fly if a big enough wind comes up. Rachel!"

The car squeals to a halt. The driver's door opens and is slammed shut violently. Rachel runs to Celia and screams. Celia keeps pulling on Rachel's hair and giggling.

"What have you done? Oh my God, why did you do it? Oh, why couldn't you leave things as they were? We were getting along all right; we were getting along—"

Celia crosses her arms and a glaze creeps over her eyes. "Would you look in that mirror? Now, Rachel, you got to get your hair cut like mine so we can keep on with the game. Okay? Promise? Denny—Denny'll fix it for us so we can get this mirror back into shape." Celia shines a big smile on Denny. "See, I'll tell you how it is. There's really only one of us. She's the woman looking in the mirror. I'm her reflection. See, I'm not real. That's why Daddy preferred me to her."

Denny starts to shake like a wino with the D.T.'s.

Celia laughs and runs to the house.

Rachel starts after her, her wedgies clomping on the pavement.

He puts his hand on her arm. "What's wrong with her, Rachel?"

Rachel stops, her hand on the screen door. She turns and looks at him, the man from Montana. His alien features are brown from the sun. "You wouldn't understand, I don't think. I think maybe you'd better leave. For good. I'm sorry." She rubs one eye and leaves a mascara scar across one cheek. The door slams shut behind her.

Denny notices all the gold hair on his body. He sneezes and he brushes at his body furiously. That just makes it worse. Celia looks out the open kitchen window that faces the driveway. No, she's gaping, a mindless grin plastered over her mouth.

All those night visits had been made by Rachel, not Celia. Maybe he knew it all the while. Maybe he'd been enchanted. But that's not how it is now. He keeps itching and he coughs, a hair caught in his throat.

✦ ✦ ✦

She didn't know that he'd stolen the gun from her nightstand before he left on his Honda. She didn't know because she never thought about it because he was leaving and they'd all be safe again, safe from the big bad man. When she used him, he was okay; that was okay.

Denny feels the cold metal in his pocket and inches forward in the rude shelter of the October night. So he had to come back to see them. He's thought and thought about it; he's tried to put them out of his mind. Now he spies on them. They're in Rachel's room, in her bed. Rachel's cut her hair to match Celia's. Once again he can't tell them apart. Celia's summer color has faded. They both wear baggy robes that remind him of the cocoons the tent caterpillars have made in their big pecan tree out in the back by the garage apartment he never used. They're eating crackers and cheese. A bowl of green grapes sits on the nightstand. They're laughing softly. He can barely hear the TV on the chest of drawers spitting and snarling out some detective show.

One of them sits up, then gets out of bed, revealing the pear shape of full pregnancy. Denny moves closer. His child, she's carrying his child. The other sits up and reveals the same shape. Denny gasps without thinking. He sits back on the balls of his feet, snapping a twig.

One of them stares out the window, apprehensive. She can't see him but she looks like she knows someone is out there. The other one gets out of bed and laboriously pulls down the shade.

Denny goes to the front porch. Piles of dead leaves clutter the grey slats and the swing creaks when he sits down in it. The wind has gotten inside him. His coat is no protection. Nothing is. He stiffens still more when she comes out and sits down beside him.

"You weren't supposed to come back."

"Both of you?" he says through teeth that won't stay gritted.

"No, just me. Celia likes to playact with the sofa cushion. It's harmless and makes her happy."

"My baby—" Denny whispers. The knowledge keeps hitting him like a persistent fist, a child's fist, an angry child's—one that he wants to kiss.

"No, *ours*."

Denny tries to touch her, hug her, show her his thanksgiving. She pushes away and the swing starts. She stops it with her foot. "You don't understand. It's mine and Celia's, to replace the one Daddy took away from us. You've got to understand. You're not as bad as the other ones. You're really kind of nice. We didn't have to do all the things—I mean, you didn't hurt me."

The numbness had begun in his feet and now creeps up his legs. She talks too fast, talks like she knows what she's talking about. His mind spins away in confusion.

She smooths her white robe over her submerged child. She squints at him, squeezes his hand. "How do I tell you this? Daddy mistreated my sister. He got her pregnant and then made her lose it. This baby will replace our loss."

"Her loss, not yours."

"*Ours*. We've always helped each other get through it all. We're all we've got. Celia's been crazy ever since Daddy did that to her. Now we have it back, the baby I mean, a new one, a better one, I bet. And I thank you for it. You know, after the doctor saw her after the miscarriage that bastard engineered, he said, the doctor, that she couldn't have another one, least not carry it to term. That about killed Celia. That's why she killed Daddy and why we could've killed you. But we didn't. So, why can't you just go away and leave us alone. Please?"

He gets the gun out slowly. He is going to kill Celia. He moves away from her slowly. Rachel lifts her chin and looks at him carefully. It's as if she reads his mind. He's that transparent. Her lips tremble. His hands shake with enraged bewilderment. Behind him the door opens wider. Celia has been there the whole time, listening. He leans against the railing and looks from the swing to the door. A gust of wind sends leaves spraying across his feet. They are waiting for him to kill himself so they won't have to do it. He knows he could never do that, and if he did, they'd only feel a dubious satisfaction. These are women who will never feel safe from men.

Rachel forces a sad smile. "Go on, then, leave."

It was what he was going to do anyway. Go to the police, with her or without her. But inside that mound beneath her robe is his child forming. He summons calm, shuts his eyes tightly, praying that the wetness will dry. "I took something from you. I came back to give it to you." He places the gun in her open hands, his eyes now watching her with brittle calm. "Rachel, what are you going to do if it's a boy?"

The screen door slams; Celia bursts out, her mouth wide and dark, unable to scream. Her hands reach out to hit the man but something in Rachel's face stops her. Her body arches toward her sister in a frozen and unnatural stance, her hands held tight beneath her breasts.

Rachel looks down at the pistol. Her fingers find the trigger. She aims the pistol at her womb and says nothing.

CANNIBAL CATS COME OUT TONIGHT

by Nancy Holder

Nancy Holder, daughter of a naval officer, lived in Japan for three years and at sixteen dropped out of high school to study ballet in Europe. Later, she graduated from the University of California at San Diego with a degree in communications. She sold her first book, a young adult romance, in 1981, and wrote romances for five years under various names. Seven novels placed on the Waldenbooks Romance Bestseller List, and she received several awards from *Romantic Times*. She recently completed a mainstream novel, *Rough Cut,* for Warner Books. Her short stories have appeared in *Shadows* 8, 9, and 10 and *Doom City (Greystone Bay* 2). She lives in San Diego with her husband, president of a software company, and with her two border collies, Ron and Nan.

Some time back Nancy called me up and we talked about the anthology and some of the themes of stories I'd read so far. I mentioned a few things that I was surprised to find I hadn't received yet, and within a few weeks she obliged with a tale about one of my favorite topics.

✦ ✦ ✦

Early on, Dwight Jones knew his daddy was not Ward Cleaver. Daddy liked to drink. Daddy liked to swear.

Daddy liked to hit.

"It's a dog-eat-dog world out there, son. Never forget that. *Ever*."

These were the first words Dwight could remember his dad saying to him.

His father started out in a pawn shop and moved into foreclosures. He collected debts for people with Italian last names. Dwight also suspected he killed people for money, but he was never certain of that.

One thing he was sure of was that he would grow up to be just like his old man. There was no way to prevent it; no one to stop it—certainly not his mother. No kindly teacher at school, no Cub Scout leader, no priest. He seemed to move in a shadow where no one saw what was happening to him; no one gave a good goddamn about the bruises and the missed days of school. He was a beautiful child, with huge blue eyes and curly red hair—but no one remarked on it. Even ugly kids were fawned over, adored, made pets of by old men with woodshops or by doting, childless chorus teachers. Not Dwight.

He was going to become just like Daddy, unable to love, aroused only by violence, ruthless and killing cruel; because everyone was afraid of his father.

And for some reason, they were also afraid of Dwight.

At first he used to cry over the inevitability of his fate. Even as a little boy, sobbing alone in his room after a beating—"teach you a lesson, make a man out of you"—feeling the rage build, feeling it fester and disease him, he understood the hardening process that was taking place inside. He was not to be like other boys. He was not to have a normal life. In the innocence of youth, he looked in the mirror behind the placid face, the clear eyes, and saw a monster.

Daddy was obsessed with the savagery of nature; they spent hours at the zoo, watching the big cats feasting on meat. Father took son out to the cornfields on the outskirts of town to watch the insects in the stalks devour one another.

"Dog eat dog, son," his father would say with satisfaction as insect legs kicked and struggled inside insect mouths. "For them and for us."

Dwight would grimace and clench his fists, not wanting to watch. He hated *Wild Kingdom,* Daddy's favorite show: it was a tarantula-eat-scorpion, snake-eat-rabbit, wolf-eat-doe world on TV. In his father's world, it was men beating on women; young men beating on old men; Daddy beating on everybody.

Daddy liked strength. He lifted weights and worked out at a gym. He hated weakness. He made Dwight go out for sports, and smacked him when he came home with a black eye from the school bully. But Dwight was weak, and as he grew, ugly. And stupid. He was such a loser he didn't blame Daddy for hitting him. He was pretty sure Daddy would eventually kill him.

Then something happened to Dwight.

He made a friend.

He was on the verge of puberty—wet dreams, acne, his hatred of his father spilling out into night dreams of murder and daydreams of running away. And then he met Angelo, sent by the angels themselves; a tall, dark Italian kid with big brown eyes and curved lips but for the moment zitty, like Dwight. Angelo was hip—he had a garage band, The Tokers, that was already getting gigs at after-school dances. Angelo was smart, he was rich, and he liked Dwight.

Dwight never understood why. Angelo had everything going for him. Everyone at school wanted to be Angelo's friend. The girls all lusted after him. He got straight A's but he was cool. He played the guitar like Hendrix; no, better. Dwight, on the other hand, was a loner, a dildo, a bizarro. The high school pack had cut him out long before—doesn't matter, fuck 'em, Dwight thought—but he longed to be one of the crowd—

—and Angelo Leone wanted to be Dwight Jones's best friend, and so he was.

It was Dwight who suggested they become blood brothers. He never knew why he suggested it; neither of them could remember—had it been after some funky John Wayne movie or some primo Colombian or what? But they pricked their little fingers, grinning sheepishly—Christ, they were almost fourteen!—and touched them together. How stupid, how sticky, how nothing—

Dwight's world changed. He had a best friend *and* a blood brother.

And the following year, they decided to do it the real way, cut their wrists the way the Indians did, make it official.

Only Dwight cut too deeply; at the hospital, they accused him of trying to kill himself. He always wondered if that's what he had tried to do. His old man beat the hell out of him for it.

But they tried again, with the other wrist. Angelo went first—the blood dripped onto the scarred table where they played cards and ferreted out seeds in their dope stashes and worked on music for the band—the blood dripped and Dwight bent down on impulse and licked it up; and gasped and said, "Damn, Angelo, it tastes fucking *good*!"

And it did, both of them agreed on that. And then the next year, Angelo cut the top of his finger off with the paper cutter—just the tip of his pinkie, just a tiny bit, and Dwight popped it into his mouth.

It was so terrific he fainted. It was like the best kind of acid; it was psychedelically delicious. Bullshit that it tasted like chicken—what crap; whoever said that had never tried it. It was incredible. Food from another planet, living human flesh.

Angelo agreed, after Dwight topped off his own little

finger for his benefit. It hurt like hell, but Angelo's reaction made it worthwhile.

Meanwhile, the lessons of Dwight's dad had incubated and yeasted and abscessed inside his son. Dwight's mother was buried—fell down the stairs, bruises like rotten apples on her face and breasts—and Dwight found he had nothing but contempt for her. He found himself thinking about digging her up and having a chew.

Then he knew that but for Angelo, he would've been lost by now. Angelo stuck by him; Angelo was always there. Dwight began to worry if he was gay on top of being a sicko. He, not Angelo, because Angelo was manly and strong and on the football team.

Dwight's father got meaner after his wife died. When Dwight ran to Angelo's with a bloody nose, Angelo decided it was time to get the hell out of Iowa. They wouldn't graduate with their class; but with Angelo's trust funds and allowances and boss leather jackets, who needed to?

On the road to Los Angeles, they both began to crave another psychedelically delicious snack. They admitted it to each other hesitantly—this was weird shit—and the more they talked about it, the worse the craving grew. The top of a finger was barely a nibble—think what a real man-sized bite would taste like!

"Well, we can't carve ourselves up," Angelo said. "What are we going to do?"

For a few weeks, they pretended they didn't know.

But after they set the band up and got a few gigs, and rented a house near the mansion wherein dwelt their heroes, The Grateful Dead, Dwight and Angelo had a long night of blood-brother talk and drew up two lists.

The first was:

The Pros and Cons of Eating Human Flesh

	Pro	Con
1.	It tastes good	It's hard to come by
2.	It tastes good	It hurts to cut ourselves up
3.	It tastes good	It's sick
4.	It tastes good	It's wrong
5.	It tastes *fucking* good	

They were stuck. How to continue the feed, the delirious, psychedelically delicious feed? It was too beautiful to stop doing it. (Years later, Dwight joked that sushi might have saved them, but he wasn't really serious—there was no comparison.) Yes, it hurt like hell, and it was wrong, but oh, god, god, god, the *taste*.

After a lot of talking, a lot of soul-searching, a few tears, they made a second list:

People We Want to Eat

1. Billy Idol
2. David Bowie
3. Madonna
4. Janet Jackson
5. David Lee Roth

Their idols. "Gourmet food," Angelo said, laughing.

Dwight cried all night. He had thought Angelo would save him, but no one could. He blamed himself for dragging Angelo into it—hadn't Dwight been the one to suggest they become blood brothers? And Angelo, dear Angelo, with his innocent offer of friendship, hadn't realized he was befriending a ghoul.

Dog eat dog; insects chomping each other; blood in the water as the sharks circled round—

How had Daddy known? How had the figures of his childhood, who had steered clear of a miserable boy obviously in need of rescuing, how had they known?

Right on, Pop. Right on, old guy. Old dead guy. Dwight didn't go back for that funeral, either, but that was the first night he and Angelo actually stalked someone, just followed her down the alley and took her home to the mansion and into Dwight's room. Sat her on the bed and took off her clothes—

gave her grass, fucked her—

and when she asked if there was anything else, Dwight stared helplessly at Angelo, who said, "Yeah, we want to eat you."

She grinned and lay back.

They killed her first. That was a mistake. For the magic left the flesh with the soul. Angelo theorized it had something to do with circulation; with the beating of the living heart. They also discovered the flesh had to be clean, very clean. Otherwise, it was . . . unappetizing.

Dwight swallowed an overdose of Librium. Angelo got his stomach pumped and brought him home. He fed him chicken soup—or tried to. Dwight could eat nothing Angelo offered him.

Except Angelo's little toe.

After that, they took their victims into the shower with them, or suggested a nice bubble bath. They ate only women—Daddy's doing, Dwight figured—and gradually, women were all they ate. (There was enough vegetable matter in the intestines to provide a balanced diet.)

"We're cannibal cats!" Angelo said, posing in his leathers. He wore his hair long and tumbling in curls down his back. He was a beautiful boy, a hot and nasty boy, and the girls flocked to him.

Dwight, on the other hand, looked okay. He didn't think he qualified as a cannibal cat, but he was grateful to Angelo for saying so, anyway.

They went on like this for a year or so.

Then they both fell in love.

Her name was Alice, which was, coincidentally, Dwight's mother's name. She came in for an audition as a backup singer with the band.

Offstage she was shy and sweet, despite her black spikey hair and thick eye makeup, sassy red lips, and leather skirts and corsets and boots that hugged her thighs. A little girl dressed in big girl's clothes. It was clear to Dwight that she dug both of them, and clearer still that Angelo wanted her all to himself.

Listen, he wanted to say to Angelo. Listen, you've been loved and adored. You've been *popular*. But I haven't had jackshit but my old man, who knew I was a freak, or made me into a freak, or I don't know what. Let me have her; she likes me, too. You can have any girl you want. You know it. But all I'll ever have is Alice.

Dwight loved sweet Alice. He cherished her in a way he thought impossible for him. She made his heart crack open, and he wanted to kneel before her and tell her she was a queen. When she sang, she sounded like the sweetest bird in the universe. When she smiled, he had to turn his head because he loved her so much. He didn't care if they ever made love; he wanted to keep his feelings for her pure and beautiful. It was the best thing about his life, except his friendship with his blood brother.

He truly, thoroughly loved Alice.

He agonized over their ghoulish secret, his and Angelo's. What if Alice found out? What if she knew that the lips that longed to kiss her had . . . eaten things?

And he agonized over what to do about his love for Alice, because it was clear that Angelo wasn't going to back off.

Alice, beautiful Alice. "Hi, babe," Angelo would say casually, as if speaking to her were the easiest thing to do in the world. "You're looking good."

Whenever Dwight was alone with her, he couldn't think of anything to say. She'd watch him expectantly, as if she were waiting for him to say something clever, like Angelo. But nothing came out but mumbling and bullshit. He had never been good with girls. Angelo was the one who picked them up when they went stalking.

Despairing, he finally let Angelo have her. He played weak, even though he wasn't really weak. He made Alice think he wasn't interested anymore—god, he would have cut off his right arm for her—and Angelo swooped down on her like a hawk.

Well, if it made them happy, it was okay by Dwight.

Only it wasn't, not really.

And then Angelo betrayed him.

He ate Alice.

By himself.

He ate Alice!

Dwight found him with the remains, bloody and stoned and happy, and he lost his cool. He raged, he screamed, he hit Angelo, his brother. Not since his childhood had he ranted and sobbed as he did that night.

Angelo was contrite. He said he hadn't known the depth of Dwight's feelings for Alice. "I would've backed off," he told Dwight. "After all, you're my blood brother."

After a while, Dwight found a way to forgive him. He, Dwight, had been weak. But Alice had been weaker, falling for Angelo. Trusting him—that was the ultimate weakness. Alice was a stupid, weak, trusting woman. And that was the name of that tune.

And that was the way things stood for another year. The Tokers played all over the country, Dwight and Angelo the two lead singers. Standing together on the stage in front of the lasers and strobes and fog banks of dry ice, in leather and lipstick, shocking, virile boys. Cannibal cats.

After their gigs they tiptoed out of the parties for a psychedelically delicious snack, then popped back, unsuspected and sated. And though the rift between them never quite healed, they were still close.

Things were still cool.

And then Angelo brought up the matter of the second list.

"We haven't munched any of them," he reminded Dwight. "We've got to get to work."

By that time, their musical tastes had changed. And since they'd decided to eat only women, they had some discussions and agreed on a new hit parade:

1. Tina Turner
2. Madonna
3. Cyndi Lauper
4. Janet Jackson
5. Annie Lennox

Dwight was terrified—these were major ladies—but Angelo insisted. "Don't tell me you're pussy!" he flung at his blood brother, perhaps sensing that was the equivalent of a double dare to Dwight. Dwight bucked up; they sucked each other's wrists to seal the pact, and began thinking about how they could get closer to Tina.

Then both of them fell in love again, with a beautiful Danish girl named Liss.

Oh, Liss. She was a tough, tall, ultrasexy woman who wore red leather unisuits and leopard skins around her shoulders. On stage she strutted like a panther; she moved slow and sure and dangerous. She was a strong woman, and Dwight warned Angelo that this time, he wouldn't back off.

"Ain't asking you to, man," Angelo said, smiling. "But I'm not, either."

So they both pursued Liss. Since all three of them were in music, it was easy to find out the clubs and parties she went to. The boys were so involved in courting her they forgot about their second list, which might or might not have saved Tina Turner's life.

Liss noticed them at the Grammys—or was it Angelo she noticed, Dwight wondered. She was friendly to both of them; said, in her charming, halting English, "I know you. You sing with The Tokers."

When she said it, the band's name sounded dumb and kidlike to Dwight, not cool in a retro way the way Angelo insisted it did.

"We *lead* The Tokers," Angelo corrected her saucily.

"It's Angelo's band." Now why did he have to say that?

"Oh, really? But you both sing so well." She smiled. She had dazzling white teeth and deep blue eyes. Dwight felt a pang as he thought of Alice, his sweet, lost love. Liss wasn't a bit like her. She was a bitch-fox. Thank god.

He had a talk with Angelo. For the first time in their friendship, Dwight took the upper hand. "No way do we eat her," he said. And at Angelo's casual nod, he clenched his fist and exposed his scarred wrist, saying, "Swear."

"Aw, come on, man." Angelo started to turn away, but Dwight grabbed his shoulder.

"Swear."

So they cut their wrists and held them together, slurped up the extra. Angelo's eyes softened and he said, "I'm sorry, man. You're right. We're brothers. We don't eat her. Hey, you can have her. It's wrong for me to hassle you over her."

Dwight drew himself up. "No. I want to win her fair and square." He wanted to know he was strong enough to.

So they kept after Liss. They went out, the three of them, to On the Rox and Touch and all the cool Hollywood hangouts. She let them kiss her but they didn't go to bed with her. Dwight thought he would burst with longing whenever he was around her.

Then she invited them to her place in the desert.

"It's miles from anywhere," she said. "We can play music and . . . play." She smiled at Angelo, who winked at Dwight. Dwight tried to smile, but he was too nervous. His moment was at hand. He would do whatever he had to to have Liss.

Whatever.

Almost.

They jumped in the Jaguar and flashed out to the Anza-Borrego Desert. It really was miles from anywhere. They had to bring in food—Dwight and Angelo had already thought of this, and agreed they would have to fast all weekend, faking eating so she wouldn't notice.

It was a two-story stone house in the middle of the desert, off roads and paths—how did the Jag manage it? But it was a fabulous place, stone and glass and rawhide couches and chairs. Indian art and big wood beams. A fireplace and a phone in every room. Jacuzzis and a pool that circled the house like a moat. And the biggest bed Dwight had ever seen.

Angelo nudged him. "I gave you my word, man," he whispered, when Liss bounced on it suggestively and smiled at the two of them.

They made dinner in the kitchen—blood-rare steaks and salads and fries. She ate and they talked, then cleared the table before she had a chance to notice that all the little bits of food cluttering their plates added up to full, untouched meals. They broke out guitars and grass and coke and got supremely high. She gave them things they'd never had before, Danish peyote or pastries or Copenhagen PCP. As they played, Angelo's eyes gleamed and Dwight was terrified he was going to forget his promises; either make love to Liss or eat her.

And then Dwight found himself in bed with her. In bed with Liss, whose glistening thighs and perfect, large breasts belonged to him. Whose pelvis moved in exquisite rhythms as he stroked her. She smiled and sighed and gave him permission to do whatever he wanted. Anything. She urged him on—*take me, do me,* lille skat, *oh, god, I'm yours. . .*

He was making love to a woman, to the woman he loved, and he had never been more . . .*more* . . .in his life. He felt almost human. Like the king of the jungle, a real animal.

A real one.

Then as he came, it seemed a nightmare; it seemed someone was biting him, teeth sinking into him, and he was terribly afraid. He fought back; he was Daddy's little man, his strong little man—

So this was what it was about, he thought, straining and pitching inside her. Grabbing her, holding her. Loving the way she gasped and screamed. This was the thing that saved you.

In the morning he woke and sat up quickly, still battling his dream. It was hot, and he was alone.

The air conditioning was off. He rose naked from the bed and found Angelo in the next bedroom, also naked, asleep. Dwight roused him and he woke slowly, complaining of the heat.

The house was littered with clothes and dope and pills. A broken guitar lay smashed against the stone fireplace. Beside it, the rough surface was flecked with droplets of blood.

The blood brothers searched everywhere, but they couldn't find Liss.

They did, however, find a note in the kitchen: "Forgive me," it said. That was all.

Together they ran naked—

—there was no one around for *miles*—

outside. The Jag was gone.

The electricity had been turned off. The phones were dead. It was as if nobody had been there for years.

It grew blazing hot, inside and out.

The hours passed; the shadows grew and brought chill desert air. They made a fire in the fireplace—Dwight discovered a shred of tattered red leather among the logs of mesquite.

"Someone will come, man," Angelo said.

Forgive me.

A week passed, and no one came. Two. They had plenty to drink because Liss had stockpiled cases of mineral water in the pantry. But they couldn't eat any of the food. It made them violently ill.

Days dragged on. They staggered for hours through the desert, staggered back to the house. They tried to catch rabbits or birds—they had never tried animals before—but nothing showed up in their snares.

"This can't be happening," Angelo said. "We can't die."

Dwight winced when he looked at his blood brother.

He was so thin. His eyes were sunken, and his teeth protruded from his gums. He was wasting away, his best friend. His body was eating itself; how psychedelically undelicious.

Another week passed. Still they were alone. They dragged lethargically around the house by night, after the heat had died down; but as the days wore on, they could barely move.

Flecks of blood by the fireplace. Tatters of red leather—

Forgive me.

"Listen, bro," Dwight said, swallowing hard. "You've been so good to me. My old man probably would've killed me if you hadn't come along." He took a deep breath. "I'd be dead by now anyway."

Angelo stared at Dwight. His lips parted. "Oh, no, man, no. No. It's both of us, or nothing. It's . . . someone will come."

Dwight lifted his chin. He had found his strength, his nature. After the years of doubt and hesitation, it was all coming together. Fucking Liss had done it—she was the real cat, the food from outer space.

He saw that now.

He rose in the moonlight, light and steady on his feet.

"I'll go take a shower, Angelo. There's still water in the pipes."

Angelo became hysterical. "No, man, don't do this. I'm so hungry. Don't tempt me. Don't do this."

"It's okay." Dwight patted him, then fell into Angelo's arms and embraced him. "It's okay, Angelo."

They sobbed together for a long time. Then Dwight stood and walked toward the master bathroom. He could hear Angelo wailing with grief down the hall.

He turned on the shower—he had saved the water, just

for this occasion—took off his clothes, and crept back down the hall into the kitchen. He found the biggest, sharpest knife he could; he began to salivate as he carried it back into the bathroom.

Forgive me.

He hoped she had, wherever she was now. Angelo would shit a brick if he knew the Jag was less than two miles away—hidden, well hidden. And the other weaknesses of civilization, obliterated. Phones, electricity, gas—they had taken the Wild Kingdom out of him. But now he was stripped free. Now he was the strong one, the cunning one, the cannibal cat—

"Angelo, hurry! Angelo, you'll never guess what I found!" He tried to sound as excited as he could.

And he was pretty excited, anyway.

"What? Is she back?"

"You'll never guess! Come here!" To the shower, to be cleansed—

"I'm coming!"

Now Angelo sounded excited. Hope, Dwight supposed, could do that to people.

Dwight stopped his tears and began to laugh. What a twit. What a stupid, weak, trusting twit.

It's a dog-eat-dog world, son.

Wrong, Dad. Wrong, old guy. But thanks for the lesson just the same. You had the idea right, if not the actual details—

—He heard Angelo falling against the walls as he hurried to his blood brother—

—the rift never quite healed—

He had waited until Angelo was so hungry he'd gotten careless; he, of course, had dined more recently—

Eating the weak, Dad, that's what makes you strong. But to take someone strong and make him weak, make her weak with lust, make him weak with greed—and then eat 'em, that is the ultimate, the totality—

—Hatred's better than spinach, as you well knew—

It wasn't dog-eat-dog; it was cat-eat-cat.

Dwight clutched the knife. He glanced in the bathroom mirror and saw the placid face, the clear eyes—

—oh yes, you thing they'd all been afraid of—
the monster.